A WELL-TRAINED ANIMAL

My man reached for his dagger and I slashed his right hand off at the wrist. He slumped to a sitting position on the snow, staring at the blood spurting from the stump of his right wrist.

Meanwhile, my warhorse had her man on the run. Suddenly he ducked behind a massive oak, then craftily peeked from the opposite side to see what had become of her.

As his head came round, she put a forehoof in his face. I could hear the crunch from fifty meters away.

She sniffed briefly at the body, calmly stepped on its neck, and trotted back to me. I wondered briefly how one trains a horse to do such things. Then decided I didn't want to know.

The Adventures of Conrad Stargard

THE CROSS-TIME ENGINEER

Book One in the Adventures of
Conrad Stargard

Leo Frankowski

A Del Rey Book

BALLANTINE BOOKS • NEW YORK

A Del Rey Book
Published by Ballantine Books

Library of Congress Catalog Card Number: 85-91211

ISBN 0-345-32762-4

Manufactured in the United States of America

First Edition: February 1986

Cover art by Dan Brown

Prologue

"DAMN IT! I have five doctorates!" she shouted.

He looked up from the pile of Polish government forms on his desk and surveyed the dumpy, middle-aged waitress in front of him. *Why me, Lord?*

"So?" he said dryly. "It happens that, academically, you are below average at this installation. I have nine. I am also your boss, and you are screaming at me."

"But it isn't fair!"

"Right. But then nobody ever claimed that the Service was fair—or that the universe was either, for that matter. This is your first day here. If you have a problem, you may tell me about it. But if you raise your voice one more time, I will bounce you off three of these walls before you hit the floor. One of *my* doctorates is in martial arts. Clear?"

"Yes, sir."

"Now, what precisely is your problem?" He leaned back, his fingertips touching to form an arch.

"Everything!" she shouted, and then remembered her situation and started again quietly. "This is all a mistake. I shouldn't be in twentieth-century Poland. My field is ancient Greece. And this fat forty-year-old body! Doctrine is that one should start out a tour of duty as a teenager! And having to tend tables at a bar! And—"

"Hold it and keep your voice down! Now, you say

1

there's been a mistake. Let's check the record." He touched four nondescript spots on his battered wooden desk, and a display appeared in front of him, individual letters glowing white in the air.

"Hmmm ... born in North America, 62,218 B.C. ... approved for child rearing; eleven children ... retired at forty-five, attended Museum University 62,219 B.C. to 62,192 B.C. ... doctorates in medicine, Slavic languages, psychology, and Greek literature ... accepted into the Historical Corps ...

"First assignment, Periclean Athens! God, what luck! Do you realize that I have twice petitioned to *vacation* in Periclean Athens and have been turned down both times? More people want to visit than there are natives in the city. And you get it as a first assignment!"

"Well, sir, my usual body isn't this flabby mess. And if you know the right people—"

"Humph. Then I recommend a program of diet and exercise. In any event, your record there was less than outstanding ... meddling in local politics, interfering with an assassination."

"But a hetaera was *supposed* to be interested in politics."

"Your examiners felt otherwise. Well, let's see ... After forty-one years in Athens, you returned to the university and obtained a doctorate in ancient Egyptian languages ... were turned down four times on assignments in the ninth through thirteenth dynasties, respectively ... eleven other requests denied ... eventually you volunteered for an open assignment and got twentieth-century Poland.

"Faced with this assignment, you requested the shortest possible tour of duty. It happens that your predecessor served twenty-seven years of a fifty-one-year tour, then quit."

"She quit? But that means—"

"Right. She was dismissed from the corps. What she does with the rest of her life is up to her. Most quitters end up drinking themselves to death out of boredom, although I hear the anthropology people are always looking for folks to track the migration patterns of *Homo erectus*."

"Living off the land in prehistoric Africa?" She shuddered.

"Right. Now, I don't see where you have a legitimate bitch. You volunteered for an open assignment and lucked out to the extent of indoor plumbing. You wanted a short assignment, and this one is only twenty-four years long. It obviously requires that your body match that of your predecessor, and the job fits nicely with your doctorate in Slavic languages."

"I got that when I was trying for a slot in the court of Casimir the Great."

He threw his hands up. "Damn it, young lady! Isn't it about time you grew up? We are out here writing the definitive history of mankind! The glory spots are few and far between. Most of it is plain, dirty grunt work, doing a mundane job well. And right now, your job involves serving drinks to a drunken tourist." He tapped a few places on his desk, and the display changed. "His drink is getting low. You'd better get back out there. I see that you haven't loaded the capsule yet."

"Loaded what capsule?"

"You didn't read your duty sheet? Damn, but you're inefficient! We are scheduled to ship nine tons of barley to the thirteenth century at 0227 tonight. *You* are to load it into the capsule."

"So now I'm a stevedore as well as a bar wench?"

"You think filling out government forms is a more pleasant occupation? Get out of here and get your ass to work!"

She stomped out, and he returned to his stack of forms. *What on Earth do they do with all of these things? They can't possibly have time to read them all. What is the psychology of it? Hmm—'The Psychology of Governmental Forms in Twentieth-Century Eastern Europe' ... There's a paper in that! ...*

Chastised, the waitress went about her duties in a black humor. She swore bitterly as she manhandled sacks of grain onto a primitive lift truck, too angry to notice that the slots in the wooden skids under the sacks matched the forks on the truck. "Damn! Not even a bloody antigrav field! As if the primitives could understand it even if they could find this place!"

Working in that ineffective manner, with runs up two flights of steps every fifteen minutes to check on her lone customer, it took her two hours to complete the loading. By then her uniform was torn, her nylons were in shreds, and she'd broken the heel from one of her shoes.

"Ridiculous clothing!" she muttered as she stomped up to the main floor in her stocking feet. In her anger she turned off the lights behind her but forgot to close the doors.

Chapter One

THE HIGH Tatras are magnificent in the early fall. I had arranged to spend my yearly vacation backpacking in the mountains south of Cracow, and for the most part my timing had been excellent.

The weather had been perfect, the color change was at its peak, and—since it was just past the usual tourist season—I had whole mountains to myself. The farmers were getting in the harvest, and all the children were back in school. All the teachers were back in school, too, which was unfortunate. I usually scored pretty well with school-teachers.

Vacationing, I generally ended up with some agreeable female companionship, but such had been sadly lacking this trip. I had been three weeks without; and frankly, my horns were showing.

Well. My allotted two-week holiday from the Katowice Machinery Works was almost up, and there was one small errand I had yet to perform. I lived with my mother, and she had read a magazine article about the Zakopane Agricultural and Horticultural Research Station. I was going to be near Zakopane, so it seemed reasonable to her that I should visit the station and buy her some seeds.

Just why seeds purchased at the ZAHRST should be any different from seeds purchased in Katowice was not explained. Neither was her sudden interest in gardening,

5

although I suspect that she had visions of me in the back-yard, hoeing up carrots, instead of being out with my friends. In any event, to keep peace in the family I had promised to buy some seeds.

The station was served by a hiking trail as well as a road. I took the trail because the pleasures of walking are degraded by road dust and noise and because I am not friendly with the fat, motorized tourist who says, "You mean you *walked* up here?"

The store was empty when I arrived. Empty, except for a few million seeds. It is incredible how many different kinds of plants there are. One rack had seeds for more than eighty different varieties of roses. Another had almost as many kinds of beets, lettuce, and strawberries.

The prices on everything were low—trivial, really—so the thought hit me: *The old girl wants seeds? Well, she's going to get seeds! Thousands of them! Not that I'm going to stick any of them into the ground!*

This slightly sadistic train of thought was interrupted as a magnificent pair of breasts came in from the back room. These breasts were followed by an equally magnificent young lady.

"Sorry. I didn't know anyone was out here. Can I help you?" Her eyes were a glorious pale green that floated in a field of red freckles. Her hair was that incredible natural red that you see maybe once in a decade, and, *oh yes, dear God*, she could help me in so many wonderful ways!

However, sad experience has taught me that pouncing on them tends to frighten them off. So I smiled, making sure that my mouth was closed and that I wasn't drooling.

"I expect so. My mother wanted me to buy her some seeds."

"Then you've gotten to the right place." She returned my smile. Glory! "Did your mummy give you a shopping list?" She was wearing a light print blouse and was definitely without a bra. Nothing in there but healthy Polish girl!

"Well, no. Actually, she was pretty vague about it. I was hoping to get some friendly expert advice."

"I think I qualify as a friendly expert. Where does she live?" She was still smiling, a good sign.

"We have a house just outside of Katowice."

"And what sort of soil do you have?"

"I don't know. It stays on the ground and is reasonably polite about it."

"No, silly! I mean is it sandy or clay or loam? What color is it? What's growing there now?"

"Well, it's sort of brownish. It doesn't stick to your shoes like clay, and we are presently harvesting great quantities of prizewinning crabgrass." I set my pack on the floor, using it as an excuse to edge a little closer, still smiling. She didn't retreat.

"Okay. That's something to go on. Now you have to decide on what you want."

I knew exactly what I wanted. But patience was still needed.

"I thought we might get a little of everything and let her do the choosing later."

"Sensible. Do you like strawberries?"

"I absolutely love strawberries." Strawberry blondes even more.

"Then these are definitely for you." She reached across to one of the stands and gently bumped me with her hip. First contact! And *she* had initiated it!

"Now, *this* variety is perfect for a home garden. The strawberries come in all during the growing season from early spring to frost, and it's a perennial." She wore the slightest hint of perfume.

"You've talked me into it."

"And *these* are great if she wants to do some canning— they all come in at once."

"Sold." She wore a skirt and nylons. None of this modern pants nonsense.

"And this is a new climbing variety."

"The wonders of modern science."

And so we went up and down rows, throwing seed packages into a brown paper bag. Following her was a pleasure. She was as perfect behind as she was in front.

"You're certainly enthusiastic about your job. Do you make a commission on all this?"

"Of course not, silly. This is a state-owned facility. But sales do count toward my efficiency rating."

"Well, we wouldn't want you to get a poor efficiency rating...uh, what *is* your name?"

"Anna."

"Anna. A lovely name."

"And yours?"

"Conrad."

"Hmm...Conrad has such a strong, masculine sound." She was still throwing seeds into the bag.

"Anna, what do people around here do when they're not selling seeds?"

"Not much, once the tourist season is over."

"But there must be some place where you folks hang out."

"Well, the group here at the station usually stops for a drink at the Red Gate Inn." She was still smiling.

"And where is this wonderful establishment?"

"Oh, it's not all that wonderful. But it *is* sort of quaint. It's been there for hundreds of years, and they've never even built a road to it."

"Then how do you get there?"

"You came in by the trail, didn't you? Then you must have come from the south; you would have passed it coming from the north."

"An inn on a hiking trail?"

"About half a kilometer down. You know, that trail is ancient. It shows up on the oldest maps. Once it was the only road through here. *Caravans* used to travel on it."

Caravans? Zakopane is surrounded by some of the highest mountains in the Carpathians. Unless you travel by the modern, dynamite-blasted road or you are a mountain climber or a helicopter pilot, there is only one way in or out—north. Within a hundred kilometers—to both the east and the west—there are ancient mountain passes into Czechoslovakia, but this area is one huge cul-de-sac. Nothing medieval would have traveled *through* here. The area's only natural resources are good hiking, great skiing, and magnificent scenery—none of which are particularly transportable by caravan mule.

However, I did not want to spoil her romantic notions. I wanted rather to *encourage* them.

"Amazing. I really must see this place. Is there any chance that you would be by there this evening?"

"There is an excellent chance." She winked. "I live just beyond the inn."

The world was wonderful. Anna was wonderful. And yes, I was wonderful, too, so my mood wasn't seriously dampened when she figured up the bill. It seems that while the price of a pack of seeds was trivial, 342 times trivial equals substantial. Actually, it took a fair bite out of a week's pay.

But I wasn't going to let that bother me. Not when there was an evening with Anna to look forward to.

The trail to the Red Gate Inn wound among pine forests below the High Tatras.

I had earned my engineering degree in Massachusetts, studying at the expense of a wealthy American relative. My summers had been free, and I had spent one of them hiking in the Appalachians. They were good mountains, but somehow they were never mine. These Tatras—this Poland—is my country, and I love it.

The Red Gate Inn was a surprisingly large place. Besides a restaurant and a taproom, it had rooms for rent and housing for its workers.

It was about four in the afternoon when I arrived, and I realized that I hadn't asked Anna about her quitting time. Well, she would get there when she got there.

The restaurant was tempting, but a meal with Anna was more tempting, so I went into the taproom, a lovely old cavern with huge oak beams and polished ancient furniture. Only the lighting and the taps themselves were modern.

They brewed their own beer, a rarity not to be passed up in these days of commercial fizziness. It was an excellent beer, and I was into my third stein by five-thirty. Also my tenth cigarette. I kept looking at the clock on the wall because I wasn't wearing my watch.

I owned an excellent watch, a solar-powered, solid-state, digital thing. It had a calculator with trig functions, and it played Chopin to wake me in the morning. But I was on vacation, and the whole idea of a vacation is to get away from things like clocks and timetables and delivery schedules and factories.

Not that I was complaining about my job. I worked for a healthy organization and had a decent, competent, understanding boss who generally let me do things sensibly, i.e., my way. Designers are *all* prima donnas.

We designed and built specialized industrial machinery, normally one-of-a-kind things to perform some industrial task—assembling carburetors, for example. My end of it involved designing the electronic and hydraulic controls for the machines, usually little more than specifying off-the-shelf components and programming a simple computer to run them. As a result, I rarely spent more than a few weeks on any one project, which kept things interesting. I got into all sorts of unusual processes. My job also involved a pleasant amount of business travel, finding out what the end-user really wanted and then making the machine work for him.

I asked the waitress about the workers at the station.

"Well, sir, it's hard telling. Those scientist people, they don't keep regular hours, you know. Another beer, sir?" Her Polish was quite bookish.

The restaurant was doing a surprisingly good business—I was checking it about every fifteen minutes—but only one other customer was in the taproom, another male hiker whom I certainly didn't want at my table when Anna came. If she came. I lit another cigarette.

Despite the considerable amount of beer I had drunk, I was getting irritated by seven o'clock. To give myself something to do, I decided to repack my knapsack and put all the seeds at the bottom. This got me to reading the labels on the envelopes.

For one thing, most of those seeds did *not* come from the Zakopane station. Half of them came from the Soviet Union, and at least a quarter of the envelopes read "Printed in U.S.A." That seed store was purely a commercial operation!

For another, I got to looking at what I'd spent half a week's pay on. Five kinds of strawberries, okay. Six kinds of lettuce, fine. Blueberries and raspberries, maybe. Seven kinds of potatoes? Perhaps. But that redheaded bitch had sold me six packages of wheat! Can you imagine my mother growing *wheat* in her tiny subdivision backyard? Not to mention rye, oats, barley, and four kinds of maize! And sugar beets. Bloody-be-damned sugar beets! And flowers. Fully a hundred varieties of flowers. One envelope read "Japanese Roses. Nature's fence. Absolutely impenetrable to man or beast. Grows to four meters in height and breadth. *Caution: Do not plant on small properties.*" And trees. I had fifty kinds of trees! Next year I wouldn't have to come to Zakopane. I could plant my own damned forest!

The next time the waitress came by, I asked her again about the group from the station.

"Well, sir, it's going on eight o'clock, and I'd guess that if they're not here by now, they won't be getting here. They don't always come. Another beer, sir?"

"No. No more beer, please. Vodka. A large glass."

I repacked my knapsack, seeds and all, and settled down to a monumental drunk.

Eventually the waitress got fairly adamant about my leaving—we were the last ones up—so I settled the surprisingly large bill and walked for the door with my pack on my back. I then decided that another trip to the rest room was in order. The rest room was in the basement, and I had made the trip quite a few times that evening.

But this time there seemed to be a lot more steps than before, and the lights were out. I must have stumbled around for twenty minutes without finding either the rest room or a light switch. I sat down to rest.

For the past two weeks, I had been sleeping in meadows and on rock piles. I could be comfortable anywhere. I relaxed, laid down, and fell asleep.

Chapter Two

I AWOKE with fluorescent lights shining in my face. My back and arms were simultaneously sore and numb; I had fallen asleep wearing my knapsack. My forehead was trying to split just above my eyebrows to relieve internal pressure. My bladder was painfully full, and my teeth were rusty.

I had not the slightest idea where I was, and I had to slowly and painfully rehearse in my mind the events of the previous day. Ah. Yes. The magnificent bitch. The idiot seeds. The inn. I must be in the basement of the inn.

Slowly, I got to my feet, half wishing that my head would explode and be done with it. I had been sleeping on sacks of grain, probably barley. Oh, yes. They brewed their own beer. I must be in the storeroom.

My pack seemed undisturbed. I checked my wallet, and everything was in order, though yesterday's stupid spending had left me with barely enough cash to pay my bus fare home.

The double door out was weird—thick steel like a bank vault or like something you might find in a submarine. Old buildings sometimes collect strange features. Perhaps it had been a bomb shelter.

But I couldn't waste time puzzling that out. It had become urgent that I find a rest room.

Beyond the strange doors was a large room filled with

boxes and bales; it was nothing like the hallway with the rest room. I found a staircase, which I climbed frantically. If I was in a basement, then up had to be out. I could always go in the bushes.

Through the doorway at the top of the stairs, I found myself in the familiar hallway, dimly lit with gray light from a high window. I must have been in a subbasement. As I rushed to the rest room, the door closed behind me with a solid click.

But there was no rest room, just another storage room filled with huge, foul-smelling crocks of sauerkraut.

My bladder could stand no more, and the room was dark. I walked behind the door and urinated on the wall.

Please understand that I was a civilized, educated, and profoundly housebroken young man. I felt extremely guilty about desecrating someone's storeroom. As my bladder deflated, other problems occurred to me. How was I to explain my presence in the basement? At best, the owners might demand of me the price of a night's lodging, which I didn't have. At worst, they might accuse me of being a thief, and no end of trouble would come of it all. Best to leave as quietly and quickly as possible.

I tiptoed to the ascending staircase that began directly in front of the door at the top of my previous climb. But the door that I had just come through had become a solid fieldstone wall without the slightest hint of a crack.

Well, I was severely hung over and probably still a bit drunk. I had never had hallucinations before, but I knew that such things were possible. But it was *probable* that I was in serious trouble. So, pack still on my back, I climbed the staircase, unbarred a door, and walked quickly down the trail without looking back.

I went at least a kilometer before I dared to stop, dig out my canteen, and drink it dry. As my fear of being caught lessened with each step, so did my mood become darker. Instead of returning from my vacation refreshed and eager for a new project, I was broke, sore, hung over, and horny. Hangovers always make me horny, and the "affair" with the redhead had not helped a bit. The weather had turned gray and cold, and I was not in a tolerant mood. Then a lunatic medievalist trotted toward me down the trail.

In retrospect and at a distance, he was not a bad sight. He rode a massive black stallion and wore a white surcoat with a huge black cross. His white shield also bore a black cross, which was repeated again by the eye-and-nose slit on his authentic-looking barrel of a helmet. He was sheathed in chain mail from his neck to his toes. A lance was at his back, a sword was at his waist, and various instruments of mayhem hung over his saddlebow.

As we approached each other, the idealized image faded and details became visible— The surcoat was shabby, and the shield was dirty. His chain mail was not of the fine rings seen in museums but of circles as big as a man's wedding ring and of iron that would have been better used for coat hangers. His helmet and weaponry were of poorly beaten wrought iron, and his horse was not well fed.

I must confess that Poland has its fair share of lunatics and more than its share of medievalists. Once a year, the whole city of Cracow is turned over to those strange people—mostly students—for a weekend. Actually, the Juvenalia is a pretty good party, but I was not in the mood in the Tatras.

Still, I needed to find a bus home, so I flagged him down.

"Hi there!" I waved as he drew up alongside.

He stopped abruptly, stiffened his back, and removed his dented helmet, which he balanced on top of the other ironmongery on his saddlebow. His hair, at least, was authentic. It was very long, very blond, and very greasy. His eyes were ice-blue, his nose had been broken, and scars crossed his forehead and cheek. I had the feeling that he was doing what he was doing because he could not afford a motorcycle.

He shouted at me in something that was probably German. My American was quite good, and I could speak a little English, but German was quite beyond me.

"That's very nice. You are very good at keeping in character, but would you please speak Polish?"

"I talk some Pole. What hell you want?"

"Okay, stay in character if your ego needs it, but I would like to know how far it is to the main highway to Cracow."

"You *on* road, Horse Ass."

"I'm on a trail, but I need to catch the bus to Cracow. Now, please cut out the nonsense."

"You need bashed head, you."

There comes a time when you must stop being polite to an idiot. I was a Polish Air Force Reserve Officer, and I spent some months in a basic training camp. There is a thing called a 'command voice.' It is very loud, very deep, and very penetrating. It is guaranteed to shake the socks off the average recruit. So: "Now listen up, you base-born moron! I have had quite enough of your archaic nonsense! I have asked you a simple, civil question: How far are we from the main road? Now, you *will* answer up, and smartly, or you *will* regret it! Do I make myself clear?" It is important that you never actually swear at an inferior, since this puts you down on his level. You can come *close*, however.

His eyes widened, and he started to draw his sword. Then he dropped it back into its sheath.

At the time I thought I had him buffaloed, but on more mature reflection I think that he simply didn't want to dirty his sword on me.

He searched among his ironmongery and pulled out a meter-long chain with a long stick at one end and a big iron star at the other. He swung this thing at me.

I was sufficiently startled that my reaction time was slow. I *did* manage to turn and start running, such that I caught the star mostly on my pack and only glancingly on the back of my skull. The impact was sufficient to knock me some ways from the trail and into a thorn bush. I decided to remain there until he went away.

He never looked at me again. He slung his gadget back over the saddlebow, put his helmet back on his head, and continued south.

God! He wasn't a lunatic so much as a bloody maniac!

I disentangled myself from the thorn bush and sorted through my pack for a clean cloth. The wound at the back of my head did not seem to be bleeding much, and I guessed that it would last until I could get to a hospital. Actually, it hurt less than the throbbing hangover in my forehead. I would live, but I would definitely report the homicidal moron to the police! Besides damage to my pride and person, he had punctured my tent, ripped my knapsack, dented my mess kit, and smashed my flashlight into three pieces! Damn it, I would sue the bastard!

I got everything back together, keeping the damaged equipment for evidence, and continued north.

The weather that had been bad turned absolutely foul. Overcast turned into fog and mist that turned into sleet and snow. I stopped and put on the long johns that my mother had insisted I take. I traded my tennis shoes for heavy hiking boots. Then I put on my nylon wind jacket and sweater over my sweat shirt. I soon covered this with a plastic poncho and was at last reduced to wrapping my sleeping bag about me under the poncho.

My hangover had not lessened a bit.

This was totally insane weather for mid-September.

According to my map, I should have crossed the highway hours ago. I supposed that I could be on the wrong trail, but only one was shown on the map. Nor had I seen another trail since leaving the inn. Perhaps I should have turned back to the inn and followed the gravel road down to the main highway, but there was always the chance that someone had seen me sneaking out. No. The likely solution was that, what with hangover and wounds, I was just slower than usual.

It was hard to tell, but I think it was about noon when my stomach began to protest. I was hungry.

I found a small stream forded by large rocks, which was strange; the Tourist Directorate usually bridges them. Not far from the trail was a cliff that sheltered some squaw wood from the sleet and snow. Squaw wood, for the benefit of you Polish city folk, is what my American friends called the dead, dry branches that stick out below the living branches of a tree. They are the best firewood in the forest, and taking them reduces the tree's burden, so no harm is done.

It didn't take much Sterno to get a fire going, and within a half hour I had a mixture of water and freeze-dried stew boiling in one aluminum pot and water for powdered coffee going in another.

The coffee went down well, but my stomach was still upset from the previous night's drinking. I was debating between (a) throwing away the uneaten half of the stew, (b) forcing it down anyway, since it was warm and I wasn't, (c) trying to carry it along. I then met my second lunatic of the day, this one heading north, as I was.

I decided that some sort of festival was being held to pep up off-season business. At least this person was completely in character. He was wearing a great, thick, shabby brown monk's robe with a huge cowl pulled far over his head. He carried two large purses—rather like military musette bags—made of real leather. One was securely buckled, but the other was covered with a loose flap. The food I had eaten had cheered me some, and after my run-in with the maniac knight, I didn't want to irritate anyone.

"Hello, Brother!" I shouted. "You look cold. Join me by the fire!"

The fellow jumped at least a meter. His cowl had been pulled so far down that he had not only missed seeing me sitting by the cliff but had missed the fire and smoke as well.

"What? Oh! Bless you, my son! What did you say?" His accent was strange, but I could make out what he said.

"I said welcome to my fire! And welcome to some food as well!" By this time it was necessary to shout because a full blizzard was howling through the trees.

"Bless you, my son, bless you!" He hobbled over to my small cooking fire.

Good God! The man was barefoot! With the snow, he'd probably be frostbitten in an hour and dead of pneumonia within a day. Sitting alongside the fire I was warm enough that I really didn't need the sleeping bag wrapped around me. By the time he got to the fire, I had it spread on the ground. "Come on, Brother. Sit down right here."

"You would give me your own cloak to sit on?"

"It's not exactly a cloak. Please, sit down."

"You do me a great honor, my son." He bowed before he sat down.

"I do you no honor at all. I am merely trying to save your life." I started zipping up the bag around him.

"Jesus Christi! It grows together!"

"No, it just zips up. Here, see? Now, stop making a fuss and eat this stew." A mercenary redhead and two—count 'em, two!—raving lunatics in a single twenty-four-hour period. My mother said that I should have gone to the beach.

"You give me your dinner, besides?"

"No big thing. I cooked too much and was about to throw the leftovers away. Look—you don't mind, do you? I've only got the one spoon."

"Of course not, my son. You honor me again."

"Right." The high honors of a dirty spoon. I filled the coffeepot again with water from my canteen and went out in search of more squaw wood.

I returned with an armload of wood and heaped up the fire. The monk had finished the stew and had taken the trouble to wash out the pot with snow.

"This is the lightest silver that I have ever seen."

"No, Brother. It's aluminum, and of no great value."

There was certainly nothing halfway about his psychosis. Apparently he had studied hard to get there. I mixed up some instant coffee with the hot water and poured half of it into his pot.

"Drink up, Brother. It's good for you."

"This is some infusion of herbs?"

"A close approximation. Coffee. It will warm you up."

The next step was to see just how badly his feet were frostbitten. I dug out my spare socks and the pair of light tennis shoes I carry. Then I unzipped the bag from the bottom and got my next major shock.

His feet were huge! They were rough-red and incredibly wide—half again wider than my tennis shoes. The calluses were fully a centimeter thick! I didn't know what the disease was, but it was nothing like frostbite. I touched his feet, rubbed them. They were warmer than my hands!

"And you would wash my feet besides, my son?"

In fact, the snow was melting on my poncho and dribbling all over. Score one for him.

"And you would have given me your own sandals if my feet had not been too big. But this goes too far, and the day is passing. We must be on our way if we are to find shelter tonight. Come, my son. Take back your cloak and let us go. Cracow is still a long way off." With that, he got up and started for the road.

"Hey! Wait! That's stupid! You'll get *lost* in this blizzard! We should wait here for a rescue party!"

"Those who follow God are never lost, my son," he explained slowly, as if to a child. "In any event, our way from here is down, and even a blind man can find 'down.' As to this rescue you speak of, I suspect that God will not see fit to grant that to me for some years yet." And then he was gone.

Lunatic or not, I could hardly abandon the man to die in a snowstorm. I quickly repacked my equipment, even though most of it was wet, and threw the remainder of the wood onto the fire. There was no possibility of a forest fire in this storm, and our fire *might* attract some attention. I put on my pack and took off after the madman at a trot.

His short, quick stride had taken him a remarkable distance before I caught up, but there was no missing his footprints in the shin-deep snow. I stopped to stamp out an arrow to indicate our direction of travel.

"Ah, my son, and here I had assumed that you were a good Christian."

"What? Of course I'm a good Christian, Brother. And a better Catholic, for that matter. I used to be an altar boy. Why should I not be a good Christian?"

"Why, those pagan marks you are making."

"Pagan? Goodness no, Brother. I'm simply showing the direction of our travel to aid rescue teams. The Hiking Society will be out, as will the Forestry Service, the police, and, likely, the Air Force. There must be dozens of people caught in this storm. Darned freakish weather for mid-September."

"Well, if you are only leaving a sign to your friends, I suppose it's all right. And while I quite agree that this would be strange weather for September, I must point out that today is the twenty-fifth of November."

"Brother!" We walked down the trail. I was surprised at how short the man was. He barely came up to my armpit.

"That brings up another point. While I dislike to be continually correcting a benefactor, please allow me to mention that my title is not Brother. It happens that I am an ordained priest, and perhaps Father would be more appropriate."

"As you like, Father." I don't *think* that insanity and the priesthood are mutually exclusive sets, and in any event, it would do no harm to humor him. "How did you know that I was going to Cracow?"

"Did I say that? If I did, I should not have mentioned it, since I obtained the information in the confessional. However, *before* he confessed, a good Christian knight told me that he had killed you—at least I assume that he referred to you. There can't be that many giants wandering about, and you *do* have a slight head wound. He asked me to give you extreme unction, which I agreed to do, although that sacrament no longer seems appropriate."

Giant? I was fairly tall—190 centimeters—but hardly a giant.

I stopped to stamp out another arrow in the snow. "Good Christian knight! He's a bloody homicidal maniac! He wanders around trying to murder people! He makes an unprovoked assault on me and you send him on his way to say a few Ave Marias."

"Not true. It was six dozen Ave Marias and three dozen Pater Nosters. And *he* certainly felt that he was provoked. Whatever decided you to be rude to a Knight of the Cross?"

"Oh! Nine dozen prayers for an attempted murder!"

"Please calm yourself. You appear to have suffered no great harm, and I don't imagine that the prayers will do the knight's soul any damage, either. After all, it is the *intent* that really matters."

"The actuality made a considerable difference to me."

"Certainly, my son. Now as I understand it, you were alone, on foot, and completely without armor or weapons. Without an apology, a compliment, or even a bow, you stopped a member of the Teutonic Knights and demanded information of him. You did not even offer him your name. He then answered your question, even translating it with his limited Polish, because you spoke no German at all. You then became ruder and claimed—or at least implied—that he lied. He then gave you a fair warning, and you returned this with...let me see. What were his exact words?... 'A tone of voice that I would have found objectionable had it been spoken to me by my own Holy Commander.' He then struck you. Now, my son, are these substantially the facts?"

"They may be substantially the facts, but the telling of them is most biased, and in any event they do not in any way justify attempted murder!"

"True. Violence is rarely justifiable, and it was for this reason that I bade the knight do penance after confession."

Christ. *I* had almost been murdered, and now a man whose life I was trying to save was trying to convince me that it was *my* fault. Damn! What the hell was wrong with the Air Rescue? We should at least have heard a helicopter by this time. I fished around in my shirt pocket, under the sweater and poncho, and dug out my cigarettes and disposable lighter. Only one cigarette left. I was about to pitch the package, but one must not litter, not even in a snowstorm with a lunatic. I stuffed the empty pack in my pocket. I lit the cigarette, drew deeply, and put away the lighter.

The priest's eyes grew wide, but his step never faltered. "Remarkable. You mentioned that you were a true Christian. Would you like to tell me how long it has been since your last confession?"

"About three weeks, Father."

"That is a long time. Would you like to confess now?"

"What? Here?"

"To be sure, a quiet, dark spot in church would be

preferable. Such things are good, but not necessary. It is what is in the heart that counts."

Recent events *had* troubled me considerably. To confess to a lunatic might be strange, but then, the whole last day or so had been pretty strange. There I was, walking along in September, through snow that was knee-deep in places, next to a mild-mannered barefoot man who showed not the slightest discomfort. The sane thing would be to stop, light a fire, pitch a tent, and wait for a rescue team. But there was such an incredible *toughness* about the man that I knew that I could stay with him, or leave him, but I could not possibly stop him, no matter how short he was. Confession seemed like a good idea, and—who knows?—maybe he really was a priest.

Perhaps not all of my eventual readers, if any, will be good Catholics, so I will try to explain the sacrament of confession. The times of confession are posted in the church, and usually a priest is available several times a day. When you feel the need to go, you go, often alone. Usually there are people in front of you, and you wait quietly in a pew, because confession is a private thing. The priest is in a tiny, screened room with screened confessionals on either side. Your turn comes, and you go inside and kneel. When the priest has finished with the person opposite, you hear the soundproof screen in front of you open, and you recite a short ritual that serves to "break the ice": "Bless me, Father, for I have sinned . . ."

And then you unburden your soul onto a very tough man who is absolutely forbidden to repeat anything that is said. You tell him what you have done, what you have thought. You answer his questions until the truth is obvious to both of you. He forgives you your sins and *then* tells you what your punishment, your penance, will be. This is usually to make a good act of contrition and to recite privately a certain number of prayers. But it *can* be whatever the priest feels is fitting. And you *do* it, because you *need* to do it, or you wouldn't have walked into the confessional in the first place.

In the Catholic church, there are seven sacraments.

Some—baptism, confirmation, and extreme unction—are performed only once in a Catholic's life. Some are performed seldom, if at all—marriage and holy orders. Two are performed frequently—confession and communion. Of the seven, confession is not only the most frequent but, given the nature of the human condition, the most important.

So, after a bit, I said, "Yes, Father, I would like to confess. 'Bless me, Father, for I have sinned. My last confession was three weeks ago, and since then..." I told him what had happened, and I dwelled particularly on the last thirty-six hours or so.

It was certainly my strangest confession, wading through thigh-deep snow next to a barefoot priest, and it was undoubtedly my longest, for he asked innumerable questions about every minor point that I mentioned. The sky was noticeably darker when we finished.

Finally he said, "This is a most remarkable story, and I am not quite sure what to make of it. I see several possibilities. Is it possible that you would lie in confession?"

"*What?*" One does *not* lie in confession, in the same manner that one does *not* fornicate with one's mother.

"I thought not. Two other possibilities occur to me. One—perhaps the most likely—is that you have taken a blow to the head. Such things have been known to addle a man's wits, but this explanation does not account for your very remarkable equipment. The other possibility that I see is that God has seen fit to do something... *unusual* in your case. But that is not for someone as lowly as myself to say.

"As to your sins, they are minor ones. You have been angry with your mother, but that is not uncommon for a man who is unmarried at twenty-eight; and the fact is that, nonetheless, you did obey her. You coveted a maiden, had lust for her, but then again, you were both unmarried and you took no improper action. In your disappointment, you became drunk, wrongfully, but you paid your debts and harmed none. You trespassed on your host in your drunkenness, but you caused him no harm. You insulted a knight, but you did not know the proper forms of courtesy. And you thought ill of me; indeed, you are still convinced that it is *my* wits that are addled ..."

"Father, please!"

"No, no. Please, let me finish." He took a breath. "And perhaps, considering the strange events that have transpired, you are justified in your belief. It is not for me to say. But I think, in spite of your strange tale, in spite of your giant's stature, and in spite of your mystic equipage, you are, within, a very good man. I absolve you of your sins. I want you to make a good act of contrition, and I think that we should now kneel and pray."

"Father, the snow will be above our waists."

"True. And the sky grows dark, and the cold grows more. My son, God will take us when He sees fit, and He will save us as He sees fit. All that we mortals can do, one minute at a time, is to do what appears best."

And with that, dear reader, I knelt down in snow up to my elbows and recited to myself the Apostles' Creed.

Some time later, we were walking again.

"Father, it's true what you said. I do believe that you are insane. But I have to say that in spite of your insanity, you are the most holy person I have ever met."

"Thank you, my son. But it is obvious that you have never met a truly saintly man. *I* have met Francis of Assisi, and he blessed me and took me into his order. You grow tired. Why don't you walk behind me?"

Saint Francis of Assisi! I had gone beyond being amazed at the man. I was wearing thermal underwear, sturdy blue jeans, two pairs of woolen socks, good hiking boots, a thick sweater, a windbreaker, and a poncho. I was cold. *He* was *barefoot* and in a monk's cassock! I was half again taller than he was, and *he* was suggesting that *he* should break snow for *me* to make my walking easier!

"No, thank you, Father. I can manage. What brings you into this neck of the woods?"

"'This neck of the woods!' Another good turn of phrase! Well, the answer is simplicity itself. I was in Rome, and I received an appointment in Cracow. To get from A to B, one is obliged to traverse the points between."

"Well, if you are a true Euclidean, it would seem that the route would be far to the west, through France and Germany, or at least north by the Moravian Gate," I said.

"The way through Germany might be softer, but it is much longer. Do you know nothing of maps? Further, you should know that the emperor of the Holy Roman Empire—which is not Roman, nor an Empire, nor particularly Holy—Nay! He is not even an emperor! At best he is somewhat acknowledged as the spokesman for a ragtag collection of German city-states pushing their unwanted existence into all parts of Christendom! He has inherited the Sicilies, gained dominance over Milan and Florence, and threatened his Holy Majesty Louis IX of France! Through the unbelievable stupidity of Duke Conrad of Mazovia, his German knights have been invited—*invited*, *mind you*—into the north of Poland itself! And these so-called Knights of the Cross are now murdering whole villages of poor, heathen Prussians!"

I had had the misfortune to hit his "hot button," and he went on like that for the better part of an hour. It seems that the Holy Roman Emperor, Frederick II—who was also King of the Sicilies, King of the Romans, and quite a few other things—owned most of Italy, and the Pope owned the rest. They had begun fighting, and the filthy German mercenaries in the pay of Frederick II had had the incredible effrontery to defeat the Pope's Just and Christian Warriors, who were also mercenaries, which is why there was an empty treasury and no funds to pay the way of a traveling priest. Furthermore, these Germans were insidiously, sometimes even openly, pushing their way into Poland, taking over its cities and founding monasteries that Poles were not even allowed to join!

I had an uncle who had survived being a partisan in the 1944 Warsaw insurrection. He hated Germans, but his hatred was like a dislike for cabbages compared with the hatred of the supremely mild man who walked beside me.

When we finally stopped to catch his breath, I said, "You are absolutely right. I completely agree with you. But tell me, please, why did you not go through the Moravian Gate?"

"Why, it had been my intention to come through the gate and avoid climbing the Beskids altogether. I walked across Italy and begged passage—working my way—on a ship that sailed the Adriatic Sea to Fiume, in Dalmatia. I then crossed the Dinaric Alps into Croatia, a mere twenty miles on the map but four days' walk. Then it was a matter of working on a riverboat down the Sava to the Danube, finding another boat, and then up the Danube. My intent had been to go upstream to the Morava, through the gate, then down the Odra, across to the Vistula, and so to Cracow. That is to say, the sensible way. However, the boat I was on was going up the Vah, not the Morava. It was late in the season, and I was not likely to find another boat. But by the maps I remember, it was but thirty miles from the headwaters of the Vah, across the Tatras, to the River Dunajec, which would also get me to Cracow before winter. This I did, although the crossing took six days. The Tatras are really not so bad as the Alps, but they are much farther north, and I crossed them two months later in the season."

It was now quite dark. The snow had stopped, and the cloud cover was breaking up. Any camper knows that a clear night is a cold night. Already the snow was crunching beneath my boots and his bare feet.

"You mean you crossed the Tatras alone? Barefoot? In this weather?"

The full moon broke through the clouds, and I could see on his face the expression I reserve for fat, motorized tourists. But what he said was, "You see, God provides us with light and therefore with hope. We will continue on."

I had rolled up and packed my sleeping bag when I left the fire at noon, and since then the exertion of keeping up with this short man had kept me warm enough. But now it was getting *cold*.

"Father, I'm going to break out my sleeping bag, that 'cloak' you saw earlier. Let me rip it in two and give you half."

"Do not destroy your property, my son, and do not

even break your stride to undo your equipage. We shall soon find shelter. I can smell it."

I could smell nothing but snow and pine trees. "Father, how do you do it? How do you walk barefoot on crunching snow?"

"Well, I will tell you a secret that should not be a secret. When your heart is truly pure, you really *do* have the strength of ten. And further, while it is best to have your heart pure with God's love, pure anything will do. Pure honor or pure greed. Pure hate or even pure evil. It is only the contradictions and inner conflicts that weaken a man.

"But enough of this. We have forgotten something, and soon I will have to introduce you. My name is Father Ignacy Sierpinski."

"I am most pleased to meet you, Father Ignacy. My name is Conrad." And here I faced a problem. You must understand that I am Polish. All my grandparents were Polish. And all their parents, all the way back to Noah. But in some unexplained manner, my last name is Schwartz. After Father Ignacy's hourlong tirade about Germans, I did not want to tell him that.

"Just Conrad? Well, nothing to be ashamed of. Many people still use only one name. Tell me, where were you born?"

"In Stargard." Stargard is a small town in northwest Poland. The name came about when there was a warehouse on a trade route. A castle was built to protect the warehouse, and a town grew up around the castle. The castle was originally called Store Gard, and the name drifted with time.

"Then Conrad Stargard you are. And here *we* are. *Hello, in there!* May two Christian travelers ask for shelter?"

I did not realize that we were at a dwelling until I had almost stepped on it. Barely a meter high, it looked like a peaked mat of straw. We heard some fumbling sounds from within.

"They build their winter huts mostly below ground hereabouts; it is good protection from the cold."

A section of the straw opened up. "Aye, Father, be

welcome, and your friend, too. But all I can offer is a place on the floor near the fire. No food, you understand."

"My good son, we understand. You would not be a good Christian if you did not see first to the feeding of your own family. Fear not for us; we are well provisioned. As you give us entrance, you give us life itself, for otherwise we would perish in the cold.

"I am Father Ignacy Sierpinski, and my friend is Conrad Stargard."

We felt our way down a crude ladder into a rectangular space that was lit by a small central campfire.

"I am Ivan Targ. My wife, Marie. My boys, Stashu and Wladyclaw. My baby, little Marie. Shoo! Shoo, you boys! Make a place for our guests."

The boys cleared a space maybe two meters square on one side of the fire. I spread my poncho out as a ground cover and rolled out my sleeping bag over it. The ceiling was high enough for the rest of them to stand upright, but I was nearly bent over double.

When we were seated, I whispered to the priest, "I know that we have not been offered supper. Do you think that we should offer something to them?"

"Oh, yes. That would be most polite. In fact, I was about to do so." He turned to our host. "Ivan, we thank you again for your courtesy and aid in our need. We would be honored if you would accept a very small token of our gratitude."

His words seemed to be a fixed ritual. He slowly opened one of his leather pouches, the one with the floppy cover, and drew from it a large, greasy sausage and a chunk of rather ripe cheese. Neither had been wrapped in aluminum foil or waxed paper. He drew his belt knife and cut each in two, returning half to his bag. The remainder of each he divided into seven equal pieces, giving one piece of sausage and one piece of cheese to each person present, himself included.

Everyone ate with relish and nods of thanks. Despite my misgivings at the lack of sanitary wrapping, I ate too. Ritual is ritual, and you do not offend the man who puts a roof over your head in the cold.

It was obviously my turn. I rummaged through my dwindling food supplies for something that could be divided, that wasn't freeze-dried. I came up with a big two-hundred gram bar of chocolate. I opened the package and found that the bar was conveniently divided into fourteen squares. Following the priest's ritual, I broke the bar in half, then a half into seven parts, which I passed around.

I gave a piece to the five-year-old boy, and he just looked up at me.

He didn't know what chocolate was.

In my world, there are madmen and there are saints. There are murderers and there are people who live in holes in the ground.

But there are no boys who don't know what chocolate is. Not in the twentieth century, anyway. The truth that I had been fighting off all day was forced in on me, and I could no longer defend myself against it.

"Father, you have told me that this is November twenty-fifth. Will you now, please, tell me what year it is?"

It seemed that he had been waiting for that question.

"It is, in the year of Our Lord, twelve thirty-one."

I drew my legs close to my chest and hugged them with my arms. I put my forehead on my knees. There were no policemen, no courts of law. There were no ambulances, no hospitals, and no doctors. There were no stores, no Hiking Society, and no Air Rescue teams. There was no rescue at all. There were only brutal knights, crazy saints, and Mongols.

In ten years the Mongols were coming, and they would kill everybody.

I fell asleep.

Interlude One

"GOOD LORD! You mean that one of the Historical Corps teams screwed up that badly?" We were watching a documentary on the extremely unauthorized transportation of Conrad Schwartz. This had been pieced together, in part from his diary (which he wrote in English to keep it private) and from the readouts of a large number of insect-sized probes initially developed for police work.

When a crime has been reported, our police transport a cluster of probes to the time and scene of the crime. These record everything, which doesn't do the victims much good. Time is a single linear continuum, and you can't "make it didn't happen." If a dead body was found, a human being was dead, and there was nothing that could change that fact. But our methods did assure that criminals committed only one crime and were always caught. As a result, we had an extremely low crime rate and no professional criminals at all.

The probes were eagerly put to use by the Historical Corps, whose occupation was the writing of a truly definitive history of the human race. It was one of their teams that had screwed up.

"Not one team but two. There were ridiculous breaches of security at both the twentieth-century and thirteenth-century portals," Tom said. Tom had been a drinking buddy of mine in the U.S. Air Force long before we got involved with time travel. Much later, we were both surprised to discover that he was my father. There were also certain ... problems concerning my mother, which I prefer not to discuss. Time travel is not entirely beneficial.

"Well, can't we send him back?" I asked. Anachronisms can be extremely disruptive, and we have no intention of adding to the sum of human misery.

"Impossible. He wasn't discovered, subjectively, until almost ten years later, when I was observing the Mongol invasion of Poland."

"Oh." If Conrad Schwartz had been observed in 1241, then that was an established fact, like the dead body I mentioned earlier. "So there's nothing we can do for the poor bastard."

"We can't bring him back until he has spent at least ten years there, but there are some things that could be done, and in fact, I have already done them.

"Decontamination, for example. The diseases of the thirteenth century are not the same as those of the twentieth century. Thirteenth-century Poland had neither syphilis nor gonorrhea nor acne, and I was not about to see them introduced by our drunken Conrad Schwartz.

"Then again, in the twentieth century smallpox has been eradicated, leprosy is very mild compared to the earlier strains, and the Black Death has become one of the varieties of the common cold.

"The 'fluorescent lights' he slept under in the Red Gate Inn did a lot more than light his way out of the transport capsule. They wiped out every foreign microorganism in him and gave him a complete immunization treatment as well."

One of the nice things about time travel is that it gives you the time to do things that are worth doing. I'd spent much of my life helping to build a technical civilization in the sixty-third millennium B.C. That civilization provides us with most of our personnel and some very high technology. It's also a fine place to live.

"Speaking of diseases, Tom, what was wrong with the priest?"

"Father Ignacy? Nothing. A fine man."

"But those huge, calloused feet!"

"That wasn't a disease. That's what normal human feet look like when they've spent a lifetime walking barefoot over broken rock and snow."

A smiling, nude serving wench announced lunch, and we took a break.

By one, we were back at the screen.

Chapter Three

"UP NOW, Conrad. Get up!" Father Ignacy was shaking my arm. I was in a dark, smelly, smoky hut. It had log walls, a dirt floor, and a straw roof. Memory came back. The barefoot saint. The snow. The thirteenth century.

"Yes. Yes, Father. I'm up. What's wrong?"

"Nothing is wrong. God has seen fit to grant us another day. As good Christians, we must not waste His gift. Come, we must be off."

"Oh. Yes. Certainly." I started putting my gear together. "The coals are still warm. Let's make breakfast and have some coffee before we go."

"What? Eating on waking? What a slothful habit! Come now. I have already bid our good host good-bye, and there is need of haste."

I find it hard to be assertive before breakfast, and soon we were walking north in the gray dawn. The snow grew thinner as we approached a river, the Dunajec. There we found a small wooden dock but no boat.

"What was the great hurry, Father? Has the boat left without us?"

"It has. Yesterday morning, in truth, and it was the last boat of the season. You should not have lost consciousness so early, Conrad."

"I fell asleep."

"To me, it appeared that you had fainted. Afterward,

I heard the confessions of good Ivan and Marie and said a mass for the family. They told me of the boat."

"But what good does an absent boat do us?"

"Absent, yes. But with a crew of only two. The boatman and a wandering poet, a goliard—worthless sorts. Despite the recent snow and rain, the river level is still low, and six men would make a better crew than two. It might be God's will that we shall find them snagged on a sandbar and in need of our aid." We walked along the river path.

"If you say so. The truth is that I no longer have a pressing need to go to Cracow. It is no longer on my way home. I no longer have a home. Or a mother. Or a job." The reality of being stranded was hitting me again, and I was holding back sobs with difficulty.

"We shall pray for your mother, my son. But remember that she is not dead, she is merely elsewhere. As to your home, why, it is only a material encumbrance and can be replaced at need. As to your job, that too can be replaced. You are an educated, healthy young man—if overly large—and it should not prove difficult to find gainful employment. In fact, already an idea occurs to me.

"I have told you that I have an appointment in Cracow. That appointment is to take over the copying department at the Franciscan monastery. I am ordered to expand the number of copyists and to found a proper library.

"Now, you can read and write, and you have told me that you know something of the new Arabic system of numbers and of the arithmetic that is used to manipulate them. You have knowledge of Euclid and of the *algebra*, as well."

Not to mention analytic geometry, calculus, and computer programming, I thought. "You are suggesting that I work for you as a copyist?"

"And why not? You have told me that much of your previous work was at a *drawing board*, which you describe as similar to a proper copying table."

"Hmm." The idea of a steady job did have merit. I had grown up in the arms of a reasonably benevolent government that was founded on sensible socialist principles.

While such a system discouraged the acquisition of fabulous wealth, it did ensure that all people were fairly well taken care of. But from what I remembered of my history courses, in the thirteenth century they actually allowed people—their own countrymen—to *starve to death*! "Your suggestion has merit, but I see some problems. For one thing, I do not think that I am ready to take Holy Orders."

"I agree with you, my son. You are not ready for so momentous a decision, nor need you be. You could be engaged as a lay brother, without any vows at all."

"The next problem is that I do not know if I would be competent as a copyist. It is different from what I have done."

"I don't know that either, my son, so my offer is tentative and temporary—for the winter at least."

"Then there is the question of remuneration, Father. What does the position pay?"

"I have no idea of what the rates are in Cracow. When demand is high and copyists are few, the pay can be excellent. But in any event, you are guaranteed a roof over your head and food in your belly."

"Very well, then, Father. It is agreed that I shall work for you for an indefinite time on nebulous terms." The snow was gone by then. The sky was a rich blue, and evergreens gave the landscape some color.

"Excellent! I'm glad that this is settled, for I was worried about you. Now then! I have several thousand questions to ask. Yesterday, as your confessor, I was obligated to concentrate on your sins. Today, as your fellow traveler and future employer, I have the right to ask questions to my own liking. Now, tell me if I am correct. You were born in the year of Our Lord, nineteen fifty-seven?"

"True, Father."

"The twentieth century! Tell me of the church, my son. Does the Pope still rule from Rome? Do the Germans dominate him?"

"The Pope is supreme in the Vatican; he is dominated by no secular power. The Germans have been pushed north of the Alps and west of the Odra."

"And the Pope himself—what of him?" The man was trembling with excitement.

"He is John Paul II, and—this you will love—he is as Polish as you are, and born Karol Wojtyla. A fine man and a great Pope."

"Oh, glory! My son, you make my heart rejoice!" That incredibly tough man, who could walk barefoot across the Alps and pray kneeling in chest-high snow, that man had stopped on the river path, and tears were streaking his windburned cheeks.

Some time passed before we started, once more, down the river road to Cracow. We were silent for a while. Then:

"And my own order, my son. Tell me of the followers of Francis of Assisi."

"Gladly, for this too is a happy thing. *I* know of him only as *Saint* Francis of Assisi. The Franciscans are alive and well in the twentieth century. I knew one personally and counted him a friend." He had been on my college fencing team and was a fine hand with a saber, though I could generally beat him with an épée.

Ignacy stopped, hugged me solidly, yanked my head down to his level, and kissed both my cheeks. I felt awkward about it. In the time of my birth, men were abandoning the ancient Slavic custom of kissing each other; perhaps it was because homosexuality was tolerated, if not socially acceptable, and healthy men did not want to be associated with anything that *they* did.

"I see that I have offended you, my son."

"Well, it's ckay. But, you know, customs change."

"Forgive me. What else do you remember?"

"About the Franciscans? Wait. Yes, I remember reading an ancient copper plaque that told of a great church, a cathedral almost, that had been built by Henryk the Pious for the Franciscans in 1237. That church still stood in Cracow."

His arms went out again, but he did not touch me. Then he said quietly, "And of me? Do you know anything of me?"

"I'm sorry, Father, but no. Please, understand that I know as much about this age as you know of the fifth century. If you chance-met a man of that age, what could *you* tell *him* about himself?"

"You are quite right, my son. Please forgive my asking."

"It might be that you are well known to the historians and theologians of my time."

"And it might not. Again, forgive me. Tell me instead of the wondrous mechanisms that your age has wrought. You spoke of machines that can fly in the air, of ships that navigate without sails or oars, and of the varieties of mechanical land beasts, *buses* and *trains*.

So I answered his questions, and we talked out the morning. I answered all his questions truthfully but did not really tell him the *whole* truth. He never brought up the subject of the Protestant Reformation, so neither did I. And why should I want to mention the Inquisition to a living saint? Because Father Ignacy *was* a saint. He was also a powerful man, an intelligent man, and by the standards of his own age, a very well educated man.

By the standards of the twentieth century he was quite thoroughly out of his mind! He was concerned—actively worried—about how many angels could dance on the head of a pin! To him, that was a major theological dispute. He was worried about the exact anatomy of incubi and succubi, and he worried if it was proper to take communion on Friday since, by the unquestionable doctrine of transubstantiation, the baked wheat flour of the Host and the wine, after being taken, were transmuted into the body and blood of Christ. And was this not meat? And was not meat forbidden on Friday?

All I knew was that I was attracted to the man, although not at all in the same way as I had been attracted to the magnificent redheaded bitch of Zakopane.

It might have been ten o'clock when we started thinking about dinner.

"Conrad, how much food are you carrying?"

"Three, maybe four days' worth at normal rations, which is a lot more than I've had recently."

"And it is all of that *cold-dried* variety that keeps indefinitely?"

"Freeze-dried. Yes, most of it. Some candy, but it'll keep too."

"Ah, yes. I meant to ask you. What was that incredible confection you distributed last night?"

"It's called chocolate."

"Marvelous stuff. If you can make more, your fortune is made without recourse to being a copyist."

What an incredible thought! Conrad Schwartz, the capitalist confectioner! Maltreating the women and children slaving away in my chocolate factory! But still, one must eat. Chocolate is what? Mostly milk, sugar, and cocoa beans, isn't it? But cocoa beans came from South America. Or was it Indonesia? I would have to look it up.

No, I would not look it up, because I *could* not look it up, because I was in the thirteenth century, and a good library here consisted of a Bible, two prayer books, and a copy of Aristotle.

"No, Father. It's impossible. It needs a kind of bean that does not grow around here."

"A pity. Well, keep the rest of it; you may someday have to impress a princely patron. For today's dinner I suggest that we finish off my supplies of cheese and sausage and keep yours for an emergency." With that, he pulled out the remains of his sausage, which might have weighed a kilo. He was about to cut it in half but reconsidered and divided it in proportion to our heights, giving me the larger piece. Half an hour later he did the same with his cheese. He refused to stop for lunch, and we ate on the march.

Again I felt queasy about the unsanitary food, but I was living in the thirteenth century and would have to get used to it. He slapped his now-empty pouch. "The last of my Hungarian food."

"Then what do you keep in the other pack, Father? Spare underwear?"

That was the first time I heard his laugh, a good sound. "Ah, Conrad, I know that you have an exalted opinion of my abilities as a traveler, and I confess that I take an improper pride in them myself. But no, I would not carry anything superfluous over the High Tatras, let alone the Alps!

"No, this is my gift to my new abbot. I have in here a copy of Euclid, a complete Aristotle, and Ptolemy in Latin, my own translation into Polish of de Bivar's *Poem of the Cid*, and letters. There are fully three dozen letters, one of them from His Holiness, Pope Gregory IX himself!

"So, you see that there can be no faltering along the way."

"You mean you have nothing at all but your cassock? It might take us weeks to walk to Cracow!"

"You worry overmuch about material things. We shall ride to Cracow and be there in five days, and we shall be well fed along the way. I can smell it."

I could smell nothing at all but more snow coming. I kept silent.

At perhaps two in the afternoon we heard the boat. A high-pitched voice was singing through the bushes:

> Despite the recent rain and snow,
> The river is still far too low!
> This tub to Cracow will not go.
> Let's plant the grain and watch it grow!

"How's that, brother boatman? It scans well, don't you think?"

"I think that if we don't get this boat off these rocks, we'll be iced in by morning and spend the winter here! My only pleasure will be in seeing you starve to death right next to me. Now *pull* on that rope, you foppish twit!"

"What? Starve while sitting on a hundred sacks of grain? That would take more ingenuity than a poet could muster. Let's see...

> While starving on a mound of rye,
> I saw a maiden floating by.
> She said..."

"Shut your goddamn trap and *pull!*"

"Hello, friends," Father Ignacy shouted.

"Who goes there?"

"A good Christian priest and a good Christian knight, come to assist you!"

As we forced our way through the brush toward the river, I whispered, "What do you mean calling me a knight? We don't even *have* knighthood!"

"And you are doubtless better off without it. But you are an officer in your military, aren't you? And a king's man besides? Knighthood would seem to be the equivalent."

"We don't have kings! There's an elected body that—"

"An excellent system. Oh, yes, don't mention the future to these men. It might frighten them. If they ask, tell them that you're Spanish."

"With blond hair?"

"Why not? Many Spaniards have blond hair. Or better yet, tell them you are English. You could easily pass for an Englishman."

Before I could reply, we broke through the brush and were on a rocky beach. In the middle of the river, a boat was securely wedged between two large rocks. The boat was about eight meters long and three meters wide and was pointed at both ends. A brightly garbed slender youth, wet to the waist, was clambering on board. Another man, in a wet gray tunic, was standing at the stern and looking at us. He held a longbow in his left hand and had an arrow fitted. There was something odd about the way he held it.

"Put away your weapon, boatman! We mean you help, not harm!" Father Ignacy held his book pouch above his head and waded into the water.

I unslung my pack and belt, held them high, and followed. That water was *cold*! I would have been prepared to swear in a court of law that it was below $-10°C$, if there had *been* any courts. My legs were numb before we got to the boat. Father Ignacy put his pouches aboard and clambered on after them. I did the same.

"Good afternoon, good boatman. I am Father Ignacy Sierpinski, and this knight is Sir Conrad Stargard."

"Good afternoon, good father and good sir knight. I am Tadaos Kolpinski, and I am at your service."

"A pleasure, Tadaos Kolpinski. We are bound for Cracow. What is your destination?"

"The same as yours, Father. Down the Dunajec and up the Vistula. Always ready to take on paying passengers, that's my motto, sirs." He ignored the poet.

"Well, you must understand our means are limited." Father Ignacy sat on a sack of grain. "Sir Conrad, I believe we were talking about Saint Augustine. Now, in *The City of God*—"

"But Father," Tadaos said, "you understand that we are having this difficulty—"

"And you feel that we should work for you, to help you out of it. This is acceptable to us, and there is only a slight matter of agreement on our wages."

"Ah, Father, I am a benevolent man, and if you will both assist me on our way to Cracow, I will feed you as well as I feed myself and depend only on your generosity for my remuneration."

"But surely it is written that a workman deserves his wages, and we are hardworking men, but poor. Yet we can get to Cracow on foot without the burden of hauling your grain. Shall we say food and six silver pennies per day per man?"

Tadaos gagged. "Please understand, Father, that I too am a poor man and that I have a wife and five poor children to feed. Surely you would not want to take food from their mouths with winter coming on. But perhaps one penny."

The bargaining went on for better than twenty minutes, with the boat hung up on the rocks and all of us sitting down. I could see that it would be difficult to get the rational principles of socialism across to these people and, further, that if I wanted to survive, I had a lot to learn. In the meantime, I set my mind to the technical problem of freeing the boat.

Eventually they settled on the wages of food and three pennies a day. Much later, I discovered that this was an excellent wage for an experienced boatman, which I wasn't

but which Father Ignacy was. He turned to me and said,
"Now then, Sir Conrad, have you solved our problem?"

"No, but I know what to try. Do you have a block and
tackle? No? Then the first thing to try is brute force. We
all get into the water and try to pull it off the rocks."

This is what Tadaos had in mind, so there were no
objections except from the poet. It was mutually agreed
that his opinions didn't count, so we all went over the
side. The poet—with assistance—went head first. I mean,
Father Ignacy was already in the water when the kid, who
was standing between the boatman and me, began to make
some rhymed objection. The boatman looked at me, and
I nodded. We picked up the poet and threw him in.

It was freezing. We tried lifting from the front, but the
boat wouldn't budge. We tried pulling from the back, but
no go. We rocked. We jerked, but it was no good. Stuck.

Shivering, we climbed back aboard.

"Well, that didn't work," I said to Tadaos. "How much
rope do you have aboard? And do you have any grease?"

"I have some cooking lard and maybe a gross of yards
of good rope."

"Okay. Give me the lard and tie this rope to the back
of the boat."

"The stern."

Yachtsmen are the same everywhere. They've got to
have their own idiot language. "The stern. I'll be back
soon." I had picked out a rounded vertical rock perhaps
fifty meters upstream of the boat. I went over the side
and waded toward it. Damn, but the water was cold! Small
bits of ice were floating in it! The rock was just what I
wanted—rounded on the upstream side and slightly concave. I greased the surface liberally and pulled the rope
around it. Then I greased about ten meters of the rope,
from the rock toward the boat, keeping the rope taut.

The boatman jumped into the water and shouted, "Okay,
here we go, you men!"

"What are you doing?" I yelled. "Get back into the
boat!"

"What do you mean? We have to pull ourselves off!"

"Yes, but the place to pull from is inside the boat."

"That's stupid, sir knight! We'll add our weight to the boat and make it harder to pull!"

"True, but our weight is small compared to the weight of the boat and the grain. And if we're inside the boat, we double our leverage. Be reasonable. Do it my way."

"Okay! We try it your way, just to show how dumb you are!"

I handed the rope up to Father Ignacy, and we struggled aboard.

"What do you think we'll do when this doesn't work?" the boatman asked.

"If this fails, we unload the boat one sack at a time and carry it to the shore. Then we try this again, and if it works, we load the boat back up again."

"That would take days! We'd lose half of the grain by dropping it in the water!"

"I know. So we try this first. Line up, you men. *Pull!*"

The boat moved, a centimeter at first, then two, then ten. Once off the rocks, it moved easily. After ten meters, the boatman belayed the line around the sternpost and ran up to the bow. "She's not taking in any water!" Soon, the line cast off and hauled in, we were on our way.

I soon noticed that along with the normal oarlocks on the sides, the boat had additional locks on the bow and stern. Their function was explained when Tadaos set an oar in each. He took the stern oar and put Father Ignacy on the bow. They used these to paddle the boat sideways in order to avoid obstructions in the river. Once he was sure that all was well, the boatman motioned me over to him.

"The good father knows his job well, and as for you, sir knight, that was as fine a piece of boatmanship as I have ever seen. I hope you'll accept my apologies for the rudeness I showed to your knightship."

"No problem. We were all under stress. Your apologies are accepted, sir boatman."

"Well, hardly that, Sir Conrad, but I have had my share. Why, there was this girl from Sandomierz, a blonde she was, that . . . but that's not what I want to talk about. I want to find out why you think that we pulled twice as hard standing in the boat as we did standing on the bottom."

"I wish I had a pencil and paper."

"Huh?"

"Some way to draw pictures for you. It wasn't that we pulled twice as hard; we didn't. Look at it from the point of view of the boat. We were pulling the rope, right? So at the same time we were pushing on the boat with our feet. Right?"

"Okay."

"Also, the rope went around the rock and came back and pulled on the boat, right?"

"So, we pushed it and pulled it at the same time. We got twice as much for nothing!"

"No, we didn't. When we pulled that rope for one of your yards, the rope pulled the boat only one half a yard. We got more force but less distance."

"So we broke even."

"Less than that. We lost some power rubbing the rope against the rock. It would have been better if we could have had a wheel on the rock."

"Like a pulley, you mean?"

Now, how in hell can an apparently intelligent man know about rope and pulleys and not about mechanical advantage? "Yes, like a pulley. Would you mind if I got out of these clothes? I'm freezing."

"Do what you will, Sir Conrad." Water was running off his clothes onto the floorboards and freezing there.

I couldn't do anything to help *his* wet clothes, but it would have been stupid for me to be uncomfortable with no gain for the others. I went to my pack and dug out my tennis shoes, light trousers, spare socks, and underwear. I changed quickly and stretched my wet things out on the grain bags. Actually, most of my things were wet.

I took stock of my gear. A pair of lightweight 7 X 25 mm binoculars. A Swiss army knife. A small hatchet. A good Buck single-bladed jackknife in a leather belt pouch. A canteen. A dented cooking kit. A compass. A few days' food. A sleeping bag. A ripped knapsack. A sewing kit. A first-aid kit. A stub of a candle. A few coins that might be worth something. Some paper money that probably wasn't. A smashed flashlight that I pitched over the side. With these few things, my total worldly possessions, I was to face the brutal thirteenth century.

I laid all of it out to dry.

At the bottom of the pack, I found the idiot seeds. That incredible redhead! It seemed like years ago rather than only forty-eight hours.

Chapter Four

THE RIVER grew increasingly interesting as the afternoon wore on, and I was glad that we had our experienced men at the helm, fighting our way past rocks and rapids.

I crawled under my still-damp sleeping bag and watched the scenery, which was pretty spectacular. The River Dunajec cuts through the Pieniny Mountains, and it was one gorgeous vista after another, with white marble cliffs thrusting up through the pine forest and sudden meadows with sheep grazing.

A castle clung high up on the slopes of a three-peaked mountain. I fumbled for my binoculars.

"That's Pieniny Castle," the boatman shouted. *Pieniny Castle!* I had toured its ruins once. Now, "dunce caps" topped the towers and the drawbridge was intact. It was here—will be here?—that King Boleslaw the Bashful took refuge after he lost the Battle of Chmielnik to Batu Khan, and Poland was left open to the Mongol invaders. That was—*will be*—in the spring of 1241, nine and a half years from now.

"What is that thing you're holding in front of your face?" Tadaos asked.

"Binoculars. They make things look close. Here, take a look."

"Later, Sir Conrad. I've got my hands full."

And he did, steering that overladen boat through rapids and eddies. I was dreading my turn at those oars.

It was dusk when he finally said, "That's the worst of it. It'll be clear sailing until tomorrow afternoon. Good Father, give your oar to the poet. Sir Conrad, come take mine. Just keep her toward the middle and you'll have no problems."

It was dark half an hour later when we slid quietly past the castle town of Sacz. It was lightless, and we saw no people.

I was back into my heavy clothes, dried now to mere dampness, but the kid at the bow was still shivering. He had been silent since his dunking, and I felt sorry for him. I supposed that I was just prejudiced. I had never met a goliard poet before, but I knew the type. He was exactly the same as the Lost Generation and the hoboes and the beatniks and the hippies and—what was the current group?—punkers, I think. Every decade or so, they all adopt a stranger slang, put on a different uniform, and say that *I* am a conformist and that *they* are doing something wondrous and new!

Groups who change their names every ten years do it for a good reason. People have discovered that they are bums, and they need new camouflage. Now, I'm Slavic and proud of it. The name was given to us by our enemies in the first millennium. "Slav" means "slave," which is about as derogatory as you can get. But we have never felt the need to change it, because we have never doubted our own self-worth. Try to get a Jew to call himself something different. Same thing.

Still, it probably wasn't the kid's fault that he was worthless. So when we were relieved to eat our supper—oatmeal and beer, but a lot of it—I sat down next to him.

"Look, kid, I'm sorry about throwing you into the river. It's just that there are times when you should not argue."

"That's okay, Sir Conrad. One gets used to insults following the muse."

"Yes . . . well. Look, are those the only clothes you have?"

"You see upon me all of my worldly possessions." He wore cheap red trousers and a thin yellow jacket with decorative buttons and worn-through elbows. He had a raggedy shirt that once might have been white. He had the tops of boots—the soles were almost completely gone—and a cap with a bent swan feather. He was as short as my other companions, but while they were thick, solid men, he was as skinny as a schoolgirl. He would have been an amusing sight if he had not been freezing to death.

"Well, maybe I can loan you something." I dug out my spare underwear and socks. Shirt and trousers. Tennis shoes and poncho.

"You'll probably swim in these, but they'll help keep you warm."

"I thank you, Sir Conrad. But don't talk of swimming, as I have done enough of that this year."

My clothes were a dozen sizes too big for him. He was awestruck by the elastic and zippers, and the buttonholes confused him.

I was boggled. His jackets had buttons all over, but he had never seen a buttonhole. How could you have buttons with no buttonholes? Was I really in the thirteenth century, or was I living a wacky dream?

My tennis shoes fit him perfectly. Did everybody back here have big feet?

When I had him dressed, he didn't look like a clown anymore. He looked like a war orphan.

We went back to our oars, and Tadaos said quietly to me, "Sir Conrad, you are too good for this world."

"Oh, he's just a kid."

"A kid who will rob you, given the chance."

"We'll see. How long is my watch?"

"Six hours; four hours to go. You have a full moon and a quiet river, so nothing much should happen; wake me if it does. Otherwise, wake me when the moon is high."

Food and warmth had cheered the kid up, and soon he launched into a monologue about himself and life. His name was Roman Makowski. He was fairly well educated for the times and had attended the University of Paris.

It seems that a student had been knifed and killed in a Paris alleyway and that the town council wouldn't do anything about it. The students, blaming the merchants, had rioted in protest and had apparently concentrated their attention on the wineshops and taverns. The town militia was called out, and the drinking and fighting spread. In the end, the king's guard had to enforce the peace. Two hundred students, including Roman, were jailed, and the university was shut down for a year.

Roman's father, who had been scrimping hard to pay for his son's education, was not amused. He paid Roman's way out of jail and then disinherited and threw him out of the house.

Roman was madly in love with three different girls without ever having touched one. He was wandering the world in search of Truth, and he hurt inside like a bag of broken glass. In short, he was a typical adolescent.

Eventually, the boatman told him to shut up.

Tadaos kept his bow and arrows in a rack near the stern oar. The bow was a huge thing, taller than the boatman and as big around as a golf ball. It took me a while to figure out what was odd about it.

Tadaos was right-handed, and the arrow rest was on the right side rather than the normal left. The arrows were well made and over a meter long. I was more than a head taller than he was, and I could only pull an 82-centimeter arrow.

The next morning I saw him use the bow while I was on watch again, waiting for dinner. Two meals a day seemed to be standard for the thirteenth century, and I was used to eating a heavy breakfast. The boatman had a fishing line over the side, and I hoped we weren't waiting for that.

"Quiet," Tadaos said in a stage whisper. He crept back to his bow while slipping a leather guard over his right thumb. He had the bow strung in an instant and fitted an arrow to the string.

But instead of drawing the bowstring in the normal way, with the first three fingers of the right hand, he used his thumb. This gave him a remarkably long draw. He elevated the bow to fully thirty degrees and let fly.

I had been so interested in his manner of shooting that it was a few seconds before I wondered what he was shooting at. We could be under attack! I looked out and saw nothing within reasonable range. Then suddenly a violent thrashing began in the bushes fully two hundred meters downstream by the water's edge.

Tadaos motioned to us, and we pulled for the bank.

"That's a remarkable bow," I said. "What kind is it?"

"Strange question coming from an Englishman," Tadaos said. "It's an English longbow. I bought it from a wool merchant."

After a little searching we found a ten-point buck with an arrow squarely in its skull. Incredible. I couldn't have made that shot with a rifle and telescopic sights!

"Well, gentlemen," the boatman said, "I can now offer better fare than oatmeal. Let's get it aboard! Quickly, now!"

Once we had manhandled the deer on board, I turned to Tadaos. "That was the finest shot that I have ever seen!"

"Thank you, Sir Conrad, but there was a lot of luck in it. Now, with a little more luck, we'll be in fine shape."

"What do you mean by that?"

"Oh, the baron hereabouts is partial to his hunting. He hangs poachers when he can catch them."

"Does he hang accessories to the crime as well?"

"That depends on his mood." Tadaos's eyes were twinkling.

The kid fainted.

I think that these people's shortness must have had a lot to do with vitamin deficiencies. They all craved that deer's internal organs. In the next three days, they ate everything in the animal but the eyeballs and the contents of the large intestine. When I asked for a steak rather than broiled lung, they thought I was crazy, but took me up on it. I also passed up the brain for some cutlets.

That evening we came to the Vistula and tied up for

the night. The trip so far had been all downstream, with little real work except at the rapids. But Cracow was upstream on the Vistula, and the next three days were drudgery. No mules were available although it seemed to me that Tadaos hadn't looked very hard.

So, we played Volga Boatmen. Three of us walked along the bank with ropes over our shoulders, while one stayed on the boat.

The work was grueling. At one point, the poet was on the boat, Tadaos was walking in front of me with his bow slung over his back, and the priest was in the rear.

"Tadaos," I said, "if you must work us like horses, you should at least provide us with horse collars."

"What do you mean?"

"You saw my backpack? Make something like that, with a strap across the chest. Tie the rope to the back and a man could at least rest his arms."

Tadaos pondered this for a while. "What if you had to let go in a hurry?"

"Tie the rope in a slipknot."

"Hmm. Not a bad thought, Sir Conrad. I'll make some up, next trip. Do you want to come along to see how they work?"

"No, thank you!"

It was late in the afternoon, and except for a tiny village at the juncture of the Dunajec and the Vistula, we hadn't seen a single habitation or another human being all day.

"I can't get over how empty this country is," I said.

"There are people," the boatman said, "but the river is too open, too dangerous. They live back in the woods in little fortified towns protected by a knight or two."

"What are they afraid of?"

"Bandits. Wolves. Mostly other knights."

"Why doesn't the government do something?"

"The government?" He spat. "Poland doesn't have a government! Poland has a dozen petty dukes who spend their time arguing with each other instead of defending the country. Poland is a land without a king!

"The last king of Poland died a hundred years ago, and he divided the country up among his five sons just so they'd each have their own little duchy to play with! And each of *them* divided it up still further, being nice to *their* children.

"Did any of them think about the land? No! They treated the country like it was a dead man's bag of gold to be divided up among the heirs."

"You paint too bleak a picture, master boatman," Father Ignacy said. "There is a strong movement afoot to unify the country. Henryk the Bearded now holds all of Silesia, along with western Pomerania, half of Great Poland, and most of Little Poland. He has the throne at Cracow, and mark my words, his son, young Henryk, will be our next king. I can smell it."

"You think Henryk's line can be kings? Does the Beard act like a king? When Conrad of Mazovia asked for aid against the Prussian raiders, did Henryk come to his aid? No! Henryk was too busy playing politics to help out another Polish duke, so Duke Conrad went and invited those damned Knights of the Cross in. They've taken as much Polish territory as they have Prussian! It was like inviting in the wolves to get rid of the foxes!"

"But politics is an essential part of unifying the country, Tadaos. At least the Polish dukes have never made war on one another the way they do in England or Italy or France."

"No, they prefer ambushes, poison, and an occasional knifing. There'll be war with those Knights of the Cross, *you* mark *my* words on that!"

There was no arguing with that statement, so the conversation died for a while.

After supper that night, I was sitting with Father Ignacy apart from the others. "You know, Father, it was the inn. It had to be the inn."

"What was what inn, my son?"

"The Red Gate Inn, on the trail near Zakopane. I must have come back in time when I slept in the inn. Those double steel doors on the storeroom—I had to have been in some kind of time machine."

"Do they make time machines in the twentieth century?"

"What? No. Of course not. But don't you see? If they had a time machine, they could be from any century."

"And you think that your being here is the result of some mechanism rather than an act of God?"

"Father, *anything* can be an act of God! God can do whatever He wants, but I have to deal with the world in the only way I know how, as an engineer. I think that I should turn back and go back to that inn. Maybe I can find the answer there."

"My son, in the first place, what you are speaking is very close to blasphemy. In the second, there is absolutely no possibility of your making it back up the Dunajec alive, not at this time of year. You could freeze to death before you were halfway there. I wouldn't try it myself except on orders from the Pope, and then I would go knowing that I was a martyr."

"Still, I must try."

"You may believe in machines, my son, but I believe in God. I think that you are here for a reason, and I think that you must find out what it is."

"But—"

"Then there is the fact that we have an agreement with the boatman to take his grain to Cracow. I'm not sure, but I think it likely that this boat of grain represents all of his wordly goods. If this boat gets frozen in, he is a ruined man."

We were silent for a while.

"Father, if you are so concerned about the boatman, why don't you worry about the kid? Tadaos is the sort who could survive almost anything. But from what Tadaos has said about Cracow, the poet isn't likely to live out the winter."

"My son, there is a vast difference between a reasonably honest workingman and a goliard poet. Don't you know anything about them? They glory in sin and drunkenness and debauchery. They mock the Church and ridicule the social order."

"Oh, he's just a lost kid. I think that if you'd give him a chance he'd turn out all right."

"Give him a chance? What do you mean?"

"Give him a job! He's fairly well educated. He's attended the University of Paris. He tells me that he's an artist as well as a poet. If you need copyists, he's a better choice than I am."

"You really think that I should let *that* into a monastery?"

"I know you should."

"Know? Is this something that you've read in your histories?"

"No, Father. Let's say that I can smell it."

"Well, I'll think on it. But I make no promises. There *is*, however, a promise I want *you* to make, my son. A promise of silence. You must tell no one—and I mean absolutely no one!—that you are a visitor from the future. I give you absolution to invent some plausible lie and to tell it to any who questions you.

"The truth of this matter must be decided by the Holy Church, and until such time as a decision is made, you will be silent."

"But why, Father?"

"Why? Well, in the first place, because I am your confessor and I am telling you to. In the second, do you have any idea of what sort of controversy would be generated by your claims? Hundreds, maybe thousands of people would plague you, wanting to know their futures. Some lunatic would likely start claiming that you were a new messiah. Others would surely denounce you as a creature of the Devil and demand your execution. Do you really want to be at the center of that sort of thing?"

"Good God! No, Father, of course not!"

"Then you will make this vow?"

"Uh, yes, Father. But what does the Church have to do with this?"

"Why, everything! I must make a full and complete report on this matter to my superiors. I am fully confident that my report, with annotations by my superiors, will eventually reach the Vatican and the Pope himself. It is likely that he will appoint commissioners to look into the matter. They will report back, and a decision will eventually be made."

"Decision? On what?"

"On what? Can't you realize that you may be a direct instrument of God, sent by Him for some special purpose?"

"I do not feel like a direct instrument of God."

"Your *feelings* have nothing to do with it."

"Hmph. Just how long will this decision-making process take?" I asked.

"Maybe two years, maybe ten. But until it is completed, you will not discuss this. I want your vow of silence!"

"What, exactly, do you want me to do?"

"You will get on your knees, and you will repeat after me . . ."

I did as he asked and made a lengthy, legalistic vow. Father Ignacy had apparently been thinking about it for some time. I am keeping that vow, but there was nothing in it that forbade me from writing a private diary, in a language that no one in the thirteenth century could possibly read.

Just before I fell asleep, I said, "Father Ignacy? What if the Church decides that I am not an instrument of God? What if it decides that I am an instrument of the Devil?"

"In that unlikely event, my son, I would expect you, as a good Christian, to obey the dictates of the Church."

Getting to sleep that night was not easy.

Chapter Five

THE NEXT morning, we began pulling the boat as soon as it was possible to see. The path along the banks of the Vistula was not good. It went up and over countless ridges, down and into hundreds of muddy rivulets. Every few hours we had to get into the boat and row it upstream past a creek or swamp that we couldn't wade through.

Still, pulling was easier than rowing, so we slogged along with ropes over our shoulders.

Thinking about it, I didn't see how mules could possibly have done the job that we did.

"Well, in the summer the water's higher and most of the swamps are covered," Tadaos explained.

"But can't you do something about improving this trail? A few thousand man-hours of work, some small wooden bridges, would cut our labor in half."

"There's been some talk about a boatman's guild to get the landlords to do something in return for the tolls we have to pay, but nothing has come of it. Guilds can work in a city, where people are close to each other; but on the river, we're too spread out. Some men work short hauls, between two points. Some work long ones. Some, like me, pick up and deliver wherever they can get a contract or make a good bargain. How could a guild work over the entire Vistula River, with all of its tributaries? I've been on this river for eight years, and I don't know half of the men who own boats."

"But can't the government do something?"

"Damn it! I've told you that there *is no government!*"

I was quiet for a while. "What's all this about tolls? I haven't seen you pay any tolls."

"You were asleep when they caught us at Wojnicz, back on the Dunajec. I would have tried to slip by at night, like we did at Sacz, but this time of year there's so little traffic that they usually don't keep a guard boat out, and I was worried that if we wasted time, the river might freeze.

"Brzesko's around the next bend, and we've got to walk by it. They'll catch us, sure."

Brzesko had tall masonry walls topped with two mail-clad crossbowmen. It also had a pompous official, who haggled with our boatman for a quarter hour before they settled on a toll of twenty-one pence.

I'd never seen a functioning castle before. I wanted to explore, but Tadaos wouldn't stand for it.

"It's bad enough paying their tolls; we don't have to support their inn as well," he said as we proceeded. "Damned bastards on the wall with their crossbows. If there were only one of them, I could have gotten three arrows into him before he got the silly thing cocked."

"You'd kill a man for twenty-one pence?" Father Ignacy asked.

"No, Father. Just talking, and anyway, I have to come by here eight or ten times a year. If I killed them, I'd be caught for sure. Still and all, you've got to admit that it's a pleasant thought."

Soon it was my turn to ride on the boat, and I could relax and think.

Languages all change, but they change at vastly different rates, and I think that English must be the most changeable of all.

When I was first learning English, I was shocked to discover that an intelligent, educated, English-speaking person of the twentieth century was unable to read Chaucer in the original without taking special college courses.

Think about it! A language changed to unintellegibility in six hundred years. No, less than that, because two hundred years later Shakespeare wrote his plays, and they *are* intelligible to the educated American.

On the other hand, any decently educated twentieth-century Spaniard can enjoy *The Poem of the Cid* without difficulty, and it was written in 1140.

The Slavic languages are among the world's most stable. The east and west Slavs—the Russians and the Poles—split off from each other around the middle of the first millennium. Yet, despite the fifteen hundred years of separate development, it is possible—by speaking slowly and listening carefully—for a Pole and a Russian to communicate.

So, despite my trouble, things could have had been much worse. Had I been dumped into thirteenth-century England, I would not have been able to make myself understood. As it was, people thought that I had a funny accent, but I could get by.

That night I was talking to Roman Makowski, the poet.

"What do you plan to do once we get to Cracow?" I asked.

"Plan? I have no plans other than to do what I have always done—follow the muse."

"But how is that going to keep you alive? Winter is coming on."

"Something will turn up. Who knows? Perhaps the keeper of a prosperous brothel will want seductive scenes painted on his walls for the encouragement of his patrons, and I shall be paid some of my fees in trade. The muse takes care of her own."

"The muse has not done well by you thus far."

"This must be admitted. Are you offering some suggestions?"

"One. Father Ignacy is in need of copyists, and you are qualified for this work. If you were to impress him with your character and ask him politely, you might be offered a job."

"Father Ignacy is already impressed with my character, though not favorably. I might better ask a job of the Devil;

at least there would be a chance of acceptance. Furthermore, the prospect of working all winter in a monastery is frightening. Consider—a whole season of sobriety! Months without touching a woman! An eternity of waking up every three hours to pray! No, the Devil would make a better offer."

"Get serious, kid. A month from now you could be dead of cold or starvation! You'd best not ignore the only iron you have in the fire!"

"The only iron in the fire! What an excellent phrase! May I borrow it?"

"Yes, and stop changing the subject. Are you going to follow my suggestion?"

"Sir Conrad, what exactly do you think I should do?"

"To start with you should ask him to confess you, and after that you might try praying a little."

"Oh, very well. It certainly can't hurt, and it might help. That artistic whoremaster could still turn up!"

I shook my head. "Go to sleep, kid."

We got to Cracow so late the next day that we walked the last kilometer by torchlight.

As we tied up to the dock, Tadaos said, "Well, lads, we made it. You can sleep on the boat tonight—at no charge—or there's a passable inn up that street on your left."

"Thank you for the invitation, but I'll never sleep on a grain sack again," I said.

"I share Sir Conrad's feelings," Father Ignacy said. "But first there's the question of our remuneration."

"But of course. I'd almost forgotten." The boatman counted out fifteen pence each to the priest and me and six pence to the poet. I guess he hadn't bargained as well.

Father Ignacy and I started off. I called back, "Tadaos, aren't you coming?"

"And leave my grain for the thieves? I shall sleep well enough here. You go, and come back in the spring if you need work!"

"I just might do that." The poet was staring at us wistfully. "Come on, kid. I'll buy you a beer." He followed us like a puppy dog.

The inn was sleazy, and the beer was sour. The food wasn't good, and the service was surly. Nonetheless, it was the first roof over our heads in five days, and it felt good to sit on something that wasn't a grain sack.

Food and lodging were a penny each, which didn't seem bad until I discovered that we all had to share the same bed.

I don't know why it felt strange getting into bed with two other men—for the past five nights, we'd been snuggling together for warmth under my unzipped sleeping bag—but somehow it did.

Three in the bed wouldn't have been so bad, but we soon discovered that we had a few thousand uninvited guests. I spent half my time scratching fleas and the other half being shaken awake as my bunkmates scratched theirs.

By midnight I'd had it with the little bastards. Tadaos's boat might be cold and lumpy, but at least it was free of vermin. My invitation was doubtless still good, so I crept out of bed, put on my pack, and felt my way down the dark hallway and out into the street.

The street was as dark as the hallway of the inn. The night was cloudy, and there were no outdoor lights at all. I fumbled through my pack until I found the candle stub. I lit it with my cigarette lighter, redonned my pack, and headed for the river.

Most of my attention was focused on keeping the candle lit while watching where I put my feet. The boats on the river were the darkest of shadows, and I couldn't tell one from the other.

"Tadaos!" I shouted, "where are you? Tadaos! Wake up!"

"Eh? What? Damn!" his familiar voice yelled. I suddenly realized that there were four figures on his boat: Tadaos at the stern and three other men who were crawling toward him with naked daggers!

"Look out!" I shouted, but the boatman was already fiercely swinging his steering oar down at the head of one of his assailants. A loud crack told of both oar and skull breaking.

I was dumbfounded. If I put down the candle and aided Tadaos, we'd be fighting in the dark. The only thing I had approaching a decent weapon was my camp hatchet, but it was deep within my pack. I fumbled out my Buck knife and was worrying it open with one hand.

Tadaos showed no such hesitation. As the first thief collapsed at his feet, he threw the broken stub of the oar into the face of the second. Even as the thief raised his hands to ward off the sharp broken wood, Tadaos had his belt knife out. He was on his man in an instant, and with a single, brutal upthrust he put his long knife under the thief's ribs and into his heart.

The third thief, seeing Tadaos's deadly efficiency in front of him—and probably my size behind him—these were all very small people—broke and ran. He shoved past me before I had my jackknife open and ran for the cover of some trees.

Faster than I would have believed possible, the boatman had his bow out and bent. As the thief ran past the first of the trees, Tadaos let fly. The arrow caught the man in the throat, knocking him off his feet and nailing him to the tree.

All this had happened in a few seconds, in horrifying silence and to the dim flickering of a single candle.

I shined the light into the boat. Tadaos was unbending his bow, obviously unhurt. The forehead of the first thief was caved in, a bloody notch centimeters wide and centimeters deep running from his nose to the top of his head, obviously a death wound.

The second was on his back with a knife buried to the hilt in his solar plexus, the hilt pointing downward. His eyes were open, his features bore an expression of astonishment, and he wasn't breathing.

The last thief was struggling feebly at the tree. I finally got my jackknife open and went to him with some vague idea about cutting him down and administering first aid.

Tadaos brushed by me.

"Thanks, Sir Conrad, but it was me they were trying

to kill, so the honors are mine." With no more concern than if he had been swatting a mosquito, the boatman put his bloody knife efficiently into the thief's jugular vein and then carefully slit the throat open to remove his arrow for reuse without damaging the fletching.

I was too shocked and horrified to do anything. "But shouldn't we call the police?"

"Police? You mean the Guard? Sir Conrad, are you absolutely out of your mind?" He searched the body and wiped his knife clean on the man's trousers "Damn, not a penny on him."

He sheathed his knife, slipped the arrow under his belt, and started dragging the corpse back toward his boat. "Would you mind getting his feet? Well, I guess you would mind, judging from your expression. Can't you understand that these cutthroats were about to rob and murder me?"

He dragged the body until he saw the knife the man had dropped. "Now that's a well-made thing," he said, handling it. "Tools of his trade, as it were. Worth thirty pence easily at either of the knife shops in Cracow. I'm tempted to keep it. Still, it might be recognized. Best to play it safe." He pitched it twenty meters into the river.

"Stop!" I said, too late. "You'll need that for evidence to prove that they came at you armed."

"Evidence? Are you still thinking about the Guard? Sir Conrad, the night must have fuddled your head. Consider our position! We are strangers here. These men are doubtless locals with dozens of friends and relatives who would swear to their honesty and good character. We'd both be in jail for six months even if they did find us innocent, which is unlikely. Personally, I have no intention of being hanged."

By this time he had the body into the river and was giving it a good shove into the current. The weapons and bodies of the other two men got the same watery grave.

My God! I had spent five days in the company of a cold-blooded murderer!

Tadaos washed his knife and arrow and said, "Well,

time I got back to sleep. Thank you for calling out when you did. You probably saved my life. But what were you doing out at this time of the night?"

"Well, uh . . . there were fleas in the inn, and I couldn't sleep."

"You're welcome to sleep on the boat, Sir Conrad."

"Uh, no . . . no. I'll head back."

"As you like. Come to me in the spring if you need work."

Eventually I crawled back into bed with the priest and the poet and the fleas.

It was a long while before I fell asleep.

At first gray light, the priest announced his intention of finding a public bath; Roman and I followed him, scratching at our new boarders.

The bath was another penny, although we got our clothes laundered in the bargain. Two huge wooden tubs were sunk into the floor: a warm one for scrubbing with a foul-smelling brown soap and a hot one for rinsing and soaking. I'd been more than a week without a bath, and it was glorious.

The public bath was just that—there were a dozen other men in with us. I heard some feminine giggles, and I looked around in the smoky gloom. Everybody had moustaches.

I eventually realized that the room and the tubs had been built twice their apparent size and that a wooden room divider had been added later. The other side was for women. There were a few knotholes in the wood.

"A good thing, that wall," Father Ignacy said. "The Church had to threaten the bathhouse keepers with excommunication before they put them up."

"You mean that bathing used to be both sexes together?"

"Yes. A disgusting barbarism."

I kept my opinions to myself and turned my attention to shaving. In my mirror, I saw Roman wander with extreme casualness over to the partition and quickly peek through a knothole. Later, I sat down next to him in the hot tub.

"I saw you at the knothole," I whispered. "Father

Ignacy might have seen you as well. Have you forgotten that you are trying to impress him with your good character so he'll give you a job?"

"No, sir, but temptation is a hard thing to resist."

"Agreed. Did you see anything worthwhile?"

"All I saw was another eye staring back at me."

When we left the bathhouse, the sun was bright and the church bells were ringing.

"Ah, tierce already," Father Ignacy said. "I must go and report to my new abbot. Sir Conrad, I suggest that you spend the day amusing yourself in the city and then visit me at the Franciscan monastery a little after none."

"Tierce?" I asked. "None?"

"When the sun is there," he said pointing to a midafternoon position, "and you hear the bells, it will be none." He left without mentioning Roman.

I said, "Well, we have some time to kill. Shall we start with some food?"

"Some food would be welcome, Sir Conrad, but then I must leave you and search for a way to make a living. I compute that my week's wages will be gone by tomorrow morning."

"I thought that we'd decided that you were going to work at the monastery."

"*We* have decided, but Father Ignacy has not."

The dock area was incredibly sleazy, with shabby wooden huts crowding an unpaved road. The road was ankle-deep in shit. Human shit, horse shit, dog shit, pig shit, cow shit, and doubtless other varieties that did not immediately impinge on my consciousness. I tried to maintain a stoic attitude as the foul, oily stuff squished and sucked at my boots,

"If we eat here, we'll likely pick up a new set of fleas," I said. "Let's go within the city walls to find our dinner; it must be cleaner there."

"It won't be cleaner, Sir Conrad, but it might be drier."

The city walls were brick. They were only four meters high and in poor repair. They could not be of any military use, but their purpose was evident when a sleepy guard demanded a toll of us.

After a few minutes of haggling, he let us both through for a penny.

It was no cleaner inside the city. People threw their garbage directly into the streets, and pigs ran loose, scavenging through it. Dogs fought each other for scraps, and chickens picked at the leavings. How people determined the ownership of the animals was beyond me.

Yet in juxtaposition to this unbelievable filth, men and women in gorgeous finery rode tall horses through the fetid mire, ignoring the shit as they ignored those of us on foot. I soon found myself ignoring those haughty, velvet-covered visions right back.

We found an inn that looked fairly clean, or at least cleaner than the first four we had looked into. After more dickering with the innkeeper, during which time he insisted on seeing our money, we settled on a halfpenny each for all we wanted of pork stew, bread, and ale.

As we sat down at the table, a female voice asked, "Would you like some company?"

She looked to be about twelve years old and underfed. Her dress was dirty and patched, and she was not clean. She was barefoot, and she was trying to smile and keep her eyes off the steaming bowl of stew in front of me.

"Why not?" I asked. "You look hungry. Would you like some dinner?"

"Well..."

"Innkeeper, bring a third meal to our table!"

"Yes, Sir Conrad!" he shouted from a back room. But when he arrived with a tray of food and drink, he saw the girl and said, "You again! How many times must I chase you out of here? Sir Conrad, surely you can't expect me to serve beggars and prostitutes."

"Surely I *can* expect you to show a bit of Christian charity! This is a little girl who is hungry. Now, put the food on the table."

"But you don't know what she is!"

"I know that she's hungry."

"But the cost—"

"I ordered it, and I'll pay for it. Now do as I say."

He left the tray on the table and walked off, grumbling. I stood and served the girl myself. "All of this haggling and argument is beginning to spoil my disposition."

"A thing to be guarded against," Roman said. "It spoils the digestion, and that can be ill afforded when good food is available in plenty."

"Yes, Sir Conrad. Please, sit down," the girl said.

So I sat. Introductions were made. Her name was Malenka. She was an orphan and had lived in Cracow for two years. Conversation drifted in the course of the meal, and it was soon obvious that she survived by renting her body to all comers.

"And what do you charge for this?" Roman asked.

She looked at me, trying to smile. "I was hoping you'd ask. A day and a night for only a penny."

I saw Roman fumbling among his dwindling supply of coins, and I thought it best to nip this in the bud. I took three pennies from my pocket and put them in front of her. "Do you go to church?"

"Yes, my lord. Every morning." Her eyes were downcast. "It's a good place to find customers."

"Well, next time I want you to do some praying."

"Yes, my lord. But I am yours for the next three days. Where shall we go?"

I had been a long time without a woman, and I confess that I was tempted. But this brutal century had not yet deprived me of my morals, and Conrad Schwartz was not a molester of children.

"*I* shall go to the Franciscan monastery, and *you* shall stay right here. It seems that you have offended the innkeeper somehow. You will make it up to him by working for him for three days."

"The innkeeper!" she cried.

"You will wash his dishes, sweep his floors, and sleep alone."

"What?" Roman exploded. "Sir Conrad, this is a foul jest! If you won't make use of her, then by the muse, I will!"

"By God, you will not! What will you tell Father Ignacy

when you next confess to him? That you took an adolescent girl by force?"

"What force? She offered, and you paid!" Roman stood.

"She was forced by hunger and poverty, which are more persuasive than any sword or club. And a good deal more brutal! Now, sit down and finish your beer."

The innkeeper came over. "Forgive me, Sir Conrad, but I couldn't help overhearing much of what was said. What is it that you are planning?"

"I'm going to give you a servant for three days. Put her to honest work. If she's useful, you might consider some more permanent arrangement with her. Is this acceptable to you?"

"Well, yes. But why are you doing this?"

"Call it an act of faith. Look, here's the money for the meal. Come on, Roman. It's time to go."

Once out on the street, Roman said, "Sir Conrad, you are a very strange man."

We wandered through the city's mixture of squalor and barbaric splendor for several hours, stopping to pray at Saint Andrew's Church.

Despite its missing the familiar baroque towers, the church seemed somehow bigger than when I had visited it in the twentieth century. Perhaps it was the lack of more imposing structures around it. I looked up wistfully at the round towers of Royal Wawel Castle and the cathedral. But Roman shook his head.

"That's not for the likes of us, Sir Conrad."

"Surely they wouldn't turn away honest visitors," I said. "Anyway, I'm a knight."

"You are a knight without a horse, or armor, or even a sword. Try if you like. I'll wait for you down here."

"Perhaps you're right. Anyway, it's time we found the Franciscan monastery."

The monastery was austere, but it was at least clean, gloriously clean by comparison to the festering slime that surrounded it. A brown-robed monk led us to a room where we could spruce up, and I began to understand all the biblical references to the washing of feet. A few hours of walking in shit does amazing things to them.

When we were presented to Father Ignacy, he welcomed me profusely and told me that my appointment as a copyist had been confirmed, at four pence a day. He showed us around and asked me if my cell was acceptable.

"It's better than some quarters I've had in the military."

"Excellent. Supper is just after vespers, and I will see you then." He turned to leave.

"Father, what about Roman?"

"I'm sorry, Sir Conrad, but I feel that his employment here would be ill advised."

"But why not give him a chance, for a few days at least?"

"That would only give him time to spread his ungodly attitudes."

Father Ignacy left, and Roman looked wilted.

"Cheer up, kid. Come back tomorrow and ask him again. He'll soften up eventually."

"Tomorrow I shall be penniless."

"Not quite." I gave him the eight pence I had left. "I won't be needing this. You pay me back when you can."

"Thank you, Sir Conrad. And bless you. But he won't see me."

"Ask him to hear your confession. He can hardly deny you that. See me afterward."

The next day, the poet was still dejected.

"It's no use, Sir Conrad. He won't give in. I can't find any other work in town, either."

"All I can say is, try again tomorrow."

The next day he was again rejected, and broke as well. I'd earned a day's pay by then; I drew it from the Brother Purser and gave it to the kid.

This went on for four more days before Father Ignacy called me to him.

"What's this business of your drawing your pay daily and giving it to that goliard poet?"

"Well, Father, I can hardly let the kid starve, can I?"

"It's embarrassing. You're outdoing the Church with your charity!"

"There is an easy solution to your problem, Father."

"Yes?"

"Hire him. Show some Christian charity yourself."

"But . . ." You could see that he wanted to swear. "Very well! But if this goes wrong, I'll hold you responsible!"

"Thank you, Father."

Chapter Six

I WAS not cut out to be a copyist.

Some of the problems centered on my lack of skill. Please understand that I spent years at a drawing board. My technical drawing was good, and my engineering lettering was considered excellent. I had seventeen years of formal schooling and am quite literate.

But I was not literate *in Latin.* And engineering lettering on mylar with a Japanese mechanical pencil has *nothing* in common with doing Gothic "Black" lettering on parchment with a goose quill and ink.

Furthermore, parchment is a kind of leather and is hideously expensive. The only technique they had for erasing an error was to wait a week for the ink to dry and then sand it off with a stone.

They did accept my suggestion to use a T square and triangle to lay out pages. They were thankful for this. They also considered me to be a monumental klutz.

Then there were the working conditions. You sat on a bench in a cold, dark scriptorium. The only windows in the room were covered with oiled parchment and might as well have been bricked over. This light was supplemented by an oil lamp at your elbow that in fact burned pig fat, under protest.

Most of my fellow copyists didn't speak much Latin either, so the straw boss—excuse me—*author*—read it off one letter at a time. He said "A," and you wrote "A." He said "B," you wrote "B." He said "C" . . . This went on for two and a half hours, until it was time to go and pray again.

Four such sessions made for a ten-hour day, which was not so bad by itself. In the twentieth century, I often worked longer than that when we were behind schedule. But when added to the time spent praying, it became excessive.

I had always considered myself a religious man. Going to mass before work is not such a bad idea. But in addition, going to the chapel another eight times a day to pray is a *bit much*. Especially when those eight times are spread out at three-hour intervals—Compline at 9 P.M., Matins at midnight, Lauds at 3 A.M., and then up again at 4:30 to catch 5 A.M. mass . . .

I was not sufficiently sinful to need that much prayer. Oh, since I hadn't taken any vows, I wasn't *required* to do all this, but they liked to wake me up anyway, just in case I wanted to beef up my soul a little.

Actually, it had been seven weeks or so since I had touched a female human being, and I *wanted* to do a little sinning. I was making an allegedly excellent salary—four pence a day—but was unable to spend much of it because I only had Sunday afternoons off, when the inns were closed.

It did not help matters that the goliard poet kid was an excellent calligrapher. Working his way through the University of Paris, he'd made his living expenses copying books. In addition, in the two weeks that he'd been at the monastery, the kid had gotten religion. He'd taken vows as a novice so that he could continue doing precisely the same job as before, but without pay.

The overnight conversion from professed sinner to religious fanatic is a fairly common one, but I've never understood it.

In any event, when I was notified right after five o'clock mass that Father Ignacy wanted to speak to me privately, I knew that I was going to be fired. I *deserved* to be fired, and one part of me *wanted* to be fired.

Another part of me wanted to continue eating regularly.

"Good morning, Father. I know what you have to say, so do not agonize yourself. I know that I am incompetent as a copyist."

"You've shown much improvement, my son. You would, in time, become a competent copyist. But you would never be a *happy* copyist, so I have found you another position. I know a merchant who requires someone skilled in keeping ledgers of purchase, sales, profits, and that sort of thing. This man travels constantly all over Europe, and you would be his companion. Do you think that you would be qualified for such a position?"

I'd had a few basic accounting courses, double-entry bookkeeping, and so on. Seeing more of the world would be pleasant. Getting out of the monastery would be a joy. "For that I know I would be qualified."

"Excellent. He often carries large sums of cash, and part of your duties would be to defend him if necessary. But no man not a fool would attack a giant such as yourself, so I expect that this will be only a formality. Still acceptable?"

"Yes."

"Good. Your salary will be doubled, to eight silver pennies per day. You will be required to provide yourself with horse, arms, and armor, but he will advance you the price of this and deduct it from your pay."

"Armor! What do I need with armor?"

"Sir Conrad, *I* can travel freely and safely because I am protected by the Church and obviously penniless. You lack this protection and will be escorting a wealthy man. Enough said?"

"Oh, whatever you say, Father."

"Good. He's waiting in the next room. If he likes you, we'll consider the bargain sealed. His name is Boris Novacek, and he's eager to leave as quickly as possible."

Novacek looked me up and down, grunted, and said, "Well, he looks to be the type. Sir Conrad, I understand that you are an officer. How many men have you commanded?"

"At one time, Mr. Novacek? The most was a hundred

and seven." I had been in charge of electronics maintenance at an airport, but why complicate matters?

"I see. And the terms are acceptable to you?"

"Eight cents a day, with you to advance my horse and armor. I assume that you will pay traveling expenses, food, and lodging?"

"Of course. But often lodging is not available, and half the time we sleep under a tree."

"Agreed, then." And we shook on it.

One of the glories of the thirteenth century is that there are no forms to fill out in triplicate.

Our first stop was at a used armor shop, since new armor was all custom-made, and that could take months. I quickly learned that "used armor" generally meant somebody had died in it, but I was losing my squeamishness.

The armory had a lot in common with a twentieth-century junkyard, and at first I despaired of finding things tall enough to fit me.

Except for helmets there was no plate armor at all, which was just as well because fit is not so important with chain mail. The stuff stretches better than double-knit. But you have to wear a heavily padded garment, a gambeson, under the mail, and they didn't have anything close to my size. I decided to trust my thermal underwear, sweater, blue jeans, and windbreaker to protect myself.

I found a mail shirt, a hauberk, that seemed to be of fair quality. It was of a good grade of wrought iron, and each individual link was riveted, not just bent in a circle. It was made for a man as wide as I was but a good deal shorter. The sleeves were intended to be full-length but went barely past my elbows, and the knee-length skirt barely covered my crotch.

Some long mailed gauntlets took care of my forearms, and I needed gloves anyway. The clerk scrounged up a sort of skirt that went from waist to knees. Some "full-length" leggings served as shin guards, greaves.

I rejected the full barrel-style helmet—you can't *see* out of the things—and found an open-faced casque that gave some neck protection without having more chain mail jingling around. Under the casque, one wore a thick rope skullcap.

It was a mismatched set, but I wasn't entering a beauty contest.

When the shopkeeper, a German, totaled up the bill, I felt my testicles tighten. For thirty pounds of wrought iron, this man was asking for two years' pay!

I said to my new boss, "Mr. Novacek, you are more familiar with shopkeepers than I am. Could I persuade you to see about arriving at a more equitable price?"

"With pleasure, Sir Conrad." He smiled with delight and then launched into the shopkeeper, who was obviously and hopelessly outclassed. I thought Father Ignacy was a good bargainer, but here I was seeing a genius practice his own special art form. He used an incredible mixture of politeness, bombast, pleading, and outright abuse. He criticized the armor I had selected until I was embarrassed for having picked it out. They started at fifty-five hundred pence. He had gotten the shopkeeper down to fifteen hundred pence when he suddenly screamed in anguish and stomped out of the shop. I had brains enough to follow.

"That was undoubtedly the finest display of commercial persuasion that I have ever encountered." His flow-eriness was wearing off on me.

"I thank you, Sir Conrad, and I compliment you on your good judgment in your choice of negotiators. But it's thirsty work, and a drop of beer is in order."

"An excellent idea, Mr. Novacek."

Drinking at 9 A.M. was not uncommon in the thirteenth century. I guess if you can't have coffee and a proper breakfast, beer is your next best bet. Some of the customers in the tavern were already in their cups.

The waitress was not pretty, but she was prompt, young, and eager.

"No time for that, Sir Conrad. Now that we have your armor selected, there is still the matter of getting you a horse with saddle and bridle, a sword, a lance, and a shield. You will also need a good, warm cloak."

"But Mr. Novacek, we don't have the armor. Surely

you recall that you left the armor shop shouting at the shopkeeper, criticizing not only his father and mother but his mother's husband as well."

"I can see that you have much to learn about commercial negotiation. I shall be back in that shop twice more this afternoon, and the final price will be seven hundred and twenty pence."

He was wrong. I got that armor for seven hundred and eighteen pence.

"Incidentally, Sir Conrad, you have a good eye for steel. You really did pick the best he had, and I quite agree with you on those barrel helmets. They're fine for a massed battle, where junk is flying from every direction and there isn't much you can do about it. But in the sorts of fights we're likely to see, hearing and eyesight are important."

But of course, we weren't likely to encounter any violence.

I'd been on a horse perhaps two dozen times in my life, always at rental stables, riding calm, tame horses that here would be called palfreys. I liked horses, but I was by no means a horseman. My boss, however, insisted on going to the only stable in Cracow that sold Chargers, exclusively. Chargers are very large, very strong, and very mean. They had eight of the things. As I walked down the line of them, one bit me, two more tried to, and I just missed being kicked. Having to ride one of the brutes for the next few years was not a pleasant prospect.

In the back of the stable was a corral with a single horse, a big red mare as big as any of the stallions. I whistled to her, and damned if she didn't come. I stroked her nose. "What's the story on this one?"

"Surely you jest, Sir Conrad! A knight in my employ riding a mare? I'd be a laughingstock!"

"And so would I, Mr. Novacek. I only asked!"

"But an excellent mount, good sirs!" the stablemaster said. "That horse has been fully battle-trained and is most intelligent."

"Battle-trained? Who in his right mind would take a mare into battle? Haw! She'd likely go into heat halfway through the fight! Would you want our good Sir Conrad on her back when a *real* Charger tries to mount her?"

"But no, my lord. That mare is completely indifferent to stallions. She shuns them, sir."

"Hah! So she's not even good for a brood mare. Still, I have a friend who's a horse breeder, and he knows of the Spanish fly. That might get her tail up! Of course, it kills them more often than not. I might give you fifty pence."

The stablemaster insisted on twelve hundred and off we went for half an hour's shouting. Actually, twelve hundred didn't seem bad, considering that the worst of the stallions went for four thousand.

This time they did settle on a price, a hundred and sixty-five pence, or at least I thought it was settled.

"Done then, stablemaster, provided that Sir Conrad likes how she handles."

"Provided? But you said..."

"I said that I'd be taking her to my stock-breeding friend in Wroclaw, didn't I? And how else are we to get her there? We'll be back soon with saddle and bridle. Come, Sir Conrad."

Novacek seemed to need to follow every bargaining session with a quick beer and a recap of the discussion.

"We really had him there—a hundred and sixty-five pence for a war-horse! I've had to pay more for a mule, and an old one at that! But you see, once a horse has been battle-trained, it can't be used for anything else. Put it to a plow and it'll likely kill you. Not many knights would take a fancy to a mare, and he was faced with feeding her all winter. We'll know about her soon enough, once you ride her. The sword shop is on the way to the saddlery.

"Oh, if she *does* go into heat with a stallion around, *jump!*"

I knew little about horses and nothing about armor. But I knew quite a bit about swords. I took fencing all the way through college and was varsity for three years. Furthermore, I was the only man on the team who used both saber and rapier. Despite the fact that "saber" is a Polish word, I prefer the Spanish rapier.

The sword shop was a comedown. It was a collection of huge hunks of wrought iron that might have been useful for breaking bones, but not much else. They were mostly hand-and-a-half bastard affairs a meter or more long. I went down the rack, hefting them and not concealing my disgust. I was about to leave and search elsewhere, when something on a back shelf caught my eye. It was a scimitar. It had a loose brass hilt, with cheap glass "jewels" set into it. The sheath was battered, and when I drew the blade, a light powder of rust puffed out. The blade was fully a meter long, much longer and heavier than a fencing saber. There was only a slight curve in the blade so that the point could be used for thrusting. The balance was poor, blade-heavy.

I took it over to the light and rubbed the blade. It was watered steel! The best sword steel is made of thousands of thin layers of hard high-carbon steel welded between layers of flexible low-carbon steel. The high-carbon steel corrodes less quickly, and the result is a surface that looks like ripples on water, hence the name. This was the first good piece of metal I'd seen in the thirteenth century.

I tried not to show my excitement. It was like finding a Stradivarius violin in a junk shop!

"This is a curious thing," I said to the shopkeeper. "Saracen, isn't it?" Very few Polish knights went on crusade, since there were plenty of heathen to kill in the immediate neighborhood.

"Aye, sir. Brought back from the Holy Wars by a great knight, sir. A holy relic, that is."

"A holy relic made by an infidel! That great knight probably gave it to his girl friend, being embarrassed to have it around the house. It's a piece of junk, and we both know it. It's too light to do any damage, and that's why I want it. I have a young nephew who's ready for his first toy sword. Something cheap that he can bash up and not hurt himself with. Shall we say five silver pennies?"

"Oh, sir, I couldn't sell that fine antique for less than fifty."

And so I went at it in the manner of my new boss, and in ten minutes we settled on fourteen, which I paid out of my own pocket.

As we left, I said, "Well, Mr. Novacek, am I learning my lessons?" Actually, they were damn strange lessons for a good socialist to be taking.

"A fair performance, for a beginner. I could have gotten him down to eleven. But what do you want with *that* silly thing?"

"You really don't know what I've got here? It's worth not eleven but eleven thousand! Would you lend me your knife even though I might damage it?" *Everybody* in the thirteenth century carried a knife.

He handed it to me. I drew my new sword and shaved a thin sliver from the edge of his knife. His eyes widened.

"That's test number one, that it can cut a lesser blade!"

"Lesser blade! This knife is first-quality steel!"

"It's good-quality wrought iron, which is about all I've seen around here. Test number two is that it can be bent, blade tip to pommel, without breaking or kinking." I put the tip to the ground and bowed the blade maybe ninety degrees, but after that I lost my nerve.

"There's a third test?"

"That'll have to wait until I sharpen it. It must be able to cut a silk scarf that's floating in the air. For now, though, do you know a smith who can tighten this hilt? And fifty grams of brass at the pommel end will improve the balance remarkably."

Saddles and bridles were sold by two different guilds, so there was no possibility that they would match. The only saddles that could fit a Charger were huge. The saddlebow and cantle came as high as my waist. An opponent could break your back, but he couldn't knock you out of that thing.

Getting into it was strange. I had to put my right foot in the left stirrup, hoist myself up, put my left foot into a special leather loop, go up higher, and then drop in without getting tangled or squashing my genitals. But I get ahead of myself.

I let Mr. Novacek pick out the saddle and bridle.

Aside from what I'd seen in the movies, I knew nothing of lances or shields. I really didn't want either of them, but the boss insisted. I picked both to be as light as possible.

"And what device on the shield, sir?" All the shields in the shop were white. Used shields were rarely resold, since they usually were destroyed just before their owners were.

"Is there time?" I looked at Novacek. What with our frequent beer stops, it was now past noon. A lot was left to be done, and he wanted to set out before first light.

"Have it done in an hour, sir, if it isn't too complicated."

Novacek nodded affirmatively.

Maybe it was the beer and no food, or maybe it was something deep inside me that yelled, "*Do it!*"

I said, "A white eagle on a red field. Put a crown on the eagle." The artist didn't react; I guessed the national insignia wasn't in common use yet.

"Is there a motto?"

"Poland is not yet dead." He didn't react to that, either, because it was the first line of the national anthem and wouldn't be written for five and a half centuries.

The saddle and harness had been delivered to the stable and installed on the horse.

I managed to clamber aboard without doing anything too embarrassing.

She was really an excellent horse: mild-mannered, obedient, not at all skittish. She was neck-trained and stirrup-trained; you could guide her with your feet alone. Of course, there was nothing at all of the fierce war-horse about her, but that was fine by me.

We hadn't bought spurs yet—still *another* guild—and it was obvious that I would not need them.

Eventually, I rode back to the inn by the monastery with my new boss walking beside me. I wore a helmet, a full suit of chain-mail armor, and a huge sheepskin-lined red cloak. I had a horse and a saddle, plus a sword and lance and an audacious shield. I would have made a truly splendid barbaric sight if my blue jeans had not been showing through my wrought-iron overalls.

Also, I was in debt for more than a year's pay.

Chapter Seven

WE WERE on the road an hour before gray dawn.

The last evening had been a frantic matter of wolfing down a meal, taking a last bath—it might be a while before the next—and collecting my gear.

Father Ignacy came to my cell to wish me good-bye and Godspeed. He gave me a letter of introduction and a list of Franciscan monasteries where I could scrounge a meal if I really got hard up. He also gave me a letter to be delivered to a Count Lambert at Okoitz.

"It's right on your way, and it will be worth at least a meal and a night's lodging to you. I carried it up from Hungary, but now you must complete its journey. God be with you, and know, my son, that you are always welcome here." He smiled. "All will be well with you, Sir Conrad. I can smell it."

The kid was waiting in the hallway with the clothes he'd borrowed. They were washed and folded. Some of them looked as if they'd been beaten between two bricks, but I didn't mention it. He also had a carefully counted pouch of silver pennies.

"I thank you for the loan, Sir Conrad, and return your property."

"Thanks, kid. Look, why don't you keep the tennis shoes. They fit you."

"Again, thank you, but they wouldn't go well with

my cassock. Have you heard the news of the prostitute Malenka?"

"No, what happened?"

"She has found a most permanent position with the innkeeper."

"Indeed?"

"Yes. They've posted banns in the church and are to be married within the month."

"I'll be damned!"

"Never that, Sir Conrad. With three pence in the right place, I believe you have saved a soul. Go with God." There was something in the way he looked at me. Envy? Admiration? But that was impossible.

I reported to Boris Novacek at the inn, where he was still drinking.

In the morning he surprised me by showing up in full armor himself. We ate a cold breakfast and left, taking with us two horses and a mule. I was on my red mare—I'd named her Anna after my lady of Zakopane—with my backpack serving as one saddlebag and a sack of food as the other. My shield rode on top. My spear fit between a socket at my right toe and a clip on the saddlebow.

Boris—we'd gotten on a first-name basis when in private, over last night's beer—rode a gray gelding, with a pair of small but very heavy saddlebags behind him. He led a mule loaded with more supplies, a leather bag of beer, and some "luxury" goods, sugar and pepper, each worth about one-fifth of an equivalent weight of silver. Both had been transported up from the Indies.

We followed a trail just north of the Vistula River, heading west. Anna was walking surefootedly on a track I could hardly see. She didn't shy at strange noises or blowing leaves. A fine animal. The plan was to follow the path until the river turned south and pick up another trail heading west again to the Odra River, then south into Moravia. With luck, and pushing it, we hoped to reach the Moravian Gate, a low pass between the Carpathian and Sudeten mountains, on the evening of the fourth day, December 26.

After that it was to be an easy trip in warmer weather

into Hungary, where we would buy 144 barrels of wine for delivery to the Bishop of Cracow in the spring. The purchase was for use in the mass and had nothing to do with the bishop's fondness for red Hungarian wines, of course.

The sun was fully up when we passed the Benedictine abbey at Tyniec, high on the white rocks across the river, but we saw not a single person from the time we left Cracow until ten o'clock in the morning.

With the sun up, Boris trotted up and rode beside me for a little conversation. Talking in the dark had been difficult because we couldn't see each other to gesticulate. He wanted to know about Arabic numbers, and I complied.

Boris caught on to the salient points quickly. He was amused by the idea of zero ("A special character that signifies nothing! Hah!"), but he soon saw its usefulness. I drew the numbers in the air in front of me as though it were a blackboard, and he memorized their shapes without difficulty. He considered the idea of positional notation to be a brilliant creation. The decimal point was still giving him trouble when we heard a rider galloping up from behind. We pulled off with me to the left side of the trail and Boris to the right to let the fellow through.

The man stopped abruptly between us and turned to my boss. He acted as if I wasn't there.

"You are Boris Novacek?"

"I am."

"You are a thief! You run out on your debts!" he said with a thick German accent.

"Who are you and why do you call me a thief?"

"I call you thief because you do not pay the twenty-two thousand pence that you owe Schweiburger the cloth merchant! And I am the man he sold the debt to!"

"I do not owe you anything, for I do not know you. As for Schweiburger, my debt is not due until Christmas, and today is only December twenty-third!"

The argument got more and more heated, and I became apprehensive. I was unsure of the legalities of the case, but it was obviously my duty to defend Boris if it came to that.

The man must have forgotten about me because while shaking one fist at my employer, he reached behind his back to draw his dagger.

I didn't want to use my sword and kill him, so I grabbed him by the back of the neck and the belt and heaved him out of his saddle. My intention was to throw him over my head and onto the ground. Then I could take my lance and stop any real violence.

But he was much heavier than I had expected. He bumped my lance free while he was airborne, and I tried to catch it with my right foot. But my high saddlebow and cantle had given me a false sense of security; it was quite possible to fall out sideways, which I did. I never claimed to be a horseman.

I was sliding off the right side of the saddle, but my hands were full of creditor so that I couldn't grab the pommel. My right foot was out of the stirrup, stopping my lance from falling. Trying desperately to find the stirrup, I let the lance go. Then there was nothing left to do but think, *Oh shit, why Me?* I hit the ground in a tangle of arms, legs, and instruments of violence.

The horses scattered, and we were untangled in an instant. He was on his feet and drawing his sword before I got up. Fortunately, his first blow was to my left, because I parried it before my sword was fully out of the sheath.

I got my sword out in time to parry a vicious chop at my head. "Hey! Stop! I don't have an argument with you!" I shouted as I blocked a blow at my right side.

"Bastard!" he yelled as he tried to bash my skull three more times.

"I'm not your enemy!" I parried a cut at my left leg. "I was only trying to stop you from committing a murder!"

Keeping him from hitting me required no great skill. A parry almost always requires less motion than an attack and so is inherently faster. Also, my opponent had little skill and no ability at subterfuge. He telegraphed every blow long before it landed.

"You ride with thieves, you!" He sent two more whacks at my right leg.

What the guy did have was a heavy sword and an ungodly amount of stamina and persistence.

"Look, I don't want to hurt you!" He was bashing at my head again. I was once the best man on campus with a saber, but I hadn't worked out in six years. Even then, I had been used to parrying a fencing saber, which weighs less than a tenth of what this guy was swinging.

"You are Polack thief and liar like everybody you know!" He kept on swinging.

"Can't we stop and talk about this? Don't you ever get tired?" My right arm was getting numb.

"Bastard!" he yelled, and started chopping faster. Had it been the twentieth century. I would have *known* that he was on some kind of dope.

Finally he got one by me, hitting my right shoulder. It broke neither skin nor bone, but it *hurt*. I knew that the defensive game could not go on forever. I had to disable him.

When next I got an opening, I beat his blade to the left. He overcompensated, and I doubled under his sword. Then, arm out, head and body vertical and in perfect fencing form, I thrust my blade into him.

In fencing, things happen too quickly to be controlled by rational thought. You practice for years so that the reflexes of your arms and legs do the right thing at the right time. That is how you score points.

That is also how I put my sword through the man's neck, severing his trachea and at least two arteries. He was probably dead before he hit the ground, but he continued bleeding. *Oh, God*, how he bled!

I stared at him, unable to believe what I had done.

"Well fought, Sir Conrad! But was that really necessary?"

"Huh?" I had never killed a man before.

"Why did you throw him out of the saddle?" Boris gathered up the horses and dismounted.

"You didn't see?" I said after a time. "He drew a knife behind his back. He meant to kill you."

"And here is the knife on the ground! My apologies, Sir Conrad. You have saved my life! I am in your debt, sir." He bent over the body and was searching it.

"Just earning my pay, and I am in your debt some three thousand pence." I was a murderer.

"Not anymore, Sir Conrad. Look here." He showed me a pouch he had removed from the body. It must have contained a kilo of gold.

"That amounts to eight thousand pence or I'm no judge. And look here! The man wears armor under his clothes! Had your sword struck elsewhere, it might have been stuck on his rings, and then he would have had your head!" Boris quickly stripped the body while I stood dumbly by. When he was done, the corpse was completely naked. "Haul that a long way off the road, will you? They get unsightly when they rot, and we wouldn't want to offend some good lady."

In his thirteenth-century way, he was telling me that one should not litter. I dragged it off. When I got back, a bundle was heaped on the stranger's horse. Boris was mounted.

"Sir Conrad, I estimate that I could sell this chance-found horse and equipment for four thousand pence. The gold is worth eight, for a total of twelve. We were together at the finding. You did the important work, but you were in my employ at the time. Therefore, I think that an even split would be equitable. Do you agree?"

"Whatever you say." Jesus Christ. I had just killed a man. Killed him and hid the body. Now I was joining in on robbing the dead.

Boris saw my expression. "Well, we can hardly leave this on the road for some thief to find! Now then, your half of twelve is six, but you owe me three, so here is your three thousand pence."

I put the money into my pouch. Added to the fifty I already had, it amounted to quite a bit. Two years' pay for killing a man.

"In addition, Sir Conrad, you saved my life. Please accept this thousand as a bonus."

I put it in my pouch and mounted up.

"One more thing," he said as we rode down the trail. "That man, whoever he was, did not have a deed of transfer on his person, and I think it probable that he was only an extortionist. But *if* he really bought the debt from Schweiburger and *if* he has no heirs, I would be forgiven the debt, saving twenty-two thousand. If these unlikely events transpire, you shall have earned an additional eleven thousand pence."

I was silent for a while. Then I said, "What is all this about your running out on your debts?"

"Well, I wasn't exactly running out on them, but it proved to be very convenient to... shall we say defer payment for a few months. You see, last summer I located some excellent Russian furs in Cracow. I knew a family in Buda that would be most interested in them. However, since I had already overinvested in amber, I could not afford to purchase the lot of furs and pay their way to Buda.

"Therefore, I left the amber with a German wool merchant of my acquaintance, and he lent me twenty-two thousand pence.

"My trading went well, and I returned to Poland with copper and samples of wine purchased near Pest, across the river from Buda."

"Wait a minute, Boris. You say you brought copper *into* Poland?" In the twentieth century, Poland is one of the world's largest copper *exporters*. Apparently, the mines near Legnica had yet to be discovered.

"Of course. There's a fair profit in copper, though nothing outstanding. You understand that I'm not wealthy enough to get involved in the really big commodities like cloth, so the best I can do is to connect individuals with diverse needs who are not aware of one another.

"This I did with a certain red Hungarian wine. It is not highly regarded in Hungary and is therefore inexpensive, but the Bishop of Cracow was quite taken with it. He ordered a huge amount at a price that will leave me well compensated for my services.

"The difficulty is that the amber market is now poor, and had I repaid Schweiburger, I would not be able to deliver the bishop's order. Discreet inquiries indicated that my lender was in no immediate need of cash, so I thought it best to delay paying him until spring. It was the profitable thing to do, even though I shall have to pay him damages."

"You mean extra interest on his money?"

"Interest? How can you say such a thing, Sir Conrad? Don't you know that the charging of interest is usury, a crime against the Church?"

"Oh. Then what did Schweiburger get for lending you the money in the first place?"

"Why, nothing. Of course, he was concerned about the safety of his money and insisted that some of his men carry it over to me. I had to agree to pay them for this work. These carrying charges amounted to twelve hundred pence, but the loan of the money was free."

"And you'll pay him no interest, but damages or other carrying charges when you pay him late."

"To the tune of one thousand to fifteen hundred pence, depending on just how late I am. It's the way things are done."

We rode in silence until noon, and then he said, "Sir Conrad, that blow you took to the shoulder, it isn't serious, is it?"

"No. I'll probably have a bruise as big as my face, but the arm works all right."

"Then why so glum? Two days in my employ and already you are a prosperous man."

"I hate killing."

"You are in a strange business to entertain that attitude."

"I seem to be good at it."

"Indeed you are! That blow you struck was remarkable. Your blade was suddenly on the other side of his sword. Then you didn't really strike him at all! You straightened your arm and sort of *pushed* into him, and your blade came out of the back of his neck!"

"That is called a beat with a double. You tap his sword, and as he moves to knock your blade away, you drop your blade under his and come up on the other side. Then

I lunged, which uses the leg instead of the wrist. Much stronger." He wanted me to recap the fight the way he recapped his haggling sessions. I was surprised that he didn't order an ale.

"Next time we're afoot, you must show me how that's done. We've lost time, and we must pass through the Moravian Gate while the weather holds. Sext already. Sext and not a drink all morning!" He unslung his leather beer sack and drank deeply. He threw the sack at me, and I found that I needed it.

"The horses were resting during the fight, Sir Conrad. What say we eat in the saddle and push on?"

"You're the boss."

We trotted on. When you're in a hurry on horseback, you don't gallop all the time unless you want to kill your mount. You gallop for a while, walk for a while, trot for a while, gallop again. Just then we were trotting.

We passed the castle town of Oswiecim when it was still light.

"We could ford the river and spend the night there, Sir Conrad, but I fear the weather. If we get snowed in before we pass the gate, the good bishop will be late in getting his wine."

"Whatever you say, Boris, though the weather has been fair all day." I was not used to riding, and I was getting sore. My mount was excellent, but ten hours in the saddle is a lot.

"Right, and the ground is hard enough for good riding. All the same, it feels wrong and I worry."

So we pushed on until dark, fed and rested the horses, and rode on again with moonrise.

Three hours later, all the horses except Anna were stumbling, and it was time to stop. I pitched camp and got some dried venison and barley stew boiling while Boris tethered and unloaded the horses.

After we were both crammed into my dome tent, he said, "That arithmetic of the Arabs, it's interesting, and I can see that once you're used to it, it would be a lot simpler than the old Roman system. But it retains one of the disadvantages of the old system."

"Eh?" God, I was tired.

"It still goes by tens and hundreds. Most of what I buy and sell goes by dozens and grosses, and a dozen is a good number. I can split a dozen into two parts, or three, or four, or even six. With ten, you can split two ways, or five, but that's all."

"There's no reason why you couldn't develop an Arabic number system to the base twelve," I said. "Just add two more symbols for ten and eleven. You'd have to memorize new multiplication tables and so on, but you haven't learned the old ones yet. I'll show you in the morning."

That was probably one of the more useful things I did in my life. It was also one of the more painful.

"As you like. Oh, you did something sensible with your newfound wealth, didn't you?"

"Yes. I tied it to my ankle." I was in the thirteenth century now, surrounded by cutthroats and thieves. I knew, because I had become one of them.

Chapter Eight

THE BEER sack was empty and I was about talked out, when it started snowing. In the twentieth century this area would be all factories and apartment houses, but we had not seen a soul all morning. We had worked out—in our heads—the tables for addition, subtraction, multiplication, and division required for base-twelve arithmetic. Boris had them all memorized and was doing long division by noon. It was an incredible display of intelligence.

In fact, almost all the people I had met in the thirteenth century were intelligent, way above average. They were ignorant, to be sure, but smart. Was intelligence a natural compensation for ignorance? Or was there something about modern education that destroys the mind? I had certainly been bored enough in school. Or were we just breeding for stupidity? You could see where the priesthood was encouraging that. The clergy was the only educated class here, and for a lot of peasant boys it was the only way up in the world. Making them celibate, as the new Gregorian reforms demanded, was biologically equivalent to killing them. The reforms had not been accepted in Poland yet, but they would be. The monasteries had been celibate for centuries.

The cities attracted the bright kids who didn't join the clergy. Filthy as the cities were, they had to be cauldrons of disease. Were seven hundred years enough to make a difference? Possibly.

I was pondering this while Anna was at her calm, steady walk. A horse is a lot like a bus in that you really don't have to pay attention to where you are going. I was thinking and sharpening my sword. Yesterday's fight had made the other guy's weapon look like a saw blade, but mine was uninjured.

The falling snow was muffling sound, and we proceeded in silence until I heard muted hoofbeats and the jingling of armor. Bemused, I looked up absently to see an armored knight galloping toward us. He rode a massive black horse that was plunging hard, its eyes wide and bloodshot. His surcoat was red with black trim. His barrel helm was polished and had an eye slit only two centimeters wide. His shield was red with a black double-headed eagle. His lance bore a red and black pennant.

And his shield was raised, and his lance was pointing directly at me!

Suddenly, Anna became completely uncontrollable. This was a game she had been taught well. She took off at a full gallop, directly at the attacking knight!

She might have known what to do, but *I* didn't. From what little I had seen of this type of fighting, I had to sheath my sword, get my shield out from in back, and level my lance at him. I was then to brace myself on the stirrups and prepare to take part in an imitation train wreck.

I dropped the sharpening stone and tried to put away my sword, wasting precious seconds; at a full gallop it is not possible to sheath a sword. The sword was the only weapon that I knew how to use, and I didn't want to drop it. I looked up, and the knight was entirely too close. No time for the shield!

With my left hand I reached across the saddle for my lance. It was riding point up with the butt in the right stirrup socket. As I swung it out, it naturally ended up with the butt forward, barely in time to beat the knight's lance away from my chest. The lance head ripped into the mail above my left elbow, but I barely felt it.

The eye slit of his helmet was the only obvious target, so I thrust at it with my sword, our left knees bashing as the horses passed to the right.

I felt the sword grate on bone and iron as my opponent flashed by, the blade was almost pulled out of my hand. I twisted, looking over my left shoulder, and saw his helmet turn fully 180 degrees before my sword was yanked out. By brute luck, I had stumbled onto a tactic for which the knight wasn't prepared.

Anna stopped and turned while the knight fell from his horse, red blood gushing on white snow as his helmet bounced off. The top of his skull with half of his brain skidded in yet another direction, leaving a third scarlet smear on the snow.

But Boris was in trouble. Two armored footmen were hacking at him with long halberds as he desperately defended himself with his sword. Without a signal from me, Anna charged to his aid.

Someone in blue ran from the forest and grabbed at my horse's reins. I slashed with my sword, dropping my lance in the process, but apparently I missed. I saw the flash of a knife swinging toward my left leg. I managed to lift my leg high while trying awkwardly to swing my sword again.

Then suddenly the blue bandit was gone, trampled beneath Anna's hind legs.

We continued toward Boris, but something felt very wrong. Still firmly in the saddle, I was slowly rotating off from the back of my horse.

The cinch strap was cut! As I tried to untangle myself from the oversized warkak, Anna turned sharply and was actually skidding sideways on the snow so that she wouldn't trample me as she had the bandit.

I came down hard and felt the saddle crack between my legs. For a moment I was stunned. I saw Anna pulling away the saddle with her teeth. I got to my feet, shaking a bit, as an axeman landed a blow on the top of Boris's gelding's neck. Blood sprayed, and the animal suddenly froze and then started to topple.

Sword in hand, I ran to my employer's aid. Anna,

without saddle or baggage, was trotting at my left side. I blessed the man who had trained her. She acted as though she really cared about what happened to me and was staying close for my protection.

Boris was still in the saddle when his horse fell on its side. The axemen jumped away from the crash and then were on him.

Boris lost his sword in the fall and was pinned under his dying mount as one of the axemen prepared to deliver a death chop.

I shouted to attract the attention of the would-be murderer, and the man turned to face me, slipping slightly on the blood-stained snow. As I ran to meet him, he swung a three-meter-long halberd down at me.

A weapon that big is much slower than a sword, although it hits a whole lot harder. If I had tried to parry it, it would have just kept coming into me, so I chopped at it with all my might and managed to cut through the hickory shaft and its iron reinforcing strips.

The axe head glanced off my back as I skidded, trying to stop on the slippery snow.

I realize now that what I had accomplished was to cut my opponent's halberd down to a quarterstaff. As it turned out, he was *very good* with a quarterstaff.

He took a quick step backward, found solid footing on Boris's chest, and gave me a quick jab in the solar plexus, which knocked the wind out of me but didn't break my momentum.

Boris grabbed the man's leg as I was skidding. I slammed into them, knocking the man down and propelling myself over the motionless body of the gelding. From flat on my back, I caught a blurred image of the second axeman coming up to take me out.

Suddenly the sky darkened and Anna's hoofs came down centimeters from my face. She had jumped entirely over our struggling bodies to bowl over the second axeman.

I lurched to my feet to see Anna taking on the second axeman in single combat. She danced aside from his axe swipes and then delivered a kick to his left arm that I was sure broke it.

Then a whack on the side of my helmet knocked me down yet a third time. The first axeman had kicked his way free of Boris and was putting his newly made quarterstaff to use.

I was hit twice more, across the back and the ribs, before I regained my feet. My opponent swung his staff in a blur of figure eights and twice parried my lunges by slapping my sword aside.

I once read that the great Japanese swordsman Musashi fought sixty duels before he was thirty years old. In most of those fights to the death, his opponents used real swords while he used a wooden stick. I put it down as a fine example of Japanese embroidery. Or perhaps Musashi's real talent was in finding incompetent opponents.

That, of course, was before I encountered a man who really knew how to use a stick.

My opponent was grinning at me through the open face of his helmet. Blood was running freely from my slashed left arm, I was staggering, and he knew I was beaten.

Well, if I couldn't get at him past that quarterstaff, I could damn well chop it up. I made it my target, focused on it, and cut the damn thing in half.

The bastard was still grinning! Suddenly he had half the quarterstaff in each hand and was fighting with two single sticks—Florentine style, I think it's called.

Something inside me snapped. He had no bloody right to be grinning at me! I was absolutely enraged, and in my rage I forgot everything I had ever learned about fencing. I snarled like an animal and started swinging like a drunken sailor.

He must have hit me three or four more times; I neither felt the blows nor cared. In moments his single sticks were reduced to pungi sticks, so he reached for his dagger. I slashed his right hand off at the wrist.

Suddenly, all fight was gone from him. He plunked down to a sitting position on the snow, staring at the blood spurting from the stump of his right wrist. The look on his face was one of astonishment.

I kicked his shoulder, and he just rolled over onto his side, still staring at the bloody stump.

I looked up and saw that Anna had her man on the run. He was dodging between the trees, both arms dangling at his sides as if broken. He ducked behind a massive oak and then peeked out around the opposite side to see what had become of her.

She outguessed him. As he stuck his head out, she put a forehoof in his face. I could hear the crunching squish from fifty meters away.

Then she looked at the body, calmly stepped on its neck, and trotted back to me.

I was just standing there, breathing hard, feeling the rage drain out of me and exhaustion take its place. Anna stopped, observed that I was reasonably alive, and then looked at the first axeman. The man was so intent on staring at where his hand had been that I don't think he noticed as she stepped on his neck.

How do you train a horse to do such a thing? I thought about it and decided that I didn't want to know.

The Black Sea. I could have gone to a nice resort on the Black Sea with girls in bathing suits and been back at my comfortable chair in the Katowice Machinery Works. My mother told me I should have gone to the beach . . .

"Uh, Sir Conrad," Boris said. "If you have a moment . . ."

This brought me back to reality. I was beaten, bloody, and certainly not unbowed, but there was work to do. I went to help Boris, still pinned under his gray gelding. The axe chop to the neck had partially severed its spine; the body was completely motionless, but the head was writhing.

"Well fought, Sir Conrad! But not me, yet. Dispatch my horse first. He has been too good a servant to leave in pain."

I opened my Buck jackknife, put it to where I thought the arteries were, and said, "Here?"

"No, no. Up a bit. That's it. Good night, old friend."

We had to tie a rope around Anna's neck and drag the carcass from Boris's leg. Dead leaves and snow had cushioned his fall; his leg was stiff, but it worked.

My knee hurt, but I could walk. I hurt all over, but no bones were broken. My arm was another matter. The cut wasn't bad, but in a world without antibiotics, a scratch can kill. I dug out my first-aid kit to dress it as Boris began methodically stripping the dead.

Somehow, that fight didn't bother me as much as yesterday's killing had. Perhaps it was because the highwaymen had been so obviously in the wrong. Perhaps it was because my soul was scar tissue and I was becoming brutal.

My saddle was destroyed, but the dead knight's was about the same size and of considerably better quality. A beautiful thing; I wondered whom he had stolen it from.

I had just finished saddling Anna when I heard a cry. "Was that a child, Boris?"

"Sounded more like a cat in heat!"

"I'm going to check it out."

"As you wish, sir knight." He had mistaken my luck in battle for prowess and was willing to forgive my squeamishness afterward.

I mounted up and rode in the direction of the cry. It sounded a few more times before I found the deserted camp. Now much there. A few brush huts, a cooking pot over a dying fire, and this kid. It must have been less than a month old, though I was no judge of age. It was wrapped up in a collection of rags and furs, with a fur flap covering its face.

I yelled to see if the mother was around. I shouted that I was friendly, but no one answered.

I could hardly leave the kid out in the snow. I yelled out my name and said that I was taking the kid west. Still no answer. I remounted with the kid in one arm and rode back to the trail.

"Not a bad haul, Sir Conrad," Boris called as I approached. He had packed up our latest loot. "Horse, equipment, three sets of armor and clothing! Five thousand worth, I'll wager. What was that you were shouting about a child?"

"I found their camp. There was a baby in it."

"Ah! Such a poor child to be alone in this heartless

world. Best baptize it and leave it with its mother, Sir Conrad."

"I tried. She must be hiding in the forest."

"You don't know? I didn't see it happen, being engaged at the time, but in your path as you came to my rescue there was a woman in a blue cloak. Trampled, she was, with a cut on her hand. Here, I'll show you."

The bodies were naked now, stripped even of their underwear. The knight's head was cut completely in two at eye level, yet his helmet was undamaged. My sword must have spun around in there like an apple slicer.

The woman might once have been pretty, but you couldn't tell. Her limbs were all broken, and there were puffy dents in her chest and stomach. Her face was a ghastly, flattened caricature. The fresh stretch marks on her belly told of recent birth.

"I didn't know," I sobbed. "I saw that you were in trouble, and I was coming to help. She grabbed my reins. I didn't know I killed a woman."

"Sir Conrad, again I am in your debt. Again you have saved my life. But you could not have done so if you had stopped for this woman. Another moment and I would have been dead."

"So she is dead instead."

"And what of it? She had a quick death, which was better than she deserved! Man, she was living with highwaymen, aiding and abetting their murders. Anyway, you didn't kill her. You only made that cut on her hand, and that's no mortal wound. It was an accident, her falling under your horse, or maybe a suicide.

"I'm going to look at that camp. You pull yourself together, man. And do what's right by that child. If you don't have water, melt a few drops of snow with your hand and see that it's baptized." He rode off on the horse that we had "found" the day before, dragging the naked axemen behind him.

In an emergency, any Catholic can perform the sacrament of baptism. I still had some water in my canteen, and I dribbled a few drops on the kid's forehead.

"I baptize thee in the name of the Father, and of the

Son, and of the Holy Ghost. Amen. I name thee..."
Whom should I name him after? Of course! "I name thee
Ignacy!"

I had the bodies off the road when Boris returned.

"Their loot, Sir Conrad! We're both rich! They had
more than a hundred thousand in silver and gold, robbed
from travelers like us! Damned if you didn't step right
over their chest!"

Somehow, I really didn't care. "I'm taking the kid with
us."

"Sir Conrad, you are the damnedest combination of
wisdom and ignorance that I have ever encountered. You
are an absolutely deadly knight yet maudlin as a pubescent
girl in a convent. But to torture a child is senseless! How
do you plan to feed it? Are your male nipples going to
spring forth with milk? How do you plan to keep it alive
this very afternoon? It's getting colder, and the snow is
deeper. It grows dark, and it's a long way to shelter."

He was right. I knew he was right. The kid would die.
Why cause needless pain? And why bother with it? "I'm
taking the kid."

"Sir Conrad, as your employer I order you to put that
child with its mother! Oh, damn you! Give it here. I'll do
it." He leaned forward.

"Boris, do you really want to fight me?"

He stopped. "Oh, all right! Keep the child if you wish.
But now we must ride if any of us is to live."

That afternoon was horrible, but the evening was worse.
The snow slashed into our faces, blown by a westerly
gale. The trail was all but invisible, and without Anna's
strength we would never have broken through the drifting
snow. I was leading the knight's war-horse, our second
strongest mount. Boris followed on his captured horse,
leading the mule.

I wrapped the kid up with my cloak, at the expense of
my legs. Hours later, I reached inside his bundling, and
his body was as cold as my hand. This wouldn't do.

Working under my armor, I unzipped my close-fitting
windbreaker, stretching out the mail, my sweater, and my
underwear. I put the kid inside, next to my skin. He was

cold. I packed his bundling around me as best I could and wrapped my cloak tight.

Shortly, he returned the favor by urinating on me. I guessed that meant that he was still alive.

We floundered on in the starless darkness. I couldn't even read my compass. To stop was death, and it was impossible to continue on. But we did go on. And on.

Chapter Eleven

WITH THE count's leave, I left him gazing out across his lands. I wanted to check on some things, and anyway, dinner was being skipped to leave an appetite for the feast.

My horse, Anna, was happy to see me. She was in a good stall in a big, clean stable, and she had been carefully groomed. "Are they treating you okay, Anna?"

She nodded yes.

"Anything you need?"

She shook her head no.

"Right." I didn't want to believe this.

Uneaten oats lay in the trough in front of her. I patted her neck and went in search of the kid I'd brought in.

Everyone in the bailey seemed to be hurrying about, getting last things done before the feast. Many were still in the plain gray wool that was everyday wear for most people, but some were already in their Sunday best, dyed in bright colors, with a great deal of embroidery.

Everyone seemed to know who I was. Passersby greeted me with smiles and nods. I had always thought of peasants as being brutally downtrodden, forced to grovel before their masters. I'm sure that that must have happened somewhere, but I saw none of it at Okoitz.

I was passing the mill when a man stopped me. He had a basket of food in one hand and a pail of beer in the

Interlude Two

THE SCREEN had gone from full color to black and white with poor definition, which indicated that the probes were using infrared and that the scene was in nearly total darkness. Yet the red mare was proceeding without difficulty.

I hit the pause button.

"Tom, that horse is impossible."

"What do you mean impossible? Do you think that we'd doctor a documentary?"

"I mean that that horse can see in the dark! It acts like it's got a compass in its head! And the way it killed those highwaymen! Something's wrong here."

"You mean something's right here. Yes, that's one of our horses. She's the result of many years of careful selective breeding, along with a bit of genetic engineering. She has an IQ of about sixty and understands Polish perfectly. And yes, she can see somewhat into the infrared, and she does have the same magnetic sense that a pigeon has."

"Then what was she doing for sale in Cracow?"

"She was there because I *put* her there, hoping that Conrad would have brains enough to buy her, which he did.

"Look, there are some other things about this that you should understand. You know that rich American relative who put Conrad through school? Well, I'm he. Conrad Schwartz is my third cousin, and while I've never tried to run anybody's life, I have tried to see that my relatives had a decent start in life.

"Of course, I've had to work within certain rules. Besides the physical limitations of causality, I have two partners in the time-travel business, and we have agreed on some very sensible regulations. Tampering with history is out—we don't play God. But we do permit the helping of blood relatives out to the fourth generation back and their descendants.

"I had nothing to do with getting Conrad dumped into the thirteenth century. That was a screw-up by the Historical Corps, which is under Ian's jurisdiction. But once Conrad was there, I had a perfect right to help a needy blood relative. Being without arms and money in the Middle Ages is serious!"

"You mean that you set him up to get into those fights and capture that booty?"

"Not quite. I learned about the fighting the same way you did, watching this documentary I had made. I wasn't worried about him, since I had met him ten years later, alive and healthy. But after the second fight, when he was bandaging his arm, I hit the pause button and ordered a pair of 'merchants' with a chest of gold to pass through there four days before. On being attacked by highwaymen, they abandoned their cargo and fled.

"This left Conrad with enough money to live comfortably for the ten years he'd have to spend in the Dark Ages."

"And the sword, was that your doing, too?"

"Sure, diamond edge and all. What's more, had he gone to the *Polish* armor shop instead of to that German, he would have found a good set of Turkish plate mail, exactly his size, that he could have picked up cheap."

"Huh. Well, I guess you can't win them all."

"No, you can't. But you can sure as hell try. Now, back to the blizzard."

Chapter Nine

THE DEAD knight's stallion was the first to fall. I felt it, but I couldn't see it. It got up and went on for another half hour. It fell again and didn't get up. It was crying in pain.

"Leave the beast, Sir Conrad! That sounds like a broken leg. But if we dismount to dispatch it, we'll never find our horses again."

I was learning to love our horses, and the beast's screams hurt me. But Boris was right; I left the stallion to die in pain.

We went on until we saw a tiny light ahead. Soon a great log barricade was in front of us.

"Hello in the fort!" Boris yelled. "We are two good Christians, dying in the cold!"

It seemed forever before a voice answered. "Stand close to the light! Who goes there?"

"Boris Novacek and Sir Conrad Stargard. Is that you, Sir Miesko?"

"Yes, Master Novacek!" A small gate opened in front of us. "Best go straight to the castle. I'll take care of the mule. *Hello, the castle! Visitors!*"

Our horses were taken away by a sleepy groom, and we were led into a large, warm kitchen. Four young women sat there. From their expressions, we must have looked like zombies. I certainly felt like one.

"We are sorry to meet you in the kitchen, sir knight, but—"

"First things first," I said. I pulled the kid out from under my clothes. "Do any of you know what to do with one of these?"

This caused a flurry of motion and fast feminine conversation.

"Oh, my God! Is it dead?"

"No. No! The heart beats! When did it last eat?"

"This morning at the latest," I said.

"What happened to the mother?"

"Dead," I said.

"Who, then?" She looked at the others.

"Mrs. Malinski just lost hers!"

"I'll go get her!" One of the women threw on a cloak and ran out.

Another carefully took the kid near the fire. "Diapers! The darling hasn't been changed all day!" She glared at me.

Another of them ran upstairs, presumably after diapers. The two remaining were inspecting the baby. We mere males were forgotten. I could see that the kid was in good hands.

I tried to remove my outer clothes, but my chain mail was frozen to my windbreaker. Distracted by my efforts, one of the women turned. "Oh! You men must be frozen. Come, sit by the fire." In seconds, we were handed huge mugs of wine heated with pokers glowing from the fire. We drained them.

Our mugs were refilled as the diapers arrived. Soon the three women were clustered around the kitchen table, with the baby in the middle. They were rubbing and scrubbing and making silly noises. It made me wish *I* were a month old.

"I never thought we'd make it here alive," I told them, "so just to be safe, I baptized him. I named him Ignacy."

Conversation stopped dead. All three of them stared at me as if I were a heretic.

"What a terrible thing to do!" the tall blonde said.

"What do you mean terrible? If he died without baptism, he'd go to limbo," I said.

"Limbo? You mean hell."

"So why are you mad? I saved him."

"No, silly, the name!"

"I named him for a good friend. A holy father. A Franciscan. Ignacy is a fine name!"

"For a girl?" This from the redhead.

"Oh." I'd cursed the poor thing with a name she'd hate for the rest of her life. Boris was giggling but didn't want to get involved.

"Don't you know the difference?" the tall blonde asked.

"Damn it, woman, of course I know the difference! What? You think I should have taken her clothes off in that storm just to see what flavor she was? You wanted maybe a properly named corpse?"

They were silent for a minute, and then the fourth woman came back with a buxom, motherly type. The kid was fed on the spot.

By then, the ice on my armor had melted enough for me to peel the mail off my windbreaker. I hung it up to dry. Boris did the same. Then I stripped down to my long underwear. If they could nurse a baby, I could get dry. I confess I was annoyed.

Mrs. Malinski left with the kid, and the four young ones whispered to each other.

Then the tall blonde came over and formally apologized for ignoring us and being a bad hostess. Introductions were made. The tall blonde was Krystyana, and the others were Ilona, Janina, and Natalia.

The count was asleep and not to be disturbed.

Soon things were okay; the rift with our hostesses was smoothed over. The table was washed, and a cloth was spread. Food was put out, and our mugs were refilled. I said grace, and we ate.

I'd forgotten about my wounded arm. Rather than strip in a snowstorm, I'd patched it up through the hole ripped in my clothes and armor. But the blood had soaked my long underwear to the wrist. Krystyana insisted on tending it while I ate. I probably should have refused and done it myself with my first-aid kit, but the food and wine and feminine companionship were working on me.

In the course of that meal they got every bloody detail of the trip out of Boris, who delighted in blow-by-blow accounts.

Later we were escorted to separate rooms. If Boris didn't worry about his property, then neither would I. I stripped down to shorts, T-shirt, and socks and eased my battered body between the clean sheets of a huge bed. It was comfortable enough and covered with an enormously thick feather blanket.

I blew out the oil lamp. It was Christmas Eve, and the bed was a marvelous present.

I was dozing off when I heard the door open.

Krystyana came in.

"That was a beautiful thing you did, Sir Conrad, saving that little girl." She stripped off her single garment and slid into bed beside me. "We'll just have to think up a good nickname for her."

Chapter Ten

LATE THE next morning, I was lying on my back and Krystyana was lying on my stomach with her elbows on my shoulders.

She was intently studying my T-shirt. The night before, things had been urgent and *necessary*, and I was in too much of a hurry at first and too tired afterward to remove my undershirt. Actually, I was still wearing my socks. The morning had been one of calm and wondrous delight, and I hadn't felt the need to change anything.

I couldn't honestly call Krystyana beautiful, but she was certainly pretty. She had lovely long blond hair that was draped over my shoulders. It went well with her light-blue eyes and blond, almost unnoticeable eyebrows and lashes. Her nose was perhaps a little too long, her mouth was too wide, and her teeth were not good, but there was nothing ugly about her. I mentioned that she was tall, but only in comparison to the others. Now her head was at shoulder level and her stretched-out toes brushed my shins. Her body was slender and most acceptable. She looked younger than I had thought last night. Perhaps she was sixteen.

I found out later that she was fourteen, the usual age of marriage among the people of Okoitz.

"Sir Conrad, this is the most amazing knot work! Do you know how it's made?"

She was staring at my knitted cotton T-shirt. Knot work? I studied it, too. Yes, I suppose you could call those knots. And once you thought of them as being hand-tied knots, yes, it was amazing.

"I've never thought about it. I suppose I could figure it out."

"I wish you would. I'd love to do something like this. It's fantastic!"

"You really like my shirt?"

"Oh, yes! Last night I was awfully impressed with that *sweater* thing you wore, but this is unbelievable. Everything is so *tiny!*"

"Well, if you want it, it's yours. Merry Christmas."

"Whee! But you mustn't give our Christmas presents now, Sir Conrad. Christmas presents are for this evening."

"As you like. This evening, then. For now, why don't you knock off the sir stuff. My friends call me Conrad, or just Con."

"But that would be most improper, Sir Conrad! If I hailed you not as a knight but as an ordinary man, why, it would be as though I was sleeping with a man before marriage, and that would be a sin."

I was confused. "You aren't married, are you?"

"Of course not!" She was shocked.

"Our . . . customs seem to be different. Could you please explain to me—slowly, as you would to a child—just what it is that you are talking about?"

She gave me a "mere man" look but said, "You are a belted knight. I am an unmarried wench and not of the nobility. You have the right to take any such unmarried woman who attracts you. Therefore, I have an obligation to do as you please. If one is performing an obligation, one cannot possibly be sinning. But for me to wantonly copulate out of wedlock, that would be at least a venial sin." It was the most incredible series of rationalizations—based on the right to rape!—I had ever heard.

"I have the right to take any peasant girl I want?" Accepting the favors of a lady who climbs into one's bed is one thing. Forcibly taking any woman in the fields is quite another, and not for Conrad Schwartz, thank you!

"Not only a right, Sir Conrad, but a duty! 'Sir' means 'sire,' you know. Not one man in a hundred becomes a knight, and the realm needs the children of such heroes."

Charles Darwin in a wheelbarrow! Knighthood as a eugenic program to improve the species? "But it was *you* who came to *me*."

"Nonsense, Sir Conrad. I merely lay down for some sleep. It was you who took me. If I made myself more accessible, why, it was only to save some other wench who might be less inclined. Therefore, it doubles my virtue."

What an amazing ball of tangled justifications! Good, though. I leaned back to ponder it all. She leaned forward to get at the window and hit the sore spots on my arm and shoulder. I winced loudly.

"I'm sorry, Sir Conrad. I forgot your wounds." She jumped out of bed and opened an oil-covered parchment window that let in a little light but no sight. She really had an excellent body, willowy yet rounded. "It's a wonderful day! Clear blue sky with not a cloud. But it's late! We've missed mass, and on Christmas day! And look! That steam! They're already quenching the sauna. Hurry or we'll be late!"

I sat up in bed and started fumbling for my clothes. There was absolutely no heat in the room!

"No. No, silly." She kneeled at my feet, yanked off my socks, and threw them any which way. She pulled off my T-shirt; this she folded neatly and set aside. Then she grabbed me by the hand and pulled me out the door and down the stairs. I was cold, naked, and embarrassed, but I followed her through the kitchen and out the back door to the end of a line of naked people running over cold whiteness. The snow on either side of us was more than a meter deep, but a path had been shoveled to the sauna.

Somehow, I had always thought of the sauna as a Scandinavian custom that had spread only in modern times, but there it was. Perhaps the problem is that I had always assumed that my ancestors were all stern, heroic types—and that my grandmother was a virgin.

This sauna was different from any I had seen before.

It was a brick dome with walls well over a meter thick. A small hole vented smoke at the top, and a tiny door opened at the side. To heat it, a roaring pinewood fire was kept burning inside for four hours. Then the fire was quenched and after a few minutes for the smoke to clear, the customers ran in. Once heated, the sauna stayed hot all day.

I was handed a board by the attendant. I followed Krystyana's bottom through the door, except that she only had to stoop while I had to crawl through the tiny opening.

The door closed behind me, and the smoke hole was plugged. I was enveloped in heat and darkness. Someone took my arm and led me to a place to sit down. My butt touched the hot bricks, and I jerked upward, hitting my head on the low ceiling. Someone placed my board on the brick shelf and sat me on it. As my eyes adjusted, I made out an oil lamp.

Dim shapes took form around me. We were in a room shaped like an arena that could have seated fifty, if they were friendly, but I counted only eight plus myself. They were friendly anyway. A windburned man with dark blond hair sat across from me—last night's gateman, Sir Miesko. The other man I hadn't met. He was a handsome muscular sort about my own age. He was tall, as the locals went, and blond, much blonder than I. In the twentieth century I would have suspected him of bleaching his hair. Ilona and a woman I hadn't met were sitting on either side, cuddled under his powerful arms and happy. A third woman was rubbing the muscles of his neck and shoulders.

Krystyana and Janina were sitting next to me, and Natalia sat by Sir Miesko.

We were all nude. The sight of those healthy bodies was delightful, but there is nothing sexy about female skin in a sauna. At these high temperatures, the gallant reflex does not take place

Following the blond man's example, I spread my arms, and the ladies snuggled close to me. I noticed that Sir Miesko still had his hands on his knees.

"Sir Conrad," he said, "you must realize that to have

the right to do something is one thing. To be able to get away with it is quite another."

The blond man laughed. "Sir Miesko, you astound me with your valor in battle and your meekness in wedlock. You had best take the advice of the Holy Church and never strike your wife with a stick longer than the distance from your fingertip to your elbow, nor bigger around than your thumb. Then take my advice and never use anything less! And often, Sir Miesko, to ensure your bliss, marital and otherwise."

"Your advice is always welcome, Count, though it may be that I will state certain facts at tonight's festival." He grinned.

"Hah! That *my* wife chooses to stay in Hungary and I support her there? Well met, Sir Miesko."

He turned to me. "And this must be the noble giant, Sir Conrad Stargard, who comes from a mysterious land not to be mentioned, decked with mystic equipment." His eyes twinkled, and he smiled. "A man who defeats bandits and highwaymen in droves and captures vast booty! A man who rescues maidens of the tenderest of ages, grabs them from the clutches of death and merchants, and at great personal peril transports them to safety! And a man who, exhausted from fighting the forces of evil and brute nature, still has sap enough in him to keep Krystyana here smiling all morning as she hasn't smiled in months." Krystyana threw a wet cedar branch at him, but he took no notice of it. "I trust that those wounds and bruises are the result of honest battle and were not received from the calm ministrations of our gentle Krystyana." A fistful of wet branches flew.

"Noble Sir Conrad, I am delighted to meet you and honored by your presence. Know that I am Count Lambert Piast and that I welcome you to Okoitz."

I started to rise. It was blindingly hot, and sweat cascaded off me. But on my first day in this century, I had been bashed on the head for not adhering to the proper forms of courtesy. I had determined to learn them all and follow them to the letter.

"Ah, ah. Please, do not bow. It is not that I have disrespect for formalities but that a bow implies getting up again, and I fear for the roof."

"I thank you, Count Lambert, and my skull thanks you as well," I said, trying to match his flippant yet perceptive conversation. "But I complain that your description of me far overshoots the facts."

"I know, but that really is the gist of the story that's been circulating. You're the first news in weeks, and these people need *something* to talk about. I know the story of the child is true because I have talked to the Malinski woman and seen to the girl's safety.

"Boris Novacek was being sensible, you know, in wanting to leave the child behind. It was only the purest luck that let you find Okoitz in that dark blizzard. A merchant can afford to be sensible, but a nobleman often cannot. A nobleman must think of justice and honor first, and damn the odds! You did well, Sir Conrad.

"Thirdhand information—that is, from reality to Boris to Ilona to me—has it that you killed five highwaymen on the trail. Is this true?"

"No, my lord, I killed only two. One may have been a thief, an extortionist, or only an irate creditor for all I know. He kept striking at me, and I could not dissuade him. I regret his death. The second was a knight I got with a lucky blow. Of the others—one of whom turned out to be a woman—I wounded two that my horse dispatched, and my horse struck down the last."

"Ah, yes. Your docile fighting mare. Your skinny sword and your strange tactics. But later with that. It's time to go out."

I was thankful, for my eyesight was blurring with the heat. One strange effect of the sauna is that once you are hot enough, cold doesn't bother you. I stood in knee-deep snow swishing myself down with a bundle of cedar branches, removing sweat and dirt. We were in a courtyard surrounded by buildings, but the people had absolutely no nudity taboo! Dozens of peasants were coming and going and paying no special attention to the nine of us nude in the snow. I'd never heard of such a custom in

Poland, but then, it isn't the sort of thing monks put into history books, is it?

I was musing on that when I felt a sharp whack on the buttocks. I spun around.

Krystyana was standing, facing me, with a cedar switch in her hand. Her legs were wide, her fists were on her hips, and she was grinning, daring me to do something. I was unsure of just what, but I accepted her challenge and swatted her across the obvious protuberances.

She squealed and struck back, and soon the other five girls joined in on her side. I was surrounded and getting the worst of it.

"Fear not, Sir Conrad! I come to thine aid!" The count swatted his way into the circle. "Back to back, Sir Conrad!"

"For this timely aid, much thanks, my lord. Together we may yet be victorious!" I shouted back. A crowd was gathering and cheering us on, generally favoring their own sex.

Still, the count and I were losing. We were outnumbered and were pulling our punches, or rather our swats. The opposition wasn't.

"Sir Miesko!" the count shouted. "You would show the white feather to your liege lord on the field of battle? Defend me!"

"My lord, it's not the enemy I fear but my wife! In all events, things appear to be about to fall to your advantage."

Uh, yes. In the cold, the gallant reflex was no longer impossible. Had I the time, I would have been embarrassed. The fight had the same effect on the count. As uninhibited as these people were, I was afraid that I was about to be involved in a public orgy.

"Defend me, Sir Miesko!"

"My lord, I shall support you with mine trebuchets." Sir Miesko began pelting us indiscriminately with snowballs. Some minutes later, the count stopped one with his face.

"Fair ladies," he said, "I call a truce with you that we might first dispatch our common foe."

Krystyana was, as usual, the spokeswoman (and ring-leader). "With pleasure, my lord. Ladies, demolish me that man!"

The eight of us turned instantly on Sir Miesko and buried him under our snowballs.

Seeing Sir Miesko being trounced, some of the spectators—there must have been a hundred by now—started pelting *us* with snowballs.

Suddenly the count stiffened and raised his hand. Instantly, all motion stopped. Snowballs in the air seemed to drop quickly, as if embarrassed.

"My good people!" the count intoned. There was suddenly nothing of the clown or wit about him. Here was a born commander, knowledgeable of his people, confident of their support.

"I know that this is Christmas day, but the festival does not begin for three hours. I am your liege lord, and I expect to be treated with respect." A smile flashed. "Until then."

He motioned us back into the sauna, and the crowd dispersed. A mother began to whack a boy who had thrown a snowball at us.

We went back to soaking up great quantities of heat. Once we were through, the commoners would get the sauna for the rest of the day.

For the two or three weeks after Christmas, work outside was impossible. Travel was also impossible, and so defense was unnecessary. Traditionally, on the afternoon of Christmas day, the whole countryside went on vacation.

Oh, they couldn't go anywhere, but they had fun anyway. Discipline was relaxed, almost to the point of non-existence. Food and drink were on the count, although everyone was supposed to pitch in on the preparations.

There were two days of gift giving. On Christmas night, December 25, you gave presents to the members of your own class. On the twelfth night, January 6, you gave to members of the opposite class. For purposes of gift giving, the ladies-in-waiting, Krystyana and company, were on the receiving end of both groups.

Properly warmed up, we went back to the castle. Count Lambert had "just under a gross" of knights, but these were all—save Sir Miesko—at their own manors, attending to their own festivities. Usually a half dozen or so were in attendance at Okoitz, with two dozen more guarding the trail.

With the word "castle," several pictures usually come to mind. One involves movie stars in plate armor making stately motions in a huge stone defensive complex like Malbork on the Nogat, near Gdansk. Another is the Viking longhouse, with barbaric warriors drinking mead around a long, open fire with meat roasting above it, then sleeping on the benches when they were drunk. A third has long, plastered halls tenanted by oil paintings and ladies with huge dresses and partially exposed breasts.

Okoitz was none of the above. It resembled, more than anything else, a log frontier fort in an American cowboy movie, roughly square with blockhouses at each corner. The walls were perhaps four meters high and two hundred meters long. Some two hundred peasants and an equal number of children lived in huts built against the outer wall, normally one family to a room. Half the wall was lined with stables.

Scattered in the enclosure—called a bailey—were special-purpose buildings: a smithy, a bakery, the sauna, two latrines, and a millhouse with a hand-turned stone. One of the blockhouses served as an inn. The others served as quarters for visiting knights when the castle was full.

In the center of the bailey were the castle proper and the church. Despite the fact that they formed a single, continuous building, they were always spoken of separately. Perhaps that was because the church was open to everyone but the castle was entered only by invitation.

The count could walk from his chambers directly to the choir loft and see the mass from there. He never did this, always taking a chair in the front row to set an example.

The church, castle, and almost everything else were

made of logs. Sawn lumber was used only when it was absolutely necessary, as on floors and doors. Brick and stone work were used very sparingly and metal almost not at all, except for hinges.

There was a newness about the place. Some of the cut wood had not yet weathered. I guessed its age to be about three years.

My backpack had been delivered to my room, which had a basin and water, so I dug out my shaving kit, removed three days of stubble, and brushed my teeth. My pouch of gold seemed to be missing, but I was among friends. They must have put it in a safe place.

I put on my underwear and was thinking about getting my body back into my soiled clothes, when Janina came in. Most people knocked before entering, but apparently ladies-in-waiting didn't have to. Or maybe they just didn't want to. She was carrying a big bundle of clothes.

"Sir Conrad, we haven't had time to get your clothes cleaned, and you wouldn't want to wear armor to a feast, anyway. These were made for Count Lambert, but we made them overly large. He told me to bring them to you."

"Thank you, Janina. The count is generous." She seemed to be expecting something, but this crew was socially equivalent to nobility; one did not tip them. When genuine female nobility were around, they were treated as something just a cut above regular servants.

She spread the clothes out at the foot of the bed. This bed was huge. It was two and a half meters long and more than two meters wide. It had a framework over it, hung with curtains.

"I think that these will fit you properly." She held the tunic up to me and smoothed it over my body. She did quite a lot of smoothing, and it was soon obvious just what it was that she was expecting. However, my needs were not all that pressing, and this business of legalized rape troubled me.

"Yes," I said, "I'm sure you're right. The embroidery on this is excellent. Did you women do this yourselves?"

"Yes, Sir Conrad. But we made the sleeves too long, see? But they're just right for you.

"I always feel so hot after a sauna! You don't mind, do you?" Without waiting to see if I did mind, she stripped off her outer robe and stood in a long underdress, waiting.

"Not at all, feel free to be comfortable." I rooted among the clothes she had brought. "These stockings—pants?— these are new to me." They were of a woven cloth but were like a woman's nylons in that they covered the foot. They had strings at the top.

"Oh, you can't wear them with those shorts. You have to wear this kind, with a belt." She promptly pulled down my undershorts.

"Interesting. And these boots are odd." This game was becoming fun. It was highly unusual to be pursued instead of the pursuer!

"I think they'll fit you." She was down at my knees, making sure I got a good look past her loose, low bodice. "Oh, your feet are cold! We'll have to get them warm!"

The game continued, and sometime later I was trying to figure out a belt buckle and Janina was lying nude on the bed.

"Damn it, Sir Conrad, get over here!"

So I bowed to the inevitable and permitted my body to be abused, knowing full well that she would later claim that she had been forced. She was not as pretty as Krystyana, but youth and enthusiasm make up for a lot.

Janina was promised my last T-shirt.

Over the next few days, I was visited by the other four ladies. Apparently they believed in share and share alike. A sound socialist principle but astounding when applied to one's person! If peasant women really outnumbered knights by a hundred to one, I couldn't imagine any possibility of rape in the modern sense of the word. A man would be too worn out satisfying the volunteers.

I later found out that in addition to giving the girls a socially acceptable outlet for their youthful sexuality and permitting them to mingle with the upper crust, a knight was expected to do well by his "friends" in providing them with a proper dowry and a substantial husband. Since the women seemed enthusiastic, I could find no fault with the system.

You could see where the girl's parents would go along with it, too. It was socially acceptable, it connected them with the nobility, and it saved them the price of a dowry and a wedding.

I was being dressed in my new outfit. Belted linen undershorts were topped with a pullover linen shirt. The deep blue pants—they really were plural, two separate pieces—were tied to the belt on the shorts. They were joined in the middle by a kind of diaper called a codpiece. The arrangement made a lot of sense, considering the use of outdoor latrines in the winter. A gorgeously embroidered long-sleeved tunic of rich burgundy was pulled on next. Something like shoelaces closed the neck.

Soft, black glove-leather boots—without thick soles; they were more like leather stockings—were pulled on. For outdoors, there were thick felt overshoes. Attractive but inferior to my hiking boots.

Over it all, a rich blue cape, matching the pants, was fastened to the left shoulder.

My plain leather belt spoiled the ensemble, but etiquette required one to wear a sword and a knife. My sword sheath suddenly seemed shabby and my jackknife case plain.

Janina was fitting the last of this around me when there was a knock on the door.

"Enter!" she cried, despite the fact that she was still naked.

"Sir Conrad," Count Lambert said, ignoring the naked lady, "I was hoping to see the fabulous equipment that you—I must say that that outfit suits you and fits you quite well." The whole sauna party trailed in with him.

"Thank you, my lord. It's beautiful, and the embroidery is lovely."

"Yes, isn't it? My ladies made it for me last fall, as a surprise. They were all new then and didn't know my size. But it fits you, so please take it as a gift."

"Why . . . why, thank you, my lord." Months of work must have gone into the embroidery alone.

"Please don't think that I'm giving you my castoffs. I could never wear it, and the dears were most disappointed. They seem to have taken quite a liking to you, though. He gestured at Janina's nudity.

"But . . . please, my lord, I hope I haven't—"

"Not in the least, Sir Conrad. What's the use in having things if you can't share them with your friends? Just see that you don't take *all* of them with you as you ride away. Leave a few behind to train the next bunch. It's a bloody nuisance to have to do it yourself! Now, about your mystic equipage . . ."

So I got my pack and showed them how it was worn. I unrolled the sleeping bag, and Janina crawled in. The room was not heated, and she had to be freezing. The count played a long while with the zipper and eventually came to understand it.

"A wondrous device, Sir Conrad! Could you teach our smiths the way of this?"

"Perhaps, my lord, but not in the few weeks that I shall be here."

"I see. And this? This is your pavilion?"

"Yes, my lord. Oh, I almost forgot! I have a letter here for you. It was brought up from Hungary by Father Ignacy."

He glanced at the envelope and threw it to Janina. "Bring that to me sometime when I'm already in a bad mood. There's no point in spoiling a good one."

I set up the nylon dome tent on the wooden floor. It didn't require tent stakes. The count asked all sorts of questions about the tent and cloth and floor, the fiberglass poles, the snaps and zippers and mosquito netting.

"A veritable house! And so light!"

"Heavier than it should be, my lord. It's still wet. We'll leave it out."

We went through the rest of my things. The lightness of my canteen and mess kit surprised them, but otherwise there was no great impression made. They took a mild interest in the freeze-dried food, but I don't think they realized just how long those few grams would last. The

Swiss army knife was considered an ingenious toy. They really didn't know what steel was.

My first-aid kit was treated with studied indifference by the count and Sir Miesko, at least. To worry about an injury was below their knightly dignity. The ladies showed some interest—Janina was still in my sleeping bag—but seemed to feel it best to remain silent.

"And these parchment packages, Sir Conrad?"

"Seeds. I bought them as a present for my mother."

Sir Miesko was greatly taken with my compass.

"So this needle always points to true north?"

"Not exactly. There is some error, to the west. But it always points in the *same* direction, and if you take it out on a clear night and orient the card with the pole star, you will know the amount. Also, the presence of iron will throw it off."

"Of course. Cold iron always confounds the devices of fairy."

"No, Sir Miesko! It was made by skillful men, knowledgeable in science. Science is the art of discovering the ways in which God made the world and has nothing to do with witchcraft."

"You swear this?"

"On my honor! Furthermore, if you like this compass, it is yours—my Christmas gift."

"Then on *my* honor, I accept, but keep it until this evening."

The sewing kit, especially the needles with their tiny holes, was met with great enthusiasm by the ladies. I knew what I would do about their four remaining presents.

I'd saved the binoculars for last. They caused quite a stir, with people taking them out of each others' hands. Finally, Count Lambert took them back from Janina.

"Girl, do you want to freeze to death? Get some clothes on!" He strode from the room, down the hall, and out onto a balcony, a part of the defenses. He spent some time adjusting the lenses and looking out upon his lands.

"Excuse me, Count," I said, "but I have not seen Boris Novacek all day. Do you know what has become of him?"

"He left at gray dawn with two of my grooms and five

horses. It seems that you lost a horse and its baggage last night. They went out to find them." He swept the fields with my binoculars.

"And there they are, by God! Look! The snow is so deep that the men are forced to break through in front of the horses." He lowered the binoculars.

"No, by God! You can't look, can you? This is a wondrous device, Sir Conrad!" He raised them back to his eyes. "See! Two horses drag the dead war-horse behind them. On another, the baggage. Look—that shield! A black eagle on a red field! You *got* him, Sir Conrad!"

"I got who?"

"You killed Sir Rheinburg, a foul German renegade knight who has been looting and killing my merchants for more than a year. That black eagle has killed eight of my knights, slaughtered a gross of my commoners, and stolen God knows how many cattle! But you got the bastard, damn it, you got him!" Count Lambert was slapping my back with enthusiasm.

"At the time, it seemed a matter of simple necessity," I said.

"Ah, but now it's a matter of rejoicing! What's more, Sir Conrad, the bounty on him is yours—ten thousand pence, it stands at."

Richer and richer. Thinking about it, where was my pouch? But it would not have been polite to ask.

"You seem to appreciate my binoculars, my lord," I said.

"Appreciate them? They are things of wonder! What a difference these would make on a battlefield!"

"Then you have completed my Christmas list, my lord. Please take them as my gift." Actually, since I had left my home in Katowice, six weeks earlier, I had used my binoculars exactly once and the compass not at all. Certainly they were small gifts for favors received.

other. "Sir Conrad? Could it be that you are looking for the child you saved?"

"In fact, I am."

"Then I shall take you there. I am Mikhail Malinski, and the child is with my wife."

"Then I am in your debt, Mikhail."

"No, Sir Conrad. It is *I* who am in *your* debt. Understand that two nights ago our third child died at birth. My wife grieved horribly for a day and a half. I thought it would be the death of her. But she's happy now. You understand?"

"I understand. We are in each other's debt. Let's see them."

"In a moment, sir. I have but a quick errand." He went inside the millhouse, and I followed. I was shocked by what I found. Four men were chained to a heavy "hourglass" mill, grinding grain to flour. It was the first brutal thing I'd seen in Okoitz.

"What's all this?"

"Why, the mill, Sir Conrad. Oh! You mean the men. These two were caught last week drunk, disorderly, and annoying some married women. They'll be here until the end of Christmas.

"This one's my brother. I always warned him about his poaching. He got six months for it."

"I wasn't poaching! I shot that deer on my land and tracked him to where they found us!"

"Save your lies for someone who'll believe them, brother! They found you four miles from your land, and that deer had an arrow through its heart. It couldn't have gone four yards!"

"What about this last one?"

"Oh, he's a bad one, he is. They caught him stealing from a merchant. He's worked off maybe half of the five years he got." Mikhail put down the food. "Your Christmas feast, brother. Share it if you want."

As we left, I said, "Five years for theft seemed severe."

"Had he robbed another peasant, it would have been only six months. But merchants have to be protected, you

know. If they aren't, they might stop coming, and who
would we sell our grain and hides to?"

"I see. What if someone stole from a knight?"

"Why, I can't remember such a thing ever happening,
Sir Conrad. I suppose, if the knight let him live, that it
would be far more than five years."

I ceased to worry about the location of my gold.

"What do you do when there aren't any criminals?"

"Well, the grain has to be ground to flour, doesn't it?
There's usually a spot or two open on the mill, and the
rest of us men have to take turns at it. But we keep an
eye out for lawbreakers."

"I can see where you would. You keep saying 'men.'
What do you do about female criminals?"

"Well, that's rare, Sir Conrad. Women are more law-
abiding. But there was a time, two years ago, when a
girl—only twelve, she was—stole a silver-handled dagger
from the count himself."

"What did the count do?"

"Got his dagger back and told the girl's father. *He* beat
his daughter to within a thumb's width of her life! Then
the count gave the father a month at the stone for not
bringing up his daughter right! As I said, it doesn't happen
too often."

"What if she'd been married?"

"At twelve? You shouldn't marry a girl off until she's
at least budding!"

"No, no, Mikhail. I mean, what about an older woman?"

"Why, that'd be up to her husband, of course!" Mikhail
walked up to his house.

In the twentieth century, it would have been called a
shed. It was three meters wide and five deep, and it was
one of a long row of similar log dwellings that stretched
along the outer log wall. Next to the wall and above the
sheds was a two-meter-wide wooden walkway, apparently
a place for defenders to stand. The rest of the roof was
straw.

"All this was by the count's own plans, it was. Houses
next to each other keep each other warm and take less
walls to build. The neighbors make noise, but that's not

the count's fault." The door had no hinges but was picked
up and moved aside. Mikhail went in without knocking,
and I followed.

Apparently, the lack of a nudity taboo applied to married women as well. Judging by the flush of her skin, Mrs.
Malinski was just back from the sauna. I guessed her to
be around thirty but later found out that she was only
nineteen. She was doing up her long hair and didn't bother
getting up or even covering herself.

"Sir Conrad! I am sorry that I did not speak to you
last night, but the baby . . . you know . . ."

"I quite understand, Mrs. Malinski." A campfire burned
smokily at the center of the single room. Their few spare
clothes were hung from pegs in the log walls, next to bags
of food, bunches of garlic, and a single cooking pot. Bags
of straw on the floor served as beds. Two small children
were playing on the dirt floor. Yet Mikhail was obviously
proud of his home! What had he been born in?

"We have real wooden floors going in next year, the
count says," Mikhail told me.

"He is a good lord, isn't he?"

"The best! Why, he could get a dozen men for every
man here if there was room for them."

I was pensive as I walked back past the latrines and
the grainery. These were *good* people, and there was so
much that I could help them with. But I would have to
leave as soon as the roads were clear.

One thing remained yet to do. There was a church, so
there had to be a priest. I had killed—or at least caused
the deaths of—five people. And there were two *very* young
women that I had . . . had. Damn it! They were not rapes!
I needed confession.

The church was full of commotion when I got there.
The altar had been removed, along with the candlesticks,
the relic—a lock of hair from Saint Adalbert, I found out
later—and all of the appurtenances. The church was fur-
nished with movable chairs instead of bolted-down pews;
I half suspect that the use of pews was the result of a
clerical rebellion to secular use of the church. The chairs
were being rearranged, and long, collapsible trestle tables

were being set up. The fact is that the church was the only room in Okoitz large enough to hold everybody.

Asking about, I learned that the priest, a Father John, and his wife (!) were in their chambers to the left of the altar.

I entered and discovered that the nudity taboo did apply to a priest's wife, at least to *this* priest's wife. From her accented shriek, I gathered that she was French. She was an attractive woman, better looking than any of the count's handmaidens. I turned to leave but was stopped by the priest.

"Please forgive her, Sir Conrad. She is new to Poland and not used to the local customs." His wife was still arranging a blanket around herself.

"Of course, Father. But still, I should leave."

"You may if you wish. But as a personal favor, I would prefer that you did not. You are from the west. Know that I met Francine when I was a student in Paris. She is the granddaughter of a bishop and was legitimate before the second Lateran Council forbade such marriages in the west. But these decrees were never ratified here in my native Poland, so here we are now, under God, man and wife."

He turned to his wife. "Francine, we cannot bring the word of God to these people unless we adhere to the local customs! There is no prohibition against nudity in the commandments, nor in the words of Christ. Remember the parable of the lilies of the field and care not about your raiment. Now, disrobe. Please."

She was embarrassed, probably as much as I was. The whole situation was awkward. There wasn't anything that I could say, but I tried to give her a confident smile and nod. She bit her lower lip, looked at me, and stood up. Then she slowly dropped her blanket. I think she did it slowly in order to pull it up if I disapproved rather than from a desire to entice.

She really was a beautiful woman, as fine as any you would see in modern Cracow. Her hair was black, the first black hair I had seen in the thirteenth century. Her waist was tiny, her hips were full, and her breasts were voluptuous orbs topped by tiny, coal-dark nipples.

"Thank you, love. Now, Christ also talked of the virtues of cleanliness, and the sauna grows cold," the priest said.

"Yes. Sir Conrad." She nodded to me and ran through the doorway.

"Thank you, Sir Conrad. I've been trying to get her to do that all day. She objected to their nudity, and they objected to her smell." The priest paused, and we heard a roar of applause from the crowd in the church. "*Damn*, but I wish they hadn't done that!"

This was a *far* stranger priest than Father Ignacy!

His next sermon was on the importance of being kind to people who were trying to fit in. Still, he seemed, for some unreasonable reason, to be a holy man.

"I took my sauna earlier, hoping that she would join me, but no such luck. But, Sir Conrad, you came here for a reason of your own. Can I help you?"

"Well, Father, I came here for a confession."

"Of course, my son, if you need it. The church is crowded now, but we are private enough here. Would this be adequate?"

I agreed, confessed, and told him about the people I had killed, the underaged girls I had copulated with, and lastly about coveting his wife!

He passed off the first two as not being sins at all but merely the things any sensible man would do. As for the last:

"You must learn to fight the results of your training. Had you seen her fully clothed, you might have thought her beautiful, but you would not have had these sensual thoughts. She was wearing what God gave her. The sin was in your eyes, Sir Conrad."

I thought about it, and he was right. I eventually got to know Francine as the unique and creative human being she really was. I learned that my initial impressions of her had been entirely wrong. She was not a shy and modest housewife. There was something of the whore in her and much of the bitch. But I get ahead of myself.

I went away with a penance of a single Pater Noster and three Ave Marias. I was somewhat surprised by that as I left the priest's chambers, but my surprise was increased when I saw Francine walking back, nude, through the crowded church. She smiled at me with her back straight. She strutted!

Her actions had much in common, I think, with the religious conversion of the goliard poet.

Half an hour later, we were seated behind a trestle table on the dais, near where the altar stood. There were five of us: Count Lambert, Sir Miesko, myself, Father John, and Francine. There were also six empty chairs that I found were for Krystyana's gang. They wouldn't actually be using them, since they were in charge of the banquet, but they had the right to sit at the head table even if they didn't have time for it.

Try to imagine six modern fourteen-year-olds being in charge of a sit-down banquet for two hundred people. Yet they did a fine job!

All the adult commoners were seated at long, narrow tables, sitting at only one side. A space was left between each pair of tables for the "servants" to walk. Actually, the servants were the peasant women. An elaborate schedule had been worked out such that each woman helped serve a certain course but most of the time played guest.

Everyone was there. The gate to Okoitz was not only left unguarded, it was left open! Had a known outlaw walked in, he would have been served along with the rest, until the festival was over. Afterward they might have hanged him.

The children were seated through the door in the count's hall. Part of the serving orchestration kept them fed, too. The babies were farther back, in the hallways and in some of the unused guest rooms. A stream of mothers flowed back and forth, but our six bright harem girls kept it all going and the food coming besides. Even the cooks took their turn at playing guest. The girls never did, the first night. But after, for the next two weeks, they were administrators, grand ladies!

Boris was down among the crowd with acceptable ladies seated on either side. He waved. I waved back, and the crowd applauded.

I had a normal place setting before me. There was a long tablecloth that doubled, I discovered, as a napkin. I had a spoon, a cup, a bowl, a large pitcher of wine—beer for the commons—and a salt shaker made of a hard wheat roll with a finger hole punched in the top.

We at the head table each had these to ourselves because of the six empty places. Among the commoners, each pair shared a setting, almost invariably a man and a woman. Not that there was a scarcity of place settings, it was just one of those things one *did* at a banquet. You *shared* a spoon, *shared* a cup, *shared* with your sister or your wife.

Musicians took turns playing—a recorder, a shawm, a pipe and tabor, a krummhorn, a bagpipe. Not the Scottish war pipes, of course, but the higher-pitched, more friendly Polish version. They had obviously practiced long for the occasion. Only when the banquet was over did they play in concert.

Father John said an elaborate grace.

The first course was a stew. Somebody's grandmother ladled it out to most of the people, but we at the head table were graced with Krystyana's service. I winked at her, and she winked back.

Stew was followed by broiled steaks. Janina placed before me a thick slab of bread directly on the tablecloth, and a girl named Yawalda, to whom I had not yet been introduced, put a juicy slice of meat on it. I found out much later that it was from the horse we had lost in last night's snowstorm. It wasn't bad.

Course followed course, usually a meat thing followed by a grain thing. There were no fresh vegetables at all.

On the final course, the count himself got up. He took a huge tray from Natalia and Janina and personally handed a small piece of cake to each person in the room, laughing and joking continuously. He got halfway through the church and then went into his "hall," where he personally gave a piece to each child. He went up and down the hallways, putting a small piece in each baby's hand, or at least on his bedclothes. Then he came back into the church and passed out cake to every commoner he had missed before.

He returned to the head table, where he placed a piece in front of each chair, including the vacant seats of the ladies-in-waiting. He stared as if aghast at the pieces left on the tray and then went up the table again, doubling the "nobles'" portions, to the applause of the crowd. Reaching the end, he put the five remaining cakes in his hand and pretended to count the crowd. Then he stuffed them into his own pouch, and the commons roared their approval.

I was so intent on this performance that I had not tasted the cakes. When Count Lambert sat down next to me—two empty chairs were between us—he said, "Well, eat up, Sir Conrad."

So I bowed and smiled and bit into one of them. It was good enough, but it was really only ordinary honey and nut cake. Nothing like the glories they make in modern Torun. I waved Krystyana over.

"This is excellent, my lord, but I too have something to contribute to the feast." When Krystyana got there, I said, "Now, quick like a bunny! I have a piece of brown stuff wrapped in silver and some brown paper. The last I saw of it, it was on my bed. Bring it here quickly!" She was off like an arrow.

"This is some cake of your own?" the count asked.

"Something like that. Chocolate."

As Krystyana came back, the other five girls were handing out bread rolls to the commons, without any helpers.

Seven pieces of chocolate were left. It was obvious that I couldn't share it with two hundred commoners and an equal number of children. There were five at the head table, plus six more who belonged there.

I broke each piece in two, got up, and started to put half a piece at each place.

The count stood up. "It's some foreign delicacy," he shouted. "It's only this big." He gesticulated. "So there's only enough for the head table, plus some for the king and queen!" This also met with shouted approval. Had there been elections just then, I think Genghis Khan could have been voted in.

So I went on, passing them out, not missing myself. When I sat down, three pieces were left.

"What is this business about a king and queen, my lord?"

He was tasting his chocolate and staring wide-eyed. "Why, we are about to select one of each, for the holidays at least. A king and a queen of misrule. See those small loaves they're handing out—wheat for the men and rye for the women? Well, in one of each sort of loaves there is a bean, and the two who get the beans shall be our king and queen for the festival. Further, you and I and the good Sir Miesko and Father John and wife shall become commoners!"

"You mean that the king would have the right to Francine?" I asked.

"She's married. Still, he might try; try and get away with it, perhaps, until the holiday was over. Then I'd cut the bastard's balls off! If I have no right to her, I'll be damned if any peasant can take her!"

"Uh. Yes. There are these three pieces left..."

"Well. One for the king and one for the queen. As to the last, well, rank hath its privileges." He started to put it in his pouch, and then he stopped. He waved Natalia over. "Give this to Pyotr Morocek's redheaded daughter." As she darted away, he looked at me and said, "It looks as though you are going to be robbing me of some of my ladies, Sir Conrad. I had better start restocking now!"

It evolved that Mrs. Malinski got the woman's bean and became queen. The blacksmith became king and ordered us "common swine" away from the head table. A side table had been prepared for us.

His first act was to order up his own six "ladies-in-waiting," namely, the six fattest women in the church. Mrs. Malinski demanded her right to some "boys-in-waiting," and called up three septuagenarians, who snuggled up to her. All this was greeted with great ribaldry from the crowd.

The king demanded that the count show more respect for blacksmiths and should henceforth act like one.

A leather apron was brought forth, and a hammer. Lambert put them on and went through a parody that I would have appreciated more had I known the blacksmith better.

Sir Miesko was charged with abandoning his wife, and another was named in her place. This huge matron was given a feather pillow, and he permitted her to beat him around the room, to the commons' delight. A great deal of beer was circulating.

My turn came up. The "king" said that since I was so adept at saving babies, I must be one of their breed. This had to be a setup, because all too soon three large women I had never met ran forward and pinned a huge diaper over my embroidered tunic and hose. I'd thought that the safety pin was a modern invention.

I was then forcibly presented with six large breasts to suck on, four of which were lactating. I survived. A television situation comedy would have contained higher, and considerably less coarse, humor.

Francine was then summoned. The "king" claimed that she had shown her wonders to but a few and that this was unfair. He commanded her to strip naked and walk among the crowd to show them what beauty was.

I tensed myself for a fight. I was quite willing to put up with the buffoonery with regard to the count, Sir Miesko, and myself. I would not permit them to humiliate a priest's wife, even though the whole concept of a priest having a wife confused me.

I never had a chance to draw my sword.

Francine stood up from her seat at the side and pulled herself out of her garments. The crowd cheered. I was awestruck. She strutted and wiggled her way up and down the tables of the commons, pinching a chin here, kissing a hairy peasant's lips there. The cheering rose to deafening levels, and she gloried in it! At last, she came to our side table. She gave Sir Miesko a peck on the cheek, which he accepted. The count demanded more and stroked her from armpit to knee.

At my turn, I wanted much more. I sat her on my knee and kissed her. She wiggled her body close.

"But this is all for the Church," she said with mock innocence. "One must mingle with the barbarians and follow their customs."

I didn't know if I wanted to beat her or rape her, so I handed her down to her husband. She stayed there the rest of the night, eventually permitting a cloak to be draped around her shoulders. The situation struck me as being more than slightly sick.

The priest and our six ladies were notably exempted from the hazing, as the king and queen turned on the commoners. All the musicians were playing in the hopes that they wouldn't be called out.

The various performances that the king and queen required of the commons were, if anything, even more crude than those required of the nobles. Most of them involved incomprehensible in-jokes that soon became boring. Boring to me, at least. Everyone else was having a marvelous time.

Eventually our royalty of misrule ran out of ideas and called for the dancing to start. Tables were moved out, chairs were moved back, and two barrels of beer were rolled in. The tops were removed from the barrels, and the beer was just dipped out.

Lambert, Sir Miesko, and I were required to join in the first dance. I was unsure of just what steps to try, but Krystyana dragged me out on the floor.

I'm not convinced that you could call it dancing. Okoitz had never heard of a polka or a mazurka, let alone a waltz, but people contented themselves with enthusiastically jumping up and down. They were not quite as bad as the modern punkers, but they came close.

That ordeal completed, I found myself standing at the sidelines next to the count. He tapped my shoulder and motioned for me to follow. He went to his chambers. A look of relief crossed his face as he closed the door. "I'm glad that we only have to do this once a year! Custom requires that I put on a party and play the clown, but I have as little liking for it as you do."

"It was a bit . . . raucous, my lord."

"Yes. I hope that you haven't gotten a bad opinion of us. Had you seen these people during harvest, your impression would have been different. We'll have to put in an appearance later, but for now, do you play chess? Oh, and do take off that stupid diaper."

I'm not a great player, but I'm competent. The game he played was identical to modern chess, except the pawns couldn't capture en passant. The count's game was good but extremely conservative; the strategy of play had evolved vastly in seven hundred years. That evening I won four games out of four.

"Sir Conrad, that brown cake you served—is there any more about?"

"I'm afraid not, nor is there any way of making more. I was surprised at that cake of yours."

"Good, yes?"

"Oh, yes. Delicious. But when all of that food and drink was flowing so generously, you were somewhat sparing with it."

"Of course. It had honey in it. I could have sold that honey for more than what the rest of the feast cost."

"Honey is that rare here? I'm surprised. It should be a natural product, easy to get."

"Easy enough to get, Sir Conrad, once you find a honey tree. A full-time honey hunter finds one, maybe two trees a year."

"Remarkable. What do you do then?"

"Why, you smoke the bees out and chop open the tree, of course."

"I begin to see your problem. You know, my lord, bees can't hollow out a tree themselves. They have to find a suitable place to build a hive. If you chop up every hollow tree, there isn't any place for them to live. No wonder honey is rare."

"I see. You're suggesting that we hollow out trees?"

"It doesn't have to be a whole tree. A simple wooden box will do. You know, bees are very remarkable creatures. I've read a few articles on them. Did you know that they have a language?"

"What! Insects talking?"

"Not exactly talking, but when a bee finds a field of flowers, she goes back to her hive and does a dance that tells the others where to go."

"Remarkable! You say 'she.' What of the male bees?"

So I prattled on for an hour about bees. Friends have accused me of having a garbage pit mind. Things fall in there and sort of stay around, fermenting. The upshot was that I agreed to instruct Lambert's carpenter on making beehives, a gross of them.

There would be nothing much to it, of course. Just a simple rectangular wooden box of about forty liters' capacity would do. You drilled a hole of four square centimeters near the bottom, facing south, and mounted them on a pole at least three meters in the air.

"It's been a pleasant and educational evening, Sir Conrad. Doubly so since you wouldn't wager any money on your chess playing. But now we must rejoin the buffoonery below."

The end point of the evening was the gift giving. Gift wrapping was unknown, but it wasn't missed. The only awkward moment occurred when the priest and his wife gave me a wooden crucifix and a carved rosary—the priest's own work—and I hadn't realized that they were on my Christmas list. The best return gift that I could think of on short notice was some rose seeds.

I also got a new sword belt from Sir Miesko. The harem didn't give; they just got. Well, maybe they did give. That night I was visited by Yawalda and Mary. They liked to work as a team.

Chapter Twelve

It was a relaxed afternoon.

I was giving Lambert and Sir Miesko fencing lessons. Over their strenuous objections and at my firm insistence, we were using wooden sticks instead of real swords. Boris Novacek soon joined us, praising my previous battles.

For men who lived by the sword, they had some odd attitudes. It was as if they didn't believe that a sword had a point! Their fencing was strictly hack and chop. They didn't see where the lunge had any use at all.

Finally, Boris said, "My lords, I have seen him use this thing! I saw him put that little sword entirely through a man's neck, and he killed the German knight with a single blow through the eye slit of his helmet."

"Well, I haven't seen him kill anything, Novacek," the count said. "Let's do some killing and prove this thing properly. Bring your sword, Sir Conrad."

I followed Lambert apprehensively out of the building, along with the rest of the crowd. He led us to a pen containing six pigs destined to be the next day's supper.

"Now then, Sir Conrad. You have allowed that the edge is useful on horseback but said that the point is stronger afoot. We shall see. I shall kill that boar with the edge of my sword, and you will take that sow with your point." Without further discussion, the count vaulted, sword in hand, into the pigpen.

The test was somewhat unfair in that the boar was mean. Lambert's first two-handed swing caught the pig a little in back of the "belt" line. This broke the boar's back without seriously cutting it. The boar was annoyed. Its hind legs were not functional, but it charged the count, dragging itself along on its front legs.

The pig is a very powerful animal, and its jaws can rip a man's leg off. All that meat is muscle.

Lambert was back-stepping furiously, and his second blow—to the shoulder—didn't slow down the boar at all. I was about to leap in when the count's sword crashed into the animal's skull and all motion stopped.

"You saw the power in that blow?" Lambert was actually proud of his performance. "Your turn, Sir Conrad."

I hated jumping into a pigsty with my embroidered tunic and leather stockings, but there was nothing else I could do. "That sow over there, my lord?"

The remaining pigs were all studying Lambert intently. I was trying to remember just how a pig's ribs went. I couldn't remember whether they angled back like a man's or not. I was obviously going to have to put all the power into my lunge that I could. Also, pigs being built the way they are, I was going to have to lunge downward.

This I did. Body upright, arm straight, blade out with the edge down.

The results surprised me. I had never actually stuck an animal before. My sword went entirely through the first pig and halfway through the one behind it. They both dropped dead without a squeal.

I got out of the pen and cleaned my sword in the snow. Then I started working on the pig shit on my boots, with Krystyana's help.

Sir Miesko said, "That was a great blow, Sir Conrad! But how real was the test? What if they were in armor?"

"An excellent idea!" the count said. "Krystyana, Boris brought in four sets of armor. Take Mary and bring us some hauberks. Pick two that match."

As the girls ran off, Sir Miesko shouted, "And the gambesons! Bring two equal gambesons!"

Boris's objections that we were about to chop up *his*

armor were squelched by Count Lambert: "Fear not, our smith will repair it."

The pigs were not minded to volunteer for this experiment, but a large number of commoners had gathered and manpower was available. At my suggestion, we did it outside the pigsty.

Under great protest by the pigs, two of them were dressed in armor and strung upright between horizontal poles, forelegs up and hind legs down.

The Society for the Prevention of Cruelty to Animals would have been horrified, but we were going to eat the animals anyway, and I fail to see where my sword was any worse than a butcher's knife.

Actually, the count's sword was a good deal worse. The rule being that all blows had to strike armor, it took him five hacks before the pig quit screaming. It died of internal concussions. The armor was never cut.

My watered steel blade cut the wrought-iron rings easily, and again I found the heart.

I could see Lambert's emotions in conflict. On the one hand, here was a valuable new technique. On the other, I was refuting the experience of his lifetime. I began to worry. Had I offended my host?

"Your blade, Sir Conrad. May I see it?"

"Of course, my lord."

He grasped the cheap brass grip and swung it a few times. Then he jumped into the pen with its one remaining live pig. With a single, mighty one-handed swing, he took the pig's head entirely off. Then he smiled.

"Your techniques have merit, Sir Conrad, but your sword! Your sword is magic!"

"Hardly that. But it *is* good steel."

"Could you teach my smith the way of this?"

"I could tell him how it's done, but the actual doing of it is an art form that he'd have to work out for himself. I wouldn't expect results for a year or two."

"Sir Conrad, we must talk." But he seemed uncertain.

As we went back inside, Krystyana seemed glum. "What's the matter, pretty girl?" I asked. "I'm sorry if all that killing bothered you."

"No, it's not that. The second course of tomorrow's supper was to be blood pudding, and you *men* have just splattered the blood all over the courtyard!"

It's hard to keep everybody happy.

Before supper, the count and I were playing chess at one end of the hall, and the girls had set up a loom at the other.

It wasn't much of a loom. There was a pole on top with a few thousand woolen strings wrapped around it. A pole at the bottom was used to roll up the cloth they made. In between, two girls were laboriously moving a shuttle back and forth between the vertical threads and then tightening the horizontal thread down with something like a pocket comb. They hadn't made a centimeter of cloth in an hour.

"Is that something they do as a hobby?" I asked.

"Hobby? There's always need of cloth, and my ladies are instructed to keep busy."

"Then why don't you use a proper loom?"

"You know something of looms?" The game was forgotten.

"Well, I'm not a weaver, but I know the process—"

"I know, Sir Conrad. 'But not in the few weeks I'll be here!' Have you no idea of our economic situation with regard to cloth? Don't you know that the French and Italians are making *vast* profits in the trade? Why, at the Troyes Hot Fair alone, *millions* of pence change hands, much of it Polish silver going for French cloth."

"But why not bring some weavers here?"

"My liege lord, Henryk the Bearded, did that very thing. At huge cost, he imported three dozen Walloon weavers and set them up, at his expense, in Wroclaw. Yet to this day not one Pole—save Henryk—has ever been in their building! And the price of cloth has not dropped a penny! Why, the cloth in that very tunic you're wearing was woven in Flanders and dyed in Florence."

"I don't know anything about dyeing, but I'm sure that I could build a loom," I said.

"Then that cuts it! Sir Conrad, I must have you. I want you to stay here and instruct my workmen—and women—

in the arts you've mentioned. In a scant two days, you've talked of honey and steel and cloth. You've shown me better swordsmanship, better dancing, and better chess playing than I would have thought possible. I say I want you. Now, what's your price?"

"My price? Well, I'm not sure that I need any money. I have half the booty I took, and—"

"Another thing—you have more than you think. This business of your splitting evenly with Novacek is nonsense! Despite the fact that he was your employer, you are a knight and he is a commoner; those spoils were taken entirely as the result of your sword arm. Oh, you might make him a gift of a twelfth of it, but any more than that would be absurd.

"There *is* the matter of booty being taken on my lands. By custom, I have the right to a tenth. But that is about the same amount as I gave you for killing that foul German, so we'll call it even."

"Be that as it may, Count Lambert, I still have an obligation to Boris. I agreed to accompany him, to keep his accounts, and to defend him, my lord."

"Novacek is traveling from here to Hungary for wine and then back. It happens that I must send a knight to Hungary. That letter you gave me was from my wife. She and our daughter stay with her relatives in Buda and Pest. She complains, as usual, about her need for money, so I must send it to her. Otherwise she will come back here to get it. If I must send a knight—who else could be trusted?—then that knight might as well accompany Boris and be paid by him.

"As to this accounting business, well, that's hardly a proper occupation for a belted knight."

"Uh . . . my lord, that hits on one more problem. You see, I'm not exactly a belted knight."

"What! You mean to say that you have been crossing swords with me, beating me at chess, and enjoying my ladies and that you are not a true belted knight? Sir Miesko! I need a witness! Attend me!"

"Coming, my lord!"

"But, Count Lambert, you see . . . in my country, we

don't have knighthood exactly, but I was an officer—no! *Am* an officer, and the priest said that—"

"Silence! Kneel, Conrad Stargard!" He drew his sword.

Visions of the boar's crushed skull flashed through my mind, but still I knelt. "You see—"

"Quiet!" The flat of his sword came down hard on my bruised right shoulder. This was followed by an equally rough blow above my wounded left arm. Apparently, I was being knighted, and the count did not go along with those effeminate taps on the shoulders so common in the movies.

"I dub thee knight!" The last blow came against the side of my head, and I saw a strange, web-shaped visual display. I almost fell over but managed to stay on my knees.

"Arise, Sir Conrad."

The girls at the looms were looking, whispering, and giggling.

"You two!" the count said. "This was purely a formality to remove any doubts from Sir Conrad's mind. They use a different ceremony in his country. All the same, be silent on this matter. You as well, Sir Miesko."

I managed to get to my feet.

"Well, that's settled. Now then, Sir Conrad, do you see any other problems?"

"Problems? Well, no, my lord. But what exactly is it that you expect of me?"

"I expect you to build such mechanisms as you feel would be beneficial here, and I would expect you to swear your allegiance to me."

Hmm. Actually, it didn't sound that bad. Comfortable surroundings, friendly people who really needed me, and plenty of sex. Compared to my previous position—well, Boris Novacek had been decent enough. But in two days on the road with him, I had been involved in two murderous fights. While two is not a statistically significant number, it certainly is an indication! Luck alone had kept *me* from being a naked corpse in a snowy wood.

"Very well, my lord. I will expect you to settle with Boris Novacek, to his satisfaction. I would swear allegiance, but not forever. Say, perhaps for nine years." I was leaving myself a cowardly way out. At the Battle of Legnica, which was not far from here, thirty thousand Christians fought a much greater number of Mongols. The Mongols did not leave a single survivor. Not one single Polish witness to the battle lived to tell of it. I wanted the option not to be there.

"Done, Sir Conrad. And your remuneration? If not money, then lands perhaps? People of your own?"

"Uh, let's leave that undefined for a while. Perhaps at some later date we may agree on something. For now, I will be satisfied with my maintenance in your castle.

"You understand that I agree to defend you and the people on your land if attacked, but I will not be responsible for other military duties."

"Agreed. Boris told me of your ambivalent feelings with regard to killing, and I saw your face when you stuck those pigs. You are a strange man, Sir Conrad Stargard."

Chapter Thirteen

THE NEXT night's feast was a more civilized affair than that of Christmas day. It was a sit-down dinner followed by dancing.

It seems that I was responsible for introducing the polka into Poland. My brief dancing with Krystyana had apparently impressed everyone, and that evening the count insisted on my demonstrating it again. I spent a few minutes with the musicians, humming the tune and slapping my thigh for rhythm, and they picked it up quickly. Having no written music, they all played by ear.

I shall make no attempt at describing the sound of three krummhorns, four recorders, a shawm, two drums, and a bagpipe playing the "Beer Barrel Polka."

The scheduling was less hectic, too. The common women were divided into six groups that took turns playing servant for a day; each of the groups of adults was directed by an adolescent handmaiden. Somehow, it worked.

The count seemed to feel that it was necessary and proper for a knight to have at least two young women within reach at all times. I think they were called "handmaidens" because they were always on hand. The term "maiden" was a euphemism, of course. When they got pregnant, he married them off and replaced them. I later discovered that this was not an ordinary state of affairs.

143

Most of his knights, as well as his liege lord, envied his ability to get away with it.

I was playing chess in my room with Sir Miesko when Krystyana darted in. She waved at me to follow her in an urgent, secretive way. I excused myself and followed. We went to an empty room next to the count's chambers. She put her ear next to the wall and motioned for me to do likewise. Confused, I did this.

I was shocked! Lambert and Novacek were discussing me! I pulled my head away and started back to my room, horrified that I should invade someone's privacy in this way.

Krystyana was still listening as I entered the hallway and the count stepped out beside me.

"Ah, Sir Conrad. I wanted to speak to you."

"Yes, my lord. Do you realize that your servants eavesdrop on you?"

"What? Of course! My dear Sir Conrad, either you are very naive or the servants in your own land are of a different breed of humanity. Servants eavesdrop! You might as well say that fishes swim. You can have servants or you can have privacy. You can't have both!

"But that's not what I wanted to talk to you about. Come into my chamber. I want to finalize our arrangements with Boris Novacek. Was I correct in assuming that you wished to gift Boris with a twelfth part of your captured booty?"

"Well, yes, at least—"

"Excellent, because that is precisely the amount that he decided to give me as my Christmas present."

Boris was turning purple. "My dear Count Lambert, surely—"

"No, not another word. You have already been too generous. Now, Sir Conrad, you recently purchased armor. I have decided to buy the armor that you captured. What did you pay for your armor?"

"Seven hundred and eighteen pence, my lord."

"So, then my price of one thousand pence per set is generous."

"But Count Lambert," Boris protested, "I could obtain

far more than that in Hungary! And besides the armor, there were weapons, saddles, bridles—"

"Yes, but I have decided to pay four thousand pence for the lot."

"But my lord—"

"But I have decided! So, that's settled. There was a dead horse that you brought in, which I accept as your contribution to the feast. The other captured horse—well, you lost a horse on my lands, so take it as my gift, a replacement.

"Sir Conrad, I have an errand for you. Go to the strong room; Krystyana will show you the way—Krystyana! I know you're listening! Get in here! Good. Now, go to the strong room. You will find, in addition to my own valuables, Boris Novacek's saddlebags, Sir Conrad's and the creditor's pouches, and a chest that they took from the German's camp. Pour both pouches into the chest. Then take four thousand pence from my own coffer and add it to the lot. Take three thousand pence out and put it in Boris's saddlebags, to pay for Sir Conrad's equipment. Then take one twelfth of the contents of the chest and put it in my coffers. The chest will be Sir Conrad's, and I believe we'll be square."

All of this verbal, without a scrap of documentation. I doubt if the count *knew* how much he had in his coffers. I could see that one of my services was going to be setting up a double-entry bookkeeping system for him.

"Oh, yes," he continued. "Krystyana, have all of my newly purchased equipment sent to the proper workmen. I want it all repaired and properly stored as soon as the holiday is over. The arms to the blacksmith, the horse trappings to the saddler, the clothes . . . Oh, I forgot the clothes. Well, I'll pay six hundred pence for them. Make that four thousand, six hundred pence that you throw in from my coffers.

"Well, it's good that all is settled."

"But my lord—"

"What *is* your problem, Novacek? You entered my lands with a knight and a loaded mule. You will leave with the same possessions, since Sir Miesko has graciously agreed to accompany you to Hungary and back at the same pay that you would have paid Sir Conrad. You will have enjoyed a holiday at no expense to yourself. As to the rest, you have had some adventures to talk of in the taverns. Where is your complaint?"

Boris bowed to the inevitable. It was obvious that one did not try to bargain with Count Lambert. "Well, there was the Arabic arithmetic that he was to teach me."

"Hmm. Sir Conrad, would you object to instructing Mr. Novacek while he is here, at your convenience?"

"Not at all, my lord."

"Then that's settled. Well, Krystyana, Sir Conrad? You have your orders. Go, but come back while the sun is still high. There is the matter of your oath of fealty."

Krystyana and I went down to the basement strong room. An army would have had trouble getting in there if it was defended, but a thief could have walked in if it was not. Most of the time, it was not. I would have to do something about locks.

We followed the count's instructions, and I began counting money. Krystyana looked at me strangely. She got out a balance scale and weighed the money. It seems that the coinage was not all consistent.

When we were through, I found that I was the owner of 112,200 pence. Krystyana told me that this was enough to hire every commoner in the fort for over five years!

It was absurd that a single person should have such wealth, especially a good socialist! I was dazed as we went back up to the sunlight.

At that time, throughout most of Europe an oath of fealty was taken with the vassal on his knees. His hands were placed together as if in prayer, with his lord's hands around them. The lord was seated.

That was not how it was done in thirteenth-century Poland. Here, you walked outside on a sunny day, with the biggest possible crowd of witnesses. You raised your right hand to the sun and made your oath in a loud voice. This was doubtless a thing held over from pagan days, but I still think it a more fitting ceremony.

My oath was, "I, Sir Conrad Stargard, promise to come

to the aid of my liege lord, Count Lambert Piast, if ever he or the people on his land are oppressed. I shall obey him for nine years. This I swear."

The count returned: "I, Count Lambert Piast, promise to defend my vassal, Sir Conrad Stargard, to the best of my ability. I shall see to his maintenance and will do such other things as are, from time to time, agreed. This I swear."

People applauded, and that was it. No forms in quadruplicate, no committees to be consulted. I was beginning to like the thirteenth century.

Chapter Fourteen

THE HOLIDAYS drifted by pleasantly. I often slept in, sometimes almost missing 10 A.M. dinner. The sauna was fired up daily during the Christmas season as opposed to the usual twice weekly. Commoners and nobility used it indiscriminately.

Afternoons I played instructor, teaching fencing, first aid, accounting, and arithmetic. I taught base-twelve arithmetic rather than the usual base-ten, in part because Boris Novacek insisted on it, in part because the people thought in terms of dozens and grosses rather than tens and hundreds, but mostly because they had convinced me that twelve is a more useful number than ten. Twelve has four factors; ten has only two. A circle can easily be divided into twelve parts, but it is almost impossible to divide it into ten without a protractor. Base-twelve is more condensed; you can state larger numbers with fewer digits.

In fact, the only advantage to the base-ten system is the unimportant biological fact that human beings happen to have ten fingers. I have heard that the American Maya Indians always went barefoot and so developed a base-twenty numbering system, counting on their toes as well as their fingers.

It was a simple matter to set up a base-twelve system. Zero and the numbers one through nine remained the same. Ten and eleven required new symbols; I picked the Greek letters delta and phi.

Counting went one, two three . . . nine, ten, eleven, twelve, oneteen, twoteen, thirteen . . . nineteen, tenteen, eleventeen, twenty, twenty-one . . . twenty-nine, twenty-ten, twenty-eleven, thirty, and so on. Eleventy-ten was the equivalent of decimal one hundred forty-two. Obvious, right? Then it was a matter of constructing multiplication tables and so on; again, straightforward.

I was astounded at how quickly some people picked up all this. Twentieth-century schools take eight years to teach children arithmetic, yet I had some students learn it in two weeks! It was as if their minds were dry sponges, eager to suck things in.

Class size varied between four and fifty. It was agreed that after the holidays, classes would be continued on Sunday afternoons.

The learning procedure was entirely by lecture, backed up with chanting for memorization. I had part of one wall of the hall plastered and painted black for use as a blackboard. There were no books, no paper, no pencils, no tests beyond verbal questions.

Despite those handicaps, learning proceeded well. By the end of his stay, Boris had a parchment ledger book that he understood better than I, since I was never able to learn to think in base-twelve arithmetic. I could *do* it but not *think* in it.

Boris complained that carrying and using slow-drying ink would be awkward on the road, so I suggested using a sharpened piece of hard lead. That worked fairly well, and a few years later we were producing and selling lead pencils, made with real lead instead of the modern graphite and clay mixture.

On the feast of the twelfth night, I was expected to give gifts to the commoners, and by then I knew precisely what to give them. The people were obviously suffering from a number of vitamin deficiencies. The seeds I had with me could make a valuable contribution to their diet if handled properly.

I sorted carefully through the seed packages, dividing them into six piles.

The first pile consisted of those which could be eaten and the seeds saved: the pumpkins, the squashes, the melons, the luffas, the tomatoes, etc. Those, I could give to the peasants and be sure that there would be seeds for future crops. There were ninety-two packets of those, enough to give one to each farmer.

The second pile contained those plants of which one ate the seeds themselves. Those were the really important crops: the grains, the maize, the potatoes, the peas, and the beans. It would be best if those were planted and harvested strictly for seed, at least the first year, since my understanding was that the modern varieties were more productive than the ancient ones. Those were best grown on the count's own lands since a peasant might get hungry and eat the seeds next winter. After some thought, I put the biennials, where I knew how they reproduced— the onions and garlic—in with this group.

The third pile consisted of the long-term plants: fruit trees, berry bushes, sugar maples, asparagus, grapevines, and so on. Those too were for Lambert's lands, since he could afford a long-term investment and a peasant probably could not.

The fourth pile contained plants that were decorative but had no economic use: decorative trees, flowers, and so on. Roses were nice, but I wasn't going to worry if we lost a strain. Those I would give to the women of the fort.

It turned out that I was completely wrong about the usefulness of some of these. Goldenrods were an excellent insect repellent, and people ate some of the flowers. And roses were their major source of vitamin C. The Japanese roses grew into a huge, tangled mass that became an excellent military defense, vastly superior to barbed wire! They also kept cattle out of the crops.

Then, there were plants that wouldn't grow in Poland at all. I had two packages of rice, six kinds of citrus fruits, and a package of cotton seeds. I didn't know why that redheaded bitch had sold them to me, but she had, and they were useless in Okoitz.

But Boris was going into the warmer lands of Hungary. I knew that rice and oranges would grow there, and—who knows?—maybe cotton would, too. I felt guilty about Lambert's settlement with Novacek, and the gift of seeds was a way I could help make it up to him. If he played his cards right—and Boris was no fool—those plants could make him rich.

The cotton was especially important. Cotton is better than linen, and it takes much less labor to make it into thread. In this clothing-conscious age, cotton could make Boris the vast fortune he so much desired.

Now if there had only been some tobacco seeds...

The last pile was of plants about which I had no idea how they reproduced. These were mainly root crops: carrots, turnips, radishes, and beets, along with the cabbage and its sisters cauliflower, broccoli, kale, Brussels sprouts, and kohlrabi. The last six are all really the same species and can be interbred. The best I could do with that pile was to turn it over to the count, and we'd try our luck. I was troubled because the sugar beets were in the last pile. With the incredible prices paid for sweets, sugar beets could be a very valuable cash crop for the count, but I didn't know how to make them reproduce.

The party went off fairly well. The people were all willing to try something new, and the count was willing to invest a few hectacres for seed production. The next spring, Father John and I, the only literate people in the fort, were kept busy reading and rereading seed packages for people.

It is annoying and time-consuming to be surrounded by illiterates. You can't leave a note for someone. You must find a messenger and trust his memory. You can't give written instructions. And somehow there's something *wrong* about illiteracy.

I found Father John working on a wood carving, a statue of a saint.

"Father, I think that we should start a school."

"Indeed? And teach what?"

"Why, reading and writing, of course."

"Now, what possible good would that do for my parish?"

"What possible good? These people are all illiterate! They can't write their own names, let alone read."

"And if I taught them to read, Sir Conrad, what then? What would they read?"

"Why, books, of course."

"The only books in Okoitz are a not particularly legible Bible and my own copy of Aristotle. These I can recite from memory. As for writing their names, where would they have need to sign them? On latrine walls?"

"But surely literacy is more important than a carving!"

"Indeed? Consider that the peasants tithe, but they give me only a tenth of what they sell to merchants, which is perhaps only a tenth of what they grow; they eat the rest. The count provides me with food and shelter but little else. I have a wife with . . . expectations. I can sell my carvings, and I cannot sell learning."

"Okay. I get your message, Father. How much do you earn by carving?"

"Five, six pence a week, sometimes."

"Very well. I will pay you—or, rather, donate to the Church—a penny a day for your teaching. Teach a dozen students, the bright ones, five days a week, from dinner until sundown during the winter. I especially want the Kulczynski boy, Piotr, taught. He has learned arithmetic in two weeks, and a mind like that must not be wasted."

"There will be expenses. Parchment, ink, wax tablets."

"Buy them. I'll give you a fund to pay for them. If you need other things, Father Ignacy of the Franciscan monastery in Cracow can provide them. He knows me."

"And I can still carve in the mornings?"

"Yes, damn it!"

"Then we are in agreement."

As I left Father John, I saw Count Lambert talking to a newly arrived knight. The fellow was very splendidly dressed in purple and gold. His armor was gold-washed and of very small links, the kind you see in museums. His embroidered velvet surcoat matched the velvet barding worn by his fine white charger, and the trim on his helmet and weapons looked to be solid gold.

I was just in blue jeans and sweater, but I went over to introduce myself.

"Ah, Sir Conrad," Lambert said. "I introduce you to Sir Stefan. Sir Conrad is my newest vassal; Sir Stefan is the son of my greatest vassal, Baron Jaroslav. The two of you will be serving together until Easter."

"I am honored, Sir Conrad," Sir Stefan said, somewhat taken aback by my size and strange clothing. "I had thought that I would be serving with Sir Miesko. Still, anyone who can do guard duty for the other half of a long winter's night is warmly welcome."

"Well, uh . . ." I stammered.

"Sir Miesko is on a mission for me in Hungary," Lambert said. "As for the rest, you touch upon a problem, Sir Stefan. You see, my arrangement with Sir Conrad is that he will have no military duties save in an actual emergency. I regret that this means that you will have to take the night guard by yourself."

"Dusk till dawn, seven nights a week in the winter, my lord. Surely that is excessive!"

I had to agree that he had a point. At Okoitz's latitude, there could be seventeen hours of darkness in the winter. Three months straight of night duty under those circumstances could make a man crazy and old before his time. I felt sorry for the young knight, but not enough to volunteer my time. It wasn't my job. I had my own work to do.

"Count Lambert," I said. "Can't you get another man to help him out?"

Lambert shook his head.

"For another knight to come, he would have to make arrangements with yet another warrior to look after his own estates; then that man would have to make similar arrangements, all of which would take time. It probably couldn't be done within three months, by which time it would no longer be needed. No. The lots were drawn last Michaelmas, and I won't upset the schedules for anything less than death or the threat of war."

"I resign myself," Stefan said. "But Sir Conrad, couldn't you occasionally help out?"

"Well, I'm sorry, but there are a lot of other projects I have to work on."

"Sir Conrad will have his own duties which only he can perform," Lambert said. "I am afraid that you are left with an arduous task, Sir Stefan."

"But *alone*, my lord?"

"Damn, man! I've explained it to you. Who else is there? The place must be guarded! I can't leave guard duty to a peasant. They'd start thinking that they were our equals. And surely you don't expect *me* to do it. It is more than sufficient that I must be awake during the day. I am your father's liege lord! Enough of this! *It is settled!*" I think Lambert felt as guilty as I did.

Sir Stefan glared at me as though it were all my fault and stalked off to the castle.

My first task was to get a gross of beehives built. There was really no hurry since bees don't swarm until June, but I wanted to establish a good working relationship with the carpenter before we started building a loom.

It was soon obvious that I was going to have difficulty with the man. Vitold had to be competent; he had supervised the construction of the entire fort. Yet when it came to sawing up some boards and building some simple boxes, he had a great deal of difficulty understanding what I wanted. I drew pictures on the snow, but three-view drawings were incomprehensible to him. He asked innumerable questions about bees and what it was that we were trying to accomplish. That went on for hours, and I was losing my temper by suppertime. We agreed to discuss it the next day. Admittedly, we were talking about a gross of the things and it would probably take a month or two to get them nailed together, but a box ought to be a simple thing.

The next morning, he caught me on my way to the blacksmith. If I couldn't get a box made, what was I going to do about the twenty-odd complicated steps involved in making watered steel?

"Sir Conrad?" Vitold asked. "Would it be all right with you if I just went ahead and built what I think you want? If you don't like them, we can always use 'em for firewood."

"That would be fine, Vitold." I figured that it would keep him out of my hair for a while, and once we had a sample, I could show him what he was doing wrong.

The blacksmith, Ilya, was the man who had been chosen king during the holidays. He had put me in diapers, and I did not have a favorable impression of his character.

"Ilya, the count wants me to tell you about steel."

"Well, since the count wants it, I'll listen. But I already know about steel."

He was working at his forge and didn't look up when he talked to me. This forge was a primitive affair about the size of an outdoor barbecue. It was a table-high rock pit with the back wall raised as a windscreen. A crude leather bellows forced air into one side. A roof without walls covered it and his anvil, his other major piece of equipment. A few pliers, punches, and hammers completed the smithy's small collection of tools. Charcoal in the forge burned yellow-hot.

"You know something about wrought iron. You know nothing about steel," I said.

"Huh." He still didn't look up. He was a short man, but he looked to be immensely strong. Even though we were outside in the snow, his sleeves were rolled up, revealing arms twice as thick as mine. He was repairing the armor that the pig had worn when I killed it a few weeks before. "Damned lucky work, here. You must have hit a couple of weak links."

"I did nothing of the sort! I killed that pig because my sword is good steel and that armor is cheap wrought iron!"

"Nothing wrong with this armor." He still didn't look up. He was beating an iron ring into the mail shirt draped over the anvil, working over the tip of the point.

"Damn it, look at me when I'm talking to you!"

He glanced up. "I see you." Then he went back to his work.

"Well, if you won't look at me, look at my sword!" I drew it to show him what watered steel looked like.

"Skinny little thing."

Obviously, I was going to have to get his attention. It occurred to me that chopping a hole through the mail he was working on might do the trick.

"Damn you, Ilya! You stand back or you're going to lose a hand!" I swung at the armor draped over the anvil and he got out of the way in time.

The results were surprising. Fortunately, Ilya was too busy staring at the anvil with his mouth open to notice my expression. I had cut three centimeters off the end of the anvil, and the armor was almost in two pieces, hanging by a shred. My sword was undamaged.

My experience as an officer had taught me to recover quickly. "Now fix that, Ilya," I growled. "Then you come to me after supper tonight and we'll talk." I walked off as though I knew what I was doing.

The carpenter was selecting logs from the firewood pile, about a meter long and half that thick, splitting them in half and laying the halves side by side on the snow.

I didn't want to ask.

I went back to the castle, thinking about a mug of beer. Maybe the count would want a game of chess. A noble wasn't allowed to play with commoners because he might lose.

Janina got my beer, and the girls pounced on me.

"Sir Conrad, you promised to show us how to make that wonderful knot work." Krystyana wasn't very good at playing the coquette. I think she was trying to imitate Francine, the priest's wife.

"Hmm. I don't remember promising anything, but I'll think on it." Thinking did me surprisingly little good. Understand that my mother knitted constantly. Unless she was cooking or sleeping, her needles and yarn were always out. My grandmother had done the same while she was alive.

And, you know? I had never really looked at what they were doing. I knew that there was a needle in each hand, with little loops of yarn that connected them to the fabric below. She did something complicated with them in the middle. I spent more than an hour trying to visualize what it was, and the girls drifted away, embarrassed.

Then a partial solution occurred to me. I didn't know what knitting was, but when I was seven, my grandmother had shown me how to crochet. I got some heavy slivers of wood from the carpenter, who was still splitting logs and laying them out.

Other groups were working. One bunch of men had piles of flax lying on the ground, and they were beating on them with large wooden mallets. Some women were shredding it into fiber. A few others were braiding a sort of rope. Some repair work was in progress on a straw roof. No one seemed to be in charge, but things were getting done.

I took my sticks back to my room, and in an hour I had whittled three usable crochet hooks. The lack of sandpaper was a nuisance, but if you take your time you can get things fairly smooth with just a knife. I borrowed a candle from the count's room and waxed them. I borrowed some yarn and shortly produced a pot holder that was as good as anything I had done when I was seven.

The girls were thrilled and picked it up without difficulty. Within a week I had two usable linen undershirts and Lambert was equally well equipped. The ladies were soon experimenting with variations, some of which were quite nice, and the peasant women were following their lead.

One surprising thing about technology is that very often the simplest processes and devices take the longest to develop, or perhaps I should say that it's surprising until you've been a designer. It is much easier, conceptually, to design a complicated thing than a refined simple mechanism. Those intricate machines that came out of twentieth-century Germany are really the results of lazy thinking.

Consider the evolution of the musket. The expensive and tricky wheel lock was produced for a hundred years before some nameless craftsman came up with the simple and dependable flintlock.

Or look at this crocheting business. It's hard to imagine

a simpler tool than a crochet hook. It produces a useful cloth fairly quickly, yet I do not know of a single primitive tribe that uses it. Even nomads, who must carry all their belongings with them, haul along a simple loom to make cloth.

A designer can mull over complicated designs for months. Then suddenly the simple, elegant, beautiful solution occurs to him. When it happens to you, it feels as if God is talking! And maybe He is.

After supper, Mary escorted Ilya the blacksmith into my room. He was considerably less surly than he had been in the afternoon.

"Sir Conrad, please understand that when I have the forge going, I have to work! It takes me two or three days to make enough charcoal to feed the fire for a single afternoon."

"Okay, Ilya. I'll count that as an apology if you'll excuse my temper. Now, about steel."

The door was open, and Lambert walked in. "Yes, Sir Conrad, about steel! I want to listen in on this.

"You've had a productive day! All my ladies are busily tying balls of yarn into remarkable knots, and I hear that you have invented a new technique for obtaining Ilya's attention."

In a place so small, everybody seemed to know what everyone else was doing. "I'm sorry about losing my temper, my lord. I imagine that anvils are expensive."

"Yes, but Ilya fixed it and the mail as well." His eyes twinkled. "I've occasionally considered using a similar technique on his head, but I feared for my sword. Now, tell us about steel."

"Well, the first step is to convert the wrought iron into blister steel. Wrought iron is almost pure iron; steel is iron with a little bit of carbon in it. Charcoal is mostly carbon, so the trick is to mix them.

"You start by beating the iron until it's fairly thin, thinner than your little finger. Then you get a clay pot with a good clay lid. You put the iron in the pot and pack it all around tight with charcoal, crushed fine. You put the lid on and seal it with good clay. It's important that no air gets into the pot.

"Then you build a fire around it, slowly heat it up to a dull red, and keep the fire going for a week."

"What? A whole week?" Ilya interrupted.

"Yes. A wood fire is hot enough, though. Now, if you've done this right and the pot hasn't cracked and no air has gotten in, the iron will have little pimples on it, and it will now be steel. Not a good grade of steel but good for some things. What I've just described is called the cementation process.

"You don't know anything about heat-treating, do you? No, I guess you wouldn't. Wrought iron stays soft no matter what you do with it. Well, steel can be hardened. You heat it until it's bright red, almost yellow, and dunk it in water. This will make it hard, so it can keep a good edge. The trouble is, it breaks easily.

"Then there is tempering, which makes it tougher. After hardening, you heat it to almost red, then let it cool slowly."

"That's what there is to it?" Ilya asked.

"That's what there is to making a decent kitchen knife or an axe blade, but it won't be springy enough for a sword. It might break unless you made it as heavy as the count's."

"So let's have the rest of it."

"Hey, this is going to be a lot harder than it sounds," I said. "Just learning how to cook a pot that long without breaking it is going to take a lot of tries, and tempering is an art form."

"Well, I want to hear it anyway."

"Yes, Sir Conrad, tell us the whole process," Lambert said.

"Okay. I'll tell you how they do it in Damascus." Actually, I didn't know how they did it in Damascus, but I'd seen Jacob Bronowski's magnificent television series, and he had showed how they did it in Japan, which was probably similar. "You weld a piece of this cemented steel to a similar piece of good wrought iron. You know how to weld, don't you?"

"Does the Pope know how to pray?"

"I'll take that as an affirmative. You weld them together and beat it out until it's twice as long as it was. Then you bend it over and weld it again. Then you heat it up again, beat it out long again, bend it over again, and weld it again. You repeat this at least twelve and preferably fifteen times. This gives you a layered structure thousands of layers thick."

"That sounds impossible."

"No, but it *is* difficult. Look carefully at my sword. See those little lines? Those tiny waves? Those are layers of iron and steel. It's called watering, and it's the mark of the best blades."

"That's it, then?"

"Almost. Then you beat it until it looks like a sword. Once you start playing with hardening, you'll learn that the faster the steel cools, the harder it gets. You want the edge very hard but the shank springy. You coat the sword with clay, thin near the edge and thick at the shank. You heat it, clay and all, until it's the 'color of the rising sun' and quench it in water the same temperature as your hand. Then you temper it and polish it. Soaking it in vinegar will bring out the watering."

"That's a long-winded process," Ilya said.

"But worth it, I'll wager," the count said. "Ilya, you work on it—in addition to your other duties, of course. Good night, Ilya. A game of chess, Sir Conrad?"

Lambert won one of our games that night. By spring he was beating me two games out of three.

Chapter Fifteen

I AWOKE to find that the carpenter was burning all the logs he had split and laid out the day before. Not one big bonfire, you understand, but hundreds of little fires, one in each split log. Furthermore, he had recruited half a dozen of the children to help him at this task. Two of the older boys were splitting kindling, and the rest were tending the fires under his supervision.

I *knew* that I didn't want to get involved.

I scrounged up some splinters of about knitting-needle size and retired to my room.

You see, it often happens with me that a problem that I have in the day gets solved in the middle of the night. I'd woken up in the dark with the answer, sitting bolt upright and startling Natalia.

It was obvious. I had a product sample, a sweater that my mother had knitted. All I had to do was figure out how to stick the knitting needles into it and then perform the operation backward! Taking it apart, I could tell how to put it together.

I had the needles ready by dinnertime, and I eagerly went at it as soon as the meal was over. It was not as easy as I had thought. I was not aided by the fact that my sweater was very fancy, with lots of embossing and special twists. Also, I did not know which end was up.

It was a long, frustrating afternoon. I learned little and lost a third of my only sweater.

Ladies wandered in and out, but I really didn't have time to be friendly.

The carpenter was still out there, burning his logs, with a new crew of helpers.

After supper, I was at it by the smoky light of an oil lamp when Count Lambert took the stuff out of my hands, handed it to Krystyana, and sat me down at the chess board.

"Time for recreation, Sir Conrad."

By the end of the third game, Krystyana had my sweater partially reassembled.

"You see, Sir Conrad," the count said, beaming. "Another eldritch art that you have taught my people."

"Uh . . . yes, my lord."

"By the way, do you have any idea as to just what Vitold is doing out there with all those fires?"

"In truth, my lord, he has been confusing me for the past two days."

"Now *that* is refreshing to hear. I hate to be the only one who doesn't know what is going on. Sometimes I think they play a game called confuse the count.

"Bedtime. Coming, Krystyana? Or is it someone else's turn?"

At noon the next day Vitold showed me the first sample beehive; by dusk he had completed the entire gross. In three days he had finished a job that I had assumed would take months.

It seems that boards were hard to make. They had to be sawed by hand out of tree trunks, using a poor saw. Nails were even harder. They had to be hammered one at a time out of very expensive iron.

But though a modern carpenter thinks in terms of boards and fasteners, Vitold thought in terms of taking trees and making things out of them.

As the firewood was already cut, splitting was a fairly simple job. He then burned out a hollow in each half log, carefully leaving about five centimeters untouched all the way around. An entrance hole was chopped in with an axe, and the two troughs were tied back together again with a sturdy, though crude, linen rope. To harvest, you untied the rope, removed the combs, and retied it.

Vitold's method was one of those brilliantly simple things that I was talking about earlier. There was a lot I had to teach the people of the thirteenth century. There was also a great deal that I had to learn.

I haven't talked much about children in this confession, perhaps because the subject is so painful. In modern Poland, children are cherished, as they are in all civilized countries. In the thirteenth century, this was not always true. Perhaps because so many of them died so young, you did not dare love them too much.

From puberty to menopause, if they lived that long, the women of Okoitz were almost continually pregnant. Most of them averaged twelve to fifteen births. There was no concept of birth control, no feeling that one should abstain from sex. In that small community of perhaps a hundred families, there were typically two births a week. There was also more than a weekly funeral, usually a tiny cloth-wrapped bundle without even a wooden coffin.

The adults, too, died young. Forty was considered old. The medical arts that can keep a sick person alive did not exist. You were healthy or you were dead!

And there was nothing I could do about it. I was completely ignorant of most medicine. Oh, I had taken all the standard first-aid courses. I could give mouth-to-mouth resuscitation. I could treat frostbite and heat stroke and shock. I could splint a fracture and tend a wound. But all that I had learned was learned for the purpose of knowing what to do *until the doctor arrives*.

I got into this sad subject because Krystyana's baby sister was dead. Her father had rolled on the baby while sleeping and smothered it. Because of the harsh winters and unheated houses, babies slept with their parents. It was the only way to keep them from freezing. And the father just—rolled over.

The look on the man's face—he couldn't have been much older than I was, but his face was lined and weathered, his hands were wrinkled, calloused claws, and his back was bent as if he were still carrying a grain sack— the look on that man's face was such that I couldn't stay through the all-too-brief church ceremony. I had to leave and I had to cry.

Everyone already knew that I was strange, and they left me alone.

I am not a doctor. I am an engineer. I did not know what most of those people were dying of. Hell, nobody here had cancer! People just got a bellyache and died! But I *did* know that a better diet, better sanitation, better clothing, better housing, and—damn it—a little heat would do wonders for them.

A sawmill for wooden floors and beds that got them off the floor. An icehouse to help preserve food. Looms for more and better cloth. A better stove for heating and cooking. Some kind of laundry—these people couldn't wash their clothes all winter!—a sewage system, and a water system.

These were things that I could do; these were things that I *would* do!

That and get ready to fight the Mongols.

It was just after Christmas that I started working on my master plan, or at least the first few glimpses of it started to come to me.

If we were going to accomplish anything with regard to the Mongols, we would need arms and armor on a scale unprecedented in thirteenth-century Poland. We would need iron, steel, and—if possible—gunpowder by the hundreds of tons.

That meant heavy industry, and heavy industry is equipment-intensive. A blast furnace can't be shut down for Sundays or holidays. It can't stop working for the planting or the harvest. Its workers have to be skilled specialists.

A steel works at Okoitz, or anywhere else in Poland's agricultural system, was simply an impossibility, yet the work could not be done in the existing cities, either. Not when dozens of powerful, tradition-minded guilds guarded their special privileges and were ready to fight anything new. Obviously, to have a free hand to introduce innovations, I would need my own land and my own people. Well, Lambert had said that was possible.

I would need to be able to feed my workers, and the local agricultural techniques produced very little surplus. Here the seeds I had packed in should help. Chemical fertilizers, insecticides, and better farm machinery were a ways off, but work on animal husbandry should be started immediately.

I'd already promised to get some light industry going—clothmaking and so on—which would improve my status with the powers that be as well as getting people more decent clothing.

Windmills. We could definitely use some windmills, and I hadn't seen one in this century.

I talked with Lambert about my plans for Okoitz, and while I don't think he grasped a third of what I had in mind, he gave me his blessings. "Yes, of course, Sir Conrad. These innovations are precisely what I wanted you to do. You are welcome to all the timber you can get cut and all the work you can get out of the peasants."

"Thank you, my lord."

"Just don't do anything silly like interfering with the planting or harvest."

"Of course not. Uh, you mentioned once that I could have lands of my own."

"Yes, I did, didn't I. But there's a slight difficulty there. You see, you are a foreigner—"

"I am not, my lord. I was born in Poland."

"Well, you talk funny, so it comes to the same thing. The law is that I can't assign you lands without my liege lord's permission. It's just a formality, really. I'm sure he'll grant it when next I see him, probably in the next year or two."

"The next *year or two*? That's quite a delay!"

"Oh, likely he'll be by in the spring or summer. What is your hurry? You have just outlined projects here at Okoitz that will take years to complete."

I talked for a while about Mongols, heavy industry, and blast furnaces.

"Oh, if you say so, Sir Conrad. If I must, I'll send a rider with a letter to find the duke, taking your word on faith.

"I must say that belief in a fire that is so intense that one dares not let it die—well, it stretches the mind more that transubstantiation!"

"But you'll send the letter?"

"After Easter, if necessary. You couldn't build anything on your land until the snow melts, anyway."

For the next few months, my time was divided, unevenly, four ways. One was animal husbandry. The people of Okoitz knew the basic principles of animal breeding. They produced outstanding war-horses, but somehow the techniques had not filtered down to the more mundane world of farm animals.

A modern hen produces more than an egg a day. The hens of Okoitz produced perhaps an egg a week. The sheep were small and scrawny; I doubted if there was a kilo of wool on any one of them. The milk cows looked likely to produce only a few liters a day, and then only in the spring and summer. Grown pigs were only a quarter of the size of the modern animal.

Much of the reason for this was economic. A farmer with a cow, two pigs, and six chickens was in no position to get involved with scientific breeding. Another part of the problem was that they tended to use farm animals as scavengers. Kept grossly underfed, pigs and chickens were allowed to run free and were expected to find much of their own food. That resulted in indiscriminate breeding and constant arguments about someone's pigs eating someone else's crops. It also spread shit over everything.

But the count had his own herds, and if we could improve the quality of those, the results would spread. For the most part, my program was a matter of dividing each species into a small A herd and a larger B herd. The A herd contained the best animals, most of them females. They got better food and the best available herdsman, who was expected to get to know them as individuals.

They were kept strictly apart from the B herd, except when inferior animals were demoted. The B herd was for eating. There were two A herds for cattle, one for beef and one for dairy products, but it took some time to convince Lambert that it was useful to breed separately for two desired sets of qualities.

The same was done for chickens: one A flock for eggs and one for fast growth. I concentrated on chickens because they have a shorter life cycle, and selective breeding would give faster results.

Breeding for egg production requires accounting. You have to know which chicken is producing how many eggs. This involves an "egg factory," with each hen imprisoned in a tiny cell. It was labor-intensive in that food and water had to be brought to them. I had a small rack built by each cell. When the breeders took out an egg, they put a stone in the rack. Big egg, big stone; little egg, little stone.

Once a month, the hens were evaluated. The best hens got a rooster, and the worst were demoted to the short-lived B flock. The mediocre got to keep their jobs. I got a couple of the older women interested in the project, and egg production doubled in the first year.

As time went on, most of our best animal breeders were women. They seemed to understand the concepts better.

A half dozen holidays came and went. These annoyed me because they cut down on the man-hours I had available. The holidays came to a height in a weeklong carnival, a Polish Mardi Gras, from Lenten Thursday to Ash Wednesday. "Carnival" is Latin for "good-bye, meat." Lent was not so much the religious abstinence from meat eating as the formal acknowledgment that the village was actually *out* of animal products and that those animals left had to be kept for spring and summer breeding.

The second of my time-consuming jobs was lumbering. Understand that the people of Okoitz had felled a lot of trees. Okoitz was built almost completely of logs, and in the last four years a huge effort had gone into it.

But those logs were actually the by-product of land clearance. If you want to clear land for farming, you not only have to remove the tree, you have to remove the stump. The sensible way is not to chop the tree down; you dig around the tree, cut out the roots, and then *pull* the tree down. Since you can't dig in frozen ground, tree removal was a summer job.

Lumber cut in the winter is superior to that cut in the summer. It is drier. There was some nearby hilly ground that was not suitable for farming but could do well as orchards. Leaving the stumps in would delay erosion until the orchard was established.

Projects I had in mind for the next summer were going to require a lot of wood, and that all added up to winter lumbering.

The difficulty was that the peasants were not *used* to working hard in the winter. Except for spreading manure on the snow and basic housekeeping tasks, winter was when you went to bed early and slept late and spent the time in between enjoying yourself. It took a lot of persuasion to get things done.

Incidentally, my horse, Anna, was quite willing to wear a horse collar and drag logs, provided that one was polite to her. Several peasants with whips were bitten and one was seriously kicked before the message got across. Anna developed a friendship with an eight-year-old girl, one of Janina's sisters, and those two made a very productive team. Somewhat later, it was discovered that the count's best stallion was also willing to work, provided that he was allowed to work next to Anna. Such things gave people their first new subjects of conversation since my arrival.

I was watching this strange and amusing trio dragging a huge log down the snowy hill when another log being dragged by a team of oxen broke loose and started rolling.

There were screams and shouts and people scrambling. The oxen were knocked over and probably would have been killed if the rope around the log hadn't come loose. The log bounded downhill, bouncing off some tree stumps and smashing others to splinters.

Mikhail Malinski was downhill of the rolling log. He had been taking his dull axe down to the blacksmith's temporary forge to get the cutting edge sharpened. With the wrought-iron tools, the edge wasn't ground—that was wasteful of iron—it was heated up and the edge was beaten sharp.

Mikhail heard the shouting, looked up the hill, and saw the log coming at him. Dropping his axe, he ran diagonally away. When he saw that he was clear, he stopped to watch, leaning against a large tree stump to catch his breath. The log struck another stump and spun completely around, smashing Mikhail's left ankle against the stump he was leaning on; then it bounced off and continued downhill.

I was the first to get to Mikhail. His ankle was red mush, and his foot was almost off. Blood was spurting from the wound. He was screaming; he knew he was going to die. Without thinking, I stripped off my leather belt, wrapped it around his calf, and twisted it tightly until the squirting stopped.

This was reflexes, this was training, this was what one did until the doctor arrived.

Only, deep inside me, a panicky voice was yelling at me that *I was it*! There was no impersonal institution to take Mikhail away and tell us later if he lived or died. There was only me, and I was not competent.

But as always, when I am scared and don't know what to do, the actor surfaces. I say the phony words and adopt a phony posture and try to fake it.

"Easy, Mikhail, easy. Don't worry, we'll take care of you." A crowd was gathering. I pointed to a long-legged young man. "You! You run to the castle and tell Krystyana or whoever of the handmaidens is there that I want the kitchen table clean with a fresh cloth on it. I want a big kettle of water boiling, and I want all the clean napkins she's got. Have it ready for us! Now move!" He moved.

"You! Take my cloak off. Spread it on the ground over there." I still had one hand on the tourniquet. "Now, you eight men! Get around us. The rest of you, back! Now, pick him up. Easy, now! Put him on the cloak! That's it. Now, pick up the cloak! No! Face *that* way, dummy! Now, we carry him back to the castle."

I trailed behind him, still holding the tourniquet, trying to remember what to do next. There was nothing in my training to tell me. Except ... except, once over a Christmas holiday in the dormitories, I spent two weeks improving my English by devouring Forester's Hornblower novels. There was one very graphic sequence where the excellent Mr. Bush lost a foot in combat and was tended by early nineteenth-century physicians. *Oh God*, I hoped that Forester knew what he was talking about and was not as great a phony as I was!

We got Mikhail on the kitchen table. "Okay. Now, lift him up and off my cloak; the cloak isn't clean enough. The first rule of tending a wound is to make it clean."

I started lecturing, acting as if this were a classroom demonstration, partly to reassure Mikhail, partly to rehearse to myself what I was to do, but mostly to shut out the reality of the bleeding man in front of me.

I had the count hold the tourniquet, and I cut away Mikhail's clothes with my jackknife. I washed my hands and the smashed foot, talking all the while about the importance of cleanliness. The foot felt like a bag of broken rocks. We got a few liters of wine into Mikhail, and I took a drink myself.

"One break or two could heal," I said. "This foot is going to have to come off." A stir went through the crowd. "That's not so bad. We can make him a new one later, out of wood." I washed my jackknife in wine and then in boiling water. I got a pair of scissors and cleaned them up. And a needle and thread, I remembered. I found the arteries by having Lambert loosen the tourniquet and seeing what squirted. I had to cut away flesh to find the things. Tying them off, I left long threads, as Forester mentioned. I trimmed the skin and pulled it up to the calf. It was "usual" to saw the bone, but not a saw in the town was up to it. I cleaned my sword and chopped the bone with a single hack. Then I sewed the wound almost shut. I left the strings from the arteries hanging out, as well as a twist of boiled linen. Forester had stressed the importance of draining.

Mikhail stood up to it fairly well, considering that the

amputation and all was done with no other anesthetic than wine. Most of the time he didn't have to be held down. You see, he wanted to believe my acting job. He *needed* to believe in the firm words I mouthed, and so he did.

We put Mikhail in one of the spare rooms in the castle, and the crowd dispersed.

I met Sir Stefan as he went to do his nightly guard duty, heavily bundled against the wintery night. The long, lonely hours were telling on him. He looked tired and older than he had been a month before.

"Sir Conrad, what's this I hear about you chopping off a peasant's foot on the kitchen table? What did the man do to deserve that?"

I was blood-splattered and tired. "Deserve? He didn't deserve it at all. He was hurt, and I had to amputate to heal him."

"So your witchcraft includes blood rites?"

"Witchcraft? Damn it, I—"

"Oh, I'm sorry." He held his hand up. "I spoke out of turn. You must know how tired I am, standing guard from dusk to dawn every night without relief while you are bedded safe with a young wench."

"Yeah. I know you've got a rough job. But it's only for a couple more months."

"Two more months of this without a wench of nights, just so you can play peasant carpenter during the day?"

"Look, Sir Stefan. If I hadn't been out there today, Mikhail would have lost more than his foot. He would have lost his life."

"Well, what of it? What damn use is a crippled peasant?"

"You're disgusting."

"*I'm* disgusting? You've just drenched the kitchen table with human blood! I have to eat off that table while you sleep soundly!" He stomped out.

Mikhail was a model patient. The wound was never seriously inflamed and seemed to be healing well. I visited him several times a day. His wife was tending him, sleeping beside him. The children, including the kid I had brought in from the storm, had been farmed out except during Ignacy's feeding time.

We talked about his future. He was thinking about becoming a trader. Traders were mostly on horseback, weren't they? I promised to advance him money and introduce him to Boris Novacek.

Within a month, I carefully pulled out the long strings, removed the rotted ends of the arteries, and then closed the wound. All seemed well. In a few weeks, we were talking about moving him back to his home.

Then one night he got a fever and was dead in the morning.

I don't know why.

Two weeks after the funeral, Lambert decided that it would be good if Ilya the blacksmith married the widow; a month later there was an Easter wedding.

Lambert had eleven barons subordinate to him. These men held lands from the count. Each had his own fort or manor, and all of them but one had subordinate knights, often with manors of their own. The number of their knights varied from zero to twenty-six. In addition, fifteen knights, including myself, reported directly to the count.

The great majority of the noblemen held their positions on a hereditary basis, but it was still possible for an outstanding commoner to be elevated.

And, of course, the count ran things at Okoitz. A number of specialists—the smith, the carpenter, the baker, and so on—had specific areas of responsibility and worked directly under the count. The castle itself was run by a constantly changing group of adolescent handmaidens, but on closer observation I found that the cook exerted a strong, steadying influence on them.

The farmers worked through a half dozen foremen, who in turn took directions from Piotr Korzeniewski. These leaders were neither elected nor appointed but attained their positions and got things done by a system of consensus that I never fully understood. People just talked things over for a while and then, somehow, things were accomplished.

Piotr had no official standing or title. In theory, all the farmers worked directly for Lambert. I was at Okoitz for months before I realized that Piotr was really the chief executive of the whole town.

Knowledge of Okoitz's ghost structure was to prove very useful to me over the years. Most of the nobility were interested only in fighting, hunting, and playing status games with each other. When I wanted something of a manor—sanitation measures or workers for my factories—the quickest way to do things was to have one of my subordinates talk things over with the informal executive.

But I get ahead of myself.

Chapter Sixteen

MY THIRD endeavor was the loom. The count insisted that we set up the loom as a permanent fixture in his hall. The situation in the cloth industry annoyed him, and he wanted the loom as a showpiece for his summer guests. The concept of keeping a profitable trade secret was entirely foreign to him. I never saw him really concerned about money at all. What he wanted was the prestige of being the man who cracked the strangling cloth monopoly.

Understand that the hall was a large room. It could handle a hundred people at a sit-down dinner. It took up most of the ground floor of the castle, and the ceiling was fully four meters high.

In order to use as little floor space as possible, my loom design was more vertical than horizontal. A loom, in essence, is a simple device. It has a framework to support a few thousand spools of thread that go lengthwise through the cloth produced. Whether this was the warp or woof, I didn't know. I wasn't a weaver, and in fact I made up my own terminology as I went along. We didn't have a warp or a woof. We had long threads and short threads.

There are some frames that loop around the long threads to spread them apart in the proper order so that the short threads can be passed through. The simplest number of these spreaders would be two, but I wanted the loom to be able to produce more complicated weaves, like tweeds, so I built it with six spreaders, each of which connected with one-sixth of the long threads. There is a shuttle that holds the short thread as it gets tossed back and forth, and there is a thing that beats the short threads tightly together. Finally, there is a roll for the finished cloth.

I was sure that on modern looms there is a friction device that holds the long threads tight, yet lets them advance as cloth was made. However, I couldn't think up a simple way of doing it. It would have to be *very* simple, since we needed a thousand of them.

I solved the problem by bypassing it. The carpenter drilled an array of holes, thirty-six wide by forty-eight high, directly into the wooden wall of the count's hall. Into these he pounded 1,728 pegs to hold the long spools of thread. This was a convenient number, since it was twelve cubed—a thousand in our new base-twelve arithmetic.

From there, the threads were to loop up over a pole near the ceiling, down under a suspended pole that could be raised as the threads were consumed, and then up to the four-meter ceiling again and down through the spreaders, the beater, and the cloth bolt.

This arrangement let you make eight meters of cloth before you had to loosen each of the thousand spools and lower the suspended pole again.

A working solution if not a perfect one.

The finished loom took up about four square meters of floor space, eight if you counted the area for the two operators. It produced a band of cloth two meters wide.

Sir Stefan waddled in one sunset as I was talking to Vitold about the spreaders. Sir Stefan was in full armor and heavily bundled and cloaked against the cold. "Another piece of witchcraft, Sir Conrad?" His voice was weary.

Vitold crossed himself but remained silent.

"A loom for making cloth," I said. "I wish you would knock off this nonsense about witchcraft."

"Nonsense, is it? Then how do you explain that witch's familiar of a mare you own?"

"I bought Anna in Cracow not two months ago. She's nothing but a good, well-trained horse."

"Indeed? Do you know what I saw last night? I saw your familiar leave the stables, go to the latrines, and relieve herself there! I followed her back to her stall and saw her putting the bar back in place. That's no natural horse!" He was glaring at me.

"Yeah, the stable boy told me she didn't soil her stall, but so what? If a dog can be housebroken, why not a horse? I told you she was well trained."

"Well trained? She's some manner of demon! Conrad, know that my father is Baron Jaroslav, the greatest of Lambert's vassals and well known to Duke Henryk. I swear that they will hear of your warlock's tricks!" he shouted as he stomped out into the snow.

Vitold crossed himself again.

"Damn it, Vitold, don't *you* start believing that horse-shit! You've been building this thing. You know there is nothing magic in it!"

"I can only do as my betters bid me." He returned to work, but you could tell that his heart wasn't in it.

We were a month getting the loom built, and then I asked for 1,728 spools of thread, each perhaps 500 meters long, to string it with.

I was looked on with horror. That amount of thread simply did not exist.

I said that I had to have it or I couldn't thread the loom. At least that much more would be needed for the short threads.

So the girls dug out their distaffs and went to work.

It was my turn to be horrified. The distaff was nothing more than a small wooden cross. You stretched some wool between the bars of the cross, and your hand gave the cross a spin. This twisted the thread. Then you wrapped the half meter of thread around the cross, stretched some more wool, etc.

The truly labor-intensive part of clothmaking wasn't in the weaving at all. It was in the spinning. I had taken off on a project without first knowing what all the parameters were. You might expect this of a beginner but not of a seasoned engineer.

I told the girls to put away their distaffs and went to work on a spinning wheel.

We were five weeks getting a spinning wheel working, partially because I had to come up with a wood lathe first. Also, we lost a week because I didn't realize that you have to have *two* loops of string from the wheel to the spindle, one to turn the spool and one to turn the twister a little faster.

Our first spinning wheel looked a lot like what you would see in a modern museum, because that's what I modeled it on. There were a lot of design flaws that were cleared up on subsequent models. The bench seat was uncomfortable, and one couldn't wear a long dress while using it. Our ladies wore a floor-length dress or nothing. Calf-length dresses were for field workers. The foot pedal gave the operator leg cramps, and it was discovered that if one tied a string from one's big toe to the crank of the wheel, it worked a lot easier.

I had learned a long time ago that if the operators don't approve of your engineering, your machines don't work. If they wanted a string on their big toe, they got a string on their big toe.

It was a lot easier to work if the spindle faced the operator at about an arm's length rather than being placed horizontally under her breasts.

Our third model had places for six operators, who sat facing each other in a circle. The job was boring, and they liked to talk.

It took six spinsters to keep up with the loom. Lambert solved this problem by putting on a few more ladies-in-waiting.

Also, it took two men—one holding the chisel, one turning the crank—six weeks on our new wood lathe to make enough spools to put the thread on.

I subsequently found out that spinning and weaving are two of the seven production steps necessary in making the crudest of homespun cloth. To produce the best commercial cloth required some thirty production steps.

It was going to take a while.

"Look, Sir Conrad, you'll be able to get this going by Easter, won't you?" the count asked.

"Well, the spinning and weaving at least, my lord. I don't think that we have enough washed and carded wool to keep us going for long."

"I'm ahead of you there. I've already sent word to my knights to send me all of their wool, and all of it washed and carded. Also, they are to send me two-thirds of the wool from this spring's shearing, and the acreage in flax is to be doubled."

"Excellent, my lord. You realize that weaving linen takes a slightly different loom, don't you? It takes more threads, closer together, and only two spreaders."

"What of it? Vitold can build more now that you've shown him the way. We'll have a dozen looms going by next year! You just put your mind to the problems of washing and carding."

"The washing is simple enough, but I'm still not sure of the carding."

"You will solve it." I wasn't sure if he was expressing confidence in my abilities or giving me an order. Sheep's wool is much finer than human hair and a sheep goes all year without combing it. As a result, it is incredibly tangled, and untangling it is what carding is all about.

"Sir Conrad, thus far you have seen us only as a small agrarian community. You must realize that Okoitz is the capital of a fair-sized province. After Easter, all sorts of people will be coming through, my uncle and liege lord, Duke Henryk the Bearded, among them. It is essential that we make a good impression."

"Yes, my lord. You say that Henryk is your uncle?"

"Well, of sorts. Henryk's father was Boleslaw the Tall; my grandfather, Miesko the Stumbling, was Boleslaw's brother, both sired by Wladyslaw the Exile."

Western countries give their rulers numbers. We Poles prefer nicknames. It's friendlier.

"In addition, after our father's untimely death, Henryk raised my brother Herman and me until we came of age. Being the eldest, he got the established city of Cieszyn and its environs. I got the Vistula–Odra Road and perforce have had to build my own town."

Another difference between eastern and western Europe was that in the west, inheritance was by primogeniture. The oldest son inherited everything, and the rest were out of luck. They might get a good job with the Church or in the army, but they were commoners.

In Poland, the rule was to divide things fairly evenly between the sons, with a very substantial dowry for the daughters. This was a nicer system, but it had the disadvantage of shattering the country and weakening—often destroying—central authority. A hundred years before, Boleslaw the Wrymouth, the last king of Poland, had divided the country up among his five sons, giving only nominal authority to the eldest. That is all very well unless you are about to get invaded.

"Certainly an ambitious project, my lord."

"So it is. But we are midway on the road, and Okoitz has to grow. Now that you've had time to look it over, what do you think of it, Sir Conrad?"

The place to build cities is at the end of a road, where pack mules change cargoes with riverboats, but I thought it wise not to mention this. And as a military defense, wooden walls only four meters high were a sick joke. The Mongols could take it in hours. But for now, there was nothing I could do about it, and I saw no reason to irritate my liege lord. "In many ways excellent, my lord. This business of building cottages side by side, sharing a wall and built against the outer wall, saves materials and heat. But I worry about fire. A single fire could burn down all of Okoitz. I have seen places where they build every other dividing wall out of brick to serve as a fire-stop."

"I can see that you haven't priced bricks and mortar, Sir Conrad."

"No, my lord, I haven't. But the new mill should give some protection. It will have a water tank higher than the church. I plan on having a fire hose long enough to reach any part of Okoitz."

"Then see to it."

Dismissed, I went out to the bailey just as a strange

procession was coming through the main gate. Sir Stefan
was riding proudly in the lead, followed by a dozen peasants holding on to strong chains. Between the peasants,
snarling, tugging, trying hard to get away, was a fair-sized
brown bear chained around the neck.

"What on earth—" I said to Stefan.

"A bit of sport, Sir Conrad," he said, getting down
from his horse. "We were a month trapping him and most
of the day getting him chained and out of the pit. But he's
a beauty, hey?"

"But what would you want with a live bear?"

"Why, to bait him, of course! Look you, Sir Conrad,
what would you say to a gentlemanly wager? I'll bet you
a thousand pence that that bear can kill six dogs before
it's brought down. What say you?"

I heard someone behind me whisper, "That's a sucker
bet. That bear is good for a dozen, easy." But I ignored
it.

"What do you mean, bait him?" I asked.

"You don't know the sport? Well, we'll chain him to
that post and turn the dogs on him. A good bear like this
one can go for hours before he's ripped apart."

"That's horrible!" I said, meaning it. "What a disgusting, brutal, ugly thing to do."

"Well, damn! If you don't like it, don't look!"

"But you can't do this! There are children here!"

"What of it? They've seen bear baiting before. Anyway, how do you dare tell me what I can or cannot do
with my property?"

"Then I'll buy it from you! What is a bear worth?" I
poured some silver out of my pouch and into my hand.
"Is a hundred pence enough?"

He swatted my hand aside, spraying my money onto
the snow. None of the peasants dared touch it.

"It's not for sale, damn you! Anyway, what would you
do with a bear? Make another warlock's familiar out of
it?"

Actually, discounting the stupidity about familiar creatures, Stefan had posed a good question. What *could* I
do with a bear? I couldn't possibly keep it—it might break

loose and kill somebody. I couldn't let it go—as angry as it was, it would *surely* kill somebody.

By this time, the bear had been fastened to the post, and a large crowd had gathered in a wide circle around the animal. It was on its hind legs, straining at the chains, trying desperately for vengeance.

I walked into the circle. "Blood sports are cruel and wicked!" I shouted. I looked to the priest for support, but he just looked away. "If you won't think about the bear, think about the brutality to your dogs!"

"What else are the dogs for?" Stefan smirked. "Sir Conrad, you look as funny as the bear."

The peasants had sense enough to keep quiet, to not get involved. But they didn't want to miss the action, either.

"Laugh if you want to, but I won't let you do this."

"Just how do you plan to stop it?" Stefan had an ugly laugh.

Another good question. Once the bear was chained to the post, he couldn't be unchained without getting past him, and that bear was *irate*. The only thing I could do for the animal was to give it a clean death.

"Like this," I said. I drew my sword and stepped close to the beast. On his hind legs, he was taller than I and must have weighed three times as much, swatting at me with his massive paws.

I timed his swipes and swung at him when both his paws were down, catching him horizontally at the neck a centimeter above the chain.

The head flew clear in a spray of blood, and the suddenly freed body lunged at me, almost falling on top of me. As I leaped aside, it brushed my leg.

"All right!" I shouted, trying not to show the pity that was welling up in me. "I want that carcass skinned and the hide tanned. And I want the meat served up for tomorrow's supper."

As I turned to leave, sheathing my sword, Stefan shouted, "You bloody bastard! You filthy scum. You blow by of an incestuous—"

"That's enough!" Count Lambert shouted, running up

to us. "You two are supposed to be knights, not kitchen dogs fighting over garbage! We will speak of this in private! Come with me, both of you."

"Yes, my lord," I said, following him to the castle, trying to control my emotions.

"It's not over, Conrad!" Stefan shouted, but I didn't turn.

Something heavy hit me square in the back, knocking me flat on my stomach in the dirty snow. I looked up to see the bear's head bouncing down the path toward the castle. Rage enveloped me as I got up.

As I turned toward him, Stefan hit me square in the face, almost knocking me down again.

I was too angry to fight efficiently, but Stefan didn't know anything about unarmed combat in the first place. For a few seconds we swung at each other wildly, and I gave a lot more than I got.

Suddenly, a naked sword divided the space between us. Lambert's.

"I swear, the next one of you who strikes will get this in his guts," Lambert hissed. "My own sworn knights fighting in the dirt, in front of the peasants no less! Now, to my chambers, and this time both of you walk in front of me."

In his chambers, Lambert ordered us to sit on opposite sides of the room but was so angry that he couldn't sit down himself.

"My own knights! Men who are supposed to enforce the peace, fighting each other like squalid beggars! You shame me, the both of you!

"First you, Sir Conrad! I saw you deliberately destroy the property and sport of a brother knight. I fine you two hundred pence for that and order you to pay Sir Stefan another fifty in damages."

"Yes, my lord."

"Is that all you have to say? Just why did you do such a despicable thing?"

"My lord, he was going to torture that animal, chain it to that post, and turn the dogs on it."

"So? Bears kill our people and our cattle. We have the

right to vengeance! You don't like our sports? I know you don't like our holidays. Very well! You can sleep through them, doing night guard duty before every one of them from now till Easter."

I groaned. Lately one day in three had been a holiday of one sort or another. Stefan smiled.

"Wipe that damn smirk off your face, Sir Stefan," Lambert said. "Your sins are worse than his! On slight provocation, you struck a brother knight with a dishonorable weapon—a bloody bear's head—without proper challenge and *in the back*! You did it when I had specifically ordered you to follow me immediately! Some lords would have you hung for that, and were it not for your father I'd be sorely tempted. Instead, I'll be lenient. I fine you three months' additional guard duty, from Easter to midsummer, *on the night shift*.

"Now I want no more bad blood between you two. Knights of the same lord should be like brothers! Stand up and give each other the kiss of brotherhood, then get out of my sight!"

As I kissed the smelly bastard, he whispered, "It's not over!"

Standing guard duty for fourteen hours in the dark gives you a lot of time to think. My engineering work was seriously hampered for lack of a decent system of weights and measures. In the cities, the guilds used a hodgepodge of gills and pennyweights and yards, mostly unrelated except that a pint of milk was supposed to weigh a pound. Nobody cared if the specific gravity of milk varied by five percent, with richer milk being lighter.

Here in the country, things were even worse. The blacksmith and the baker did things until they felt about right. The saddler just cut and trimmed until it fit. The carpenter did a bit of measuring—in cubits and spans and finger widths—but he used *his* cubit, from his elbow to his fingertips.

We didn't even have a meter stick.

Of course, I could invent my own system of weights

and measures easily enough, and it would at least have the advantage of consistency.

But I would lose a lot doing it. Every person, and certainly every engineer, knows hundreds of numbers. I knew the speed of light and the diameter of the earth and the distance from the earth to the sun. I knew the tensile strength of wrought iron and what could be expected of concrete and, well, all sorts of things.

But I knew all these values in terms of the metric system. Without a meter stick, I was stuck with guess-work. With one, I could derive all of the weights and measures and from there translate the data I remembered into any other system at all.

But none of my equipment contained a single reliable measurement. I had nothing that I knew was a definite length or weight.

At gray dawn, the answer hit me. I had my own body! My weight might not be reliable—I had put on muscle and lost some fat since arriving—but surely my height hadn't changed. I was precisely 190 centimeters tall. I had only to measure myself in stocking feet, divide by nine-teen, multiply by ten, and I had my meter stick. With that, a cube of cold water ten centimeters to the side has a volume of a liter and a mass of a kilogram.

From there it was simple arithmetic to translate it into the base-twelve system that these people could use.

Dead tired, I got Krystyana out of bed and had her standing on a chest, marking my height on the wall with a piece of charcoal.

"Sir Conrad," Lambert said as he saw us. "Just what are you doing now?"

I tried to explain how I was developing a standard meter and about engineering constants. Some things I had to repeat three times, perhaps because I hadn't slept in twenty-four hours and Lambert was just out of bed and bleary-eyed.

"So by measuring yourself, you will somehow know the distance from earth to moon? My dear Sir Conrad, God may have spanned the universe to his own measure, but it is rank blasphemy and profound hubris for a mere mortal to do so. In all events, the standard of measure here is the Silesian yard, not this foreign *meter* thing. I won't have you changing it."

"Yes, my lord." After yesterday the last thing I wanted was to irritate Lambert. "Uh, how long is a Silesian yard?"

"I'll show you." Taking Krystyana's charcoal, he marked it on the wall. With his head turned left, it was the distance from his nose to his right fingertip.

"Thank you, my lord," I said, and he left.

Forever after, I used yards instead of meters rather than offend my liege lord. I soon knew the *ratio* of yards to meters and that was enough to save my data.

My fourth endeavor was engineering the mills.

Understand that I had no reference books, no instruments, and no measuring devices. I had no drawing equipment and darned little parchment. These last two wouldn't have done me much good anyway, because I didn't have anyone who could read a blueprint.

For the comparatively small items I'd had to build thus far, it was possible to give instructions like "We need a piece of wood that's *this* long, and it's got to have holes in it so it can fit into *this* thing and *that* thing."

This technique was not suitable for building a mill, and we needed two of them; I built one-twelfth scale working models, because the people had to see how things moved in order to understand them.

Okoitz didn't have a stream suitable for damming, so that left wind power. The problem with wind power is that it works only when the wind is blowing. This is not a great complication on something like a flour mill, because only one operator is required and he can work strange hours if the situation requires it. But a lot of processes—beating flax and sawing wood—are both energy- and labor-intensive. If a crew is working and the wind stops, twenty people are left standing around, which is blatantly inefficient. An intermediate energy shortage device is needed, and we had water.

The first windmill was a water pump and some storage tanks. Actually, it was two sets of water pumps. One set of four pumps pumped water from a new well to a tank near the top of the mill. We needed a new well anyway because the old well was entirely too close to the latrines. The top tank provided fresh water to the community and supplied the lower, working tanks. I used four small pumps because I did not know how much power the mill would produce. If we only had enough torque to operate two pumps, the other two could be disconnected and used as spares. Also, if one pump malfunctioned, it could be repaired while the others continued in operation.

This is called contingency planning, or in the colorful language of my American friends, "keeping your ass covered."

Four larger pumps operated between the lowest tank and the middle tank. These provided water power to several machines in a circular shed that ringed the base of the windmill.

The sawmill, for example, had a straight saw blade operating vertically between two ropes. These ropes were connected by a pulley system to two short, fat barrels mounted at the ends of long pivot arms. A barrel, reaching the top of its stroke, pushed open a weighted door that allowed water from the middle tank to fill it. Filled, it descended, pulling the saw blade and raising the other barrel. Reaching the bottom, a fixed peg pushed up another weighted door on the bottom of the barrel, which drained the water into the lowest tank. At the same time, the second barrel was filling and the process reversed itself.

This "wet mill" was a fairly big thing. The body of it was a truncated cone twenty-four yards across at the bottom and twelve at the turret. The walls were vertical logs flattened on two sides. The cone shape resulted from the natural taper of the logs. I was learning.

The foundations went a full story into the ground, and from the ground to the top of the highest blade the thing was as tall as a nine-story building.

A windmill must be kept facing the wind, so the turret has to rotate. Ours did this on ninety-six wooden ball bearings, each as big as a man's head. One of my college professors had shown us a device to accomplish this auto-

matically. A second, much smaller windmill was built on
the back of the large turret, with the blades at right angles
to the main blades. This was geared down to rotate the
turret if the small windmill wasn't parallel to the wind.
He claimed it was the world's first negative feedback
device.

I could have made the turret manually rotatable, but I
wanted the mill to operate unattended at night.

One of the engineering problems I faced was that the
weight of the water tanks, besides pushing downward,
also pushed outward. Some crude calculations indicated
that a wrought-iron band strong enough to hold the middle
tank together would have weighed eight tons. I wasn't
sure that there *was* that much iron available on the market, and in any event the cost would have been fabulous.

My solution was exactly the same as that used by my
contemporaries, the Gothic cathedral builders. These
cathedrals have purely decorative internal stone arches
that produce an outward thrust. I say purely decorative
because the cathedrals were topped by wooden truss roofs
that kept the rain out and didn't touch the arches. They
actually built the outer walls and wooden roof first and
then built those magnificent arches later, working indoors
out of the rain.

I used the circular work shed as a flying buttress, leaning into the tower and squeezing it together.

Between the high-water level of the lowest tank and
the bottom of the middle tank was a space of four yards.
This was at ground level, but the area would be dark and
wet, and I could think of no good use for it. I didn't bother
putting a floor there.

This resulted in the lowest tank being used, over my
protestations, as a swimming pool.

By the time I got the model of the wet mill done, the
weather had broken. The bitter cold of winter was over,
the snow had melted, and the first warm breezes kissed
the land.

A mood of wondrous relief and joviality filled the community. It was so glorious that I had to rip my shirt off
and stand in the warm sunshine, soaking up the vitamin

D. I wasn't alone in doing this; Krystyana and Natalia were suddenly standing naked next to me.

This mood lasted for about a day, and then it was time for spring plowing and planting, an all-out effort for those people, who got up before dawn and performed fifteen or sixteen hours of grueling labor before collapsing exhausted, only to repeat the process the next day.

The count kept equal hours supervising, and the carpenter and the smith were kept busy repairing tools. There were only three or four weeks to complete the task, and if the planting didn't get done, next winter we would starve.

I seemed to be the only one at loose ends—as a knight, I was not allowed to work—so I wandered about observing things, seeing what improvements could be made. What they needed most was a good steel plow, and I saw no way of providing one.

Lambert owned more than half the land surrounding Okoitz. Well, actually, he owned two hundred times as much besides, but much of it was farmed out to his knights, most of whom ran manors similar to, but smaller than, his.

Peasants were expected to work three days a week on his land and had the balance of their time "free" to work their own. Special workers—the bakers, carpenters, etc.— had their own separate and often quite complicated arrangements, but in general it amounted to a fifty percent taxation, with the count being the entire government.

In return, the people got what amounted to police and military protection, much of their clothing, and a fixed number of feasts per year. In addition to the Christmas season, there were twenty-two days of feasting. I estimated that twenty-five percent of the food consumed by the commons was eaten at these feasts.

Also, and very important, the count made arrangements for the sick and needy. Since Lambert was an intelligent and decent person, it really wasn't a bad system. Under a stupid or greedy lord, you could see where it could be pure hell.

Chapter Seventeen

I WASN'T accomplishing anything at Okoitz. No feast days fell during the planting season, church and state being practical about such matters. By the terms of my punishment, I didn't have to stand guard duty. I was told that right after planting and Easter there would be plenty of manpower available to start work on the mill.

There were some parts of the mill that we could not produce locally. I wanted the main rotor bearings to have brass or bronze collars riding on lead bushings. The lead we could cast in place, but the heavy collars troubled me until the count mentioned some bell casters at his brother's city of Cieszyn some thirty "miles" away to the south.

I was soon riding along the road to Cieszyn on a fine spring day. My equipment was much the same as that I had purchased in Cracow last fall, only now I wore conventional padded leather under my chain mail. I had a new scabbard for my sword, and its garish brass hilt had been replaced, a wrought-iron basket guard added. The shield and spear were as before. Anna had a new saddle and bridle of modern design, and she was happy to be traveling.

Riding a palfrey beside me, Krystyana was even happier. Three hours of her begging and pleading had persuaded Lambert to let her go along to "take care of me."

He didn't mind her going, but he hated losing another horse during spring plowing.

She was wearing her best dress, covered with a large traveling cape, and had four others—borrowed—in her saddlebags. She was taking her first trip away from Okoitz since she had moved there with her family when she was ten years old.

Krystyana was a competent person and actually handled most of the day-to-day management of the castle. But she was trying to remain on top of an unfamiliar sidesaddle—I don't think *I* could have stayed on one of the silly things—while trying to play the part of a knight's lady.

She was ludicrous at it; I decided that much of her problem was that the only "ladies" she had ever seen were seen from a distance, when she was a peasant girl. What she needed was a good role model.

I carried letters from Lambert to his brother. These he had dictated to Father John because, for all his good qualities, the count was illiterate.

I also had instructions to see if Sir Miesko's wife and lands were well since his manor was on our route. It was six hours to Sir Miesko's manor, all of it at a walk, because Krystyana could never have stayed on at a gallop. As it was, the poor kid had leg cramps all night.

I was not looking forward to meeting Lady Richeza, Sir Miesko's wife. From the events at the Christmas party, where Sir Miesko had declined the favors of Count Lambert's ladies because he feared repercussions from his wife—permitting the king of fools to brand him as henpecked—I had formed an impression of a violent, shrewish woman. I was absolutely mistaken. After meeting Lady Richeza, I decided that Sir Miesko had declined all others simply because he loved his wife. Implying that he was henpecked was simply a ruse to avoid exposing his true feelings.

In her thirties, she was not a pretty woman. She was tall as the Poles of the thirteenth century went, and overly broad in the hip. Her hair was dark, curly, and shoulder length, and her face long and rectangular, with remarkably bushy eyebrows. She had dark blue eyes, and her features were otherwise unremarkable. Even in her first bloom, I doubt any man, on seeing her from a distance for the first time, could have honestly called her pretty.

Yet after meeting her and talking with her for a few hours, it dawned on me that I was being honored by the presence of one of the world's truly beautiful women.

But I get ahead of myself.

Sir Miesko's manor was not a fort. It was a comfortable-looking six-bedroom log house located a few hundred yards from a town of perhaps forty small cottages. A few barns and outbuildings were scattered about nearby, but they were located for convenience, not defense. What fences and walls there were had been built with animals, not enemies, in mind.

At first the place seemed too peaceful for such a brutal age, but then I noticed that all the peasants in the fields were armed. Some carried spears, others had axes, and a few possessed swords in addition to the ubiquitous belt knives. Half the women had bows. Sir Miesko apparently had his own theories on defense.

As we approached the manor, two boys who had been working at a kitchen garden laid down their hoes and came to greet us. "Welcome gentles," the older of the two said. I guessed his age at twelve. Despite the hard work they'd been doing, the boys had a fresh-scrubbed look. "Stash, got tell Mother we have company. I'll take care of the horses."

"We thank you for your courtesy." I dismounted and helped Krystyana down from her sidesaddle. The poor thing could barely stand. I kept an arm around her waist for more reasons than affection.

The boy looked up at me. "Sir, can it be that I am addressing the hero, Sir Conrad Stargard?"

I couldn't help smiling. "I don't think that I qualify as a hero, but I'm Conrad Stargard. This is my friend Krystyana."

"You are a hero here, Sir Conrad. Sir Rheinburg killed my best friend's father and four other men from the village. He stole half my father's cattle. You are the knight who defeated him."

I don't think the boy was intentionally snubbing Krystyana. He was just at an age where heroes are far more important than girls. He'd learn.

A woman came out to the portch. "We'll talk later, son. I must greet your mother."

"Welcome." The smiling woman looked at me calmly while drying her hands on a towel.

"I take it that you are Lady Richeza. I am Sir Conrad Stargard, and this is Krystyana."

"Welcome, Sir Conrad." She took both my hands and squeezed them. I knew she wanted a hug, so I gave her one. Understand that I did not and never have felt any sexual attraction for the woman. She was simply the warm sort of person who automatically steps into the role of a favorite aunt or cousin.

"And a very warm welcome to you, Krystyana." As she gave my girl a hug and a kiss, I saw Krystyana tighten up. She wasn't used to this sort of thing. Lady Richeza pretended not to notice but took her by the hand and led her inside. I followed.

The furnishings were sparse by modern standards but very comfortable by those of the Middle Ages. Large chests along the walls served as chairs, and each had a comfortable cushion, a thing lacking at Okoitz. The floor had a carpet of braided rags, the first rug I had seen in the thirteenth century. Most places made do with rushes scattered on the floor. But mostly, everything—including the two small children playing on the rug—was incredibly clean. My own mother's house was no cleaner, and she vacuumed daily.

One of Lady Richeza's daughters brought in some beer and bread. "Is beer acceptable? It seemed too warm a day for wine."

"A beer would be wonderful, Lady." I downed the mug. It was flat, of course; no pressure containers in the Middle Ages. One got used to it.

I had a very pleasant evening. The food was good, the surroundings pleasant, the conversation wonderful. I felt at home. The children—eight of them, five boys and three girls—were exactly what children are supposed to be but never are: inquisitive, bubbling with energy, yet clean and well mannered.

All of them over six could read and write. Sir Miesko had a library of twenty-two hand-lettered books, most of them copied by himself. That was another side of his personality that I hadn't seen at Okoitz. He had taught his wife, and she in turn had educated not only her own children but all those in the village as well.

After the kids were in bed, Lady Richeza and I spent a few hours talking over a school system, one that would spread to every village in Lambert's county. She had the potential teachers, and I could imagine nothing better to do with my money.

Throughout the evening Krystyana was unusually stiff and quiet despite our tries at getting her into the conversation. I put it down to feminine moods, augmented by the pain of the sidesaddle.

When we were in bed in the guest room, I said to Krystyana, "Our hostess is a truly fine lady. If you grew up to be like her, you'd make some very lucky man very happy."

"You ogled her all evening long."

"Ogled? Nonsense! I was just being polite to a very gracious lady."

"She isn't even a real lady."

"Krystyana, you are talking stupid."

"She isn't a lady, and Sir Miesko isn't really a knight. They were both born peasants. Miesko was twenty-five when the duke knighted him on the battlefield. He was a clerk before that."

"Remind me tomorrow to give you a spanking. You are saying horrible things. If Sir Miesko raised himself by his own efforts, he's a better man than if he was just born to the nobility. And Lady Richeza would be a great lady whether the duke said so or not!"

"It's not the *same*."

"No. It's better."

"But—"

"Shut up and go to sleep." We stayed celibate for the night, and Krystyana had leg cramps until dawn.

We got to Cieszyn the next afternoon. It was a nice little town if you could ignore the lack of a sewage system. It had perhaps four thousand people, a great city by Krystyana's standards. At the city gate, a guard saluted us and waved us through. Apparently, a knight and his lady didn't have to bother with tolls. The outer walls were of brick, as were several charming little round brick chapels, two hundred years old.

The castle was brick as well and was exactly like what the movies told you to expect. Count Lambert had walked away from quite a bit.

Count Herman was in Cracow, along with most of his household knights, attending his liege lord, Henryk. Somehow, word of my "military" exploits had reached Cieszyn, and the ladies of the court gave me a warm welcome.

They were noticeably less cordial to Krystyana. Count Lambert's ... uh ... chosen life-style was not appreciated by those fine women, and Krystyana was available to take it out on. Conversation was somewhat strained that afternoon. I kept trying to get Krystyana into the discussion, and they kept cutting her off.

The situation became worse when we were called to supper. I was to be seated between two spreading middle-aged women, and no chair had been provided for Krystyana.

"But surely you understand," my hostess said.

"Oh, yes. I understand." I was doing a very good job of containing my temper, but I understood entirely too well. "Mistakes happen all the time, even in the best regulated of households. Page! Someone forgot a chair for Krystyana. Bring one and set it next to mine."

"But my lord ..." The rumors that the page had heard spoke of my killing twelve men in a single fight, each with a single blow. Angry with a blacksmith, I supposedly had chopped an anvil entirely in half. He had also heard an exaggerated version of the way Lambert and I had slaughtered pigs.

"Another chair. Right here." I pointed. I'm sure that my mouth was smiling, but I don't think my eyes were. A chair rapidly appeared, and after some shuffling, Krystyana sat down.

My actions caused more problems than I had intended. At Okoitz, the "share the spoon, share the cup" thing was reserved for holidays. In the castle at Cieszyn, apparently, it was for every meal. Adding one more person meant that everyone downstream of us suddenly had to change partners and that the woman at the end was all alone.

Oh, well. To hell with them! If they could be rude, so could I. It was all very well to give people fancy titles, but that's no excuse for snubbing a perfectly decent fourteen-year-old girl, especially one who happened to be my date.

"Sir Conrad," my hostess eventually said, trying to smooth things over, "please tell us of your adventures."

"Adventures? Well, I'd be happy to tell you about what I've been working on lately." I launched into a discourse on the finer points of animal breeding. I must have rattled on for ten minutes and was stressing the importance of counting eggs when I felt my hostess's hand on my arm.

"That's most educational, Sir Conrad. Was it really you who defeated the renegade Black Eagle, Sir Rheinburg?"

"I killed the lunatic if that's what you mean."

"Was he *really* insane?"

"I suppose so. People who go around attacking armed men in public generally aren't too sensible."

"And you felled him with a single blow, cutting his head in two, though he wore a helmet?"

"Look, there wasn't much time. I gather you like gory stories. I'll tell you how Mikhail Malinski lost his foot." And I told them, every bloody bit of it. Slewing and slaying on a battlefield were great fun to them, but tying off an artery was entirely too graphic. More than one person excused herself before I was done.

My hostess was a little green below the ears. "And he died in a bed in Count Lambert's castle?"

"It was easier to take care of him there. Krystyana and her friends are great nurses. Oh, did I tell you about our looms and spinning wheels? Krystyana and seven of her friends can take wool and turn it into twenty of your yards of cloth in a single day."

"Seven of her friends. Oh, dear."

The only upshot of this was that one of the guest rooms at Okoitz became "the bed where the peasant died," with something stupid and supernatural attached to it. In a way, it was beneficial because when higher-ranking guests arrived, none of them were eager to take that room. I wasn't bumped to the blockhouses as otherwise would have happened. Anyway, if Mikhail Malinski ever had a ghost, it would have been a good ghost.

Much later, our hostess suggested that Krystyana would be much more comfortable in the servants' quarters. The bitch still hadn't learned, and I was out of teaching techniques.

"Madame, that is hardly necessary. I have delivered my liege lord's letters, and we have enjoyed an excellent Lenten supper. Regretfully, duty calls and we must be off."

"But I had hoped—"

"As I said, it's regrettable, but I have my duty." I led Krystyana off to the stables.

"Page, I want our horses saddled and our personal effects gathered. Now."

The page made quick finger motions, and four men scurried off. In minutes we were riding to the postern gate, led by the page with a torch.

"But Sir Conrad, it's so dark out now," he said.

"Then I shall need the loan of your torch." I took it.

"There are thieves out there! It's dangerous."

"You're right, kid. Go tell the thieves to be careful."

Krystyana had been holding her feelings in all afternoon and evening. Once outside the gate, she bawled like the schoolgirl she should have been. There wasn't much I could do but squeeze her hand and mumble about things getting better.

I asked at a few taverns and was eventually directed

to a decent inn, the Battle Axe. The room was big and clean, and ten pence a day for food, lodging, and care of the horses didn't seem all that bad. The innkeeper was overjoyed. I had forgotten to haggle.

"You understand that I will expect excellent service, food, and drink. See that our horses are well taken care of and send a large pot of good wine to our room."

"Yes, my lord. Of course, my lord." I later discovered that we were his only guests. Business was not booming in Cieszyn, and many who were willing could not find work. That people in Okoitz should be working sixteen hours a day and people in Cieszyn should be idle—and ill fed—offended my socialist morality. This place needed organization.

As soon as we were alone in our room, Krystyana threw her arms around my neck and started crying again. "Sir Conrad, I love you!"

"I hope not, pretty girl. I'm not the marrying kind."

"No, I mean, you don't have to but, I mean, leaving all those countesses and baronesses and ladies because of me."

"Hold it. I didn't leave because of you. I left because *I* was offended by their rudeness. Also, I had no intention of bedding any one of those overaged, overweight, and profoundly married women. And certainly not when there is somebody as sexy as you around. Now have some wine and settle down."

Sometime later, she said, "I love you anyway, Sir Conrad."

The next morning I sent Krystyana out shopping with one of the innkeeper's servants to keep her safe and see that she didn't get gypped. I tipped the woman a penny a day, and she was overjoyed. I gave Krystyana a hundred pence and told her to buy presents for her family and friends. Also a wedding gift from me to Mrs. Malinski and something for the carpenter and the count.

"But what could Count Lambert possibly want?"

"Dye. Dye for cloth. And if you can find a good dyer out of work, the count would like that, too."

I was pleased to discover that the bell casters I had come to Cieszyn to see lived directly across from the inn.

The bell foundry was owned and operated by the three Krakowski brothers—Thom, Mikhail, and Wladyslaw. It had been their father's business and had been a thriving concern until a year before, when the bishop's nephew, a German, had opened up a bell foundry in Cracow. New orders to the Krakowski brothers had stopped, and their melting furnace had been cold for six months. But the information came out slowly, and I got some of it from the innkeeper. The brothers were trying to keep up appearances.

The Krakowski brothers and I spent the morning talking. I talked about the huge bushings I would need—the bore was to be a full yard, and the outside flange diameter of the blade-end bushing was to be two yards. They were each to be a yard long. Modern roller bearings would have been a tenth that size, but I had no illusions about the quality the Krakowskis could give me. In working with inferior materials, you must make things *big*.

They talked to me about bell casting. They used the lost wax method. This is *not* an ancient "lost" technology, even though I once met a twentieth-century museum tour guide who seemed to think so; it's still being used when intricate, one-of-a-kind castings are needed. To make a bell, the brothers Krakowski first dug a pit. In the pit, they fashioned by hand, from clay, a male form shaped like the inside of the bell. They then took beeswax and made a wax bell over the form, carving in wax all the exterior decorations and, being somewhat literate, the lettering. Clay was carefully molded over the wax, and the whole was left to dry for a week. Then they built a fire in the pit, small at first but growing.

In a few days the wax melted, ran out of prepared holes, and burned. A few days later, the mold was hot enough for the pour. Having carefully measured the amount of wax used, the casters knew exactly how much brass to melt. After the pour, they broke off the clay and spent a few months "tuning" the bell by chipping brass out of the inside to get it to sound right.

"That's the trick, Sir Conrad," the youngest brother said. "The mold has got to be as hot as the brass or she'll crack, or the bell will crack."

The other brothers looked at him as if he were divulging guild secrets, and maybe he was.

"I'm familiar with the process," I lied. It was now past noon, and they had not offered me dinner. I thought about that—they looked more underfed than Lent alone would account for. "This is interesting," I said. "But I grow hungry. I would like to invite you and your families to dinner. I'm staying at the Battle Axe. Could you send someone to tell the innkeeper how many are coming? Have him let us know when it's ready."

They eagerly accepted my offer, and soon we were at a sit-down dinner for fourteen. There were no babies; all three had died in the winter.

As it was Lent, the meal was meatless: bread and oatmeal, pease porridge, and small beer. Even the children drank beer. Water was unhealthy, and cows would not start producing milk for another month. My guests ate a great deal under the watchful gaze of the innkeeper, who was hovering at the back of the room to make sure everything went right. We were his biggest sale in months.

These men had skills that I needed, and they certainly needed me. They needed socialism, and I was going to socialize them—within the framework of their own society, of course. I'm not the banner-waving, gun-wielding revolutionary sort.

"Excuse me, sir knight," the oldest Krakowski brother finally said. "But are you *the* Sir Conrad Stargard? The man who killed Sir Rheinburg?"

That business again? "Yes."

"Then we owe you gratitude. That German murdered our cousin Yashu. Killed him on the road when he was weaponless and penniless."

"I'm sorry about your cousin. The German was a madman, but he's dead now."

"Still, we owe you."

"You don't owe me anything. All I did was to stop myself from joining your cousin."

The innkeeper intruded. "Excuse me, Sir Conrad, you realize that serving fourteen is more than we agreed on."

"Of course. Put the difference on my bill."

"Yes, sir. That would be twelve pence."

Small talk at the table stopped. A penny for each meatless meal!

"Innkeeper, that seems excessive. I do not like to haggle, but if I decide that you are cheating me, you will lose my business." I said this quietly and calmly but without smiling.

"Yes, Sir Conrad." Beads of sweat suddenly dotted the man's forehead. When I eventually settled the bill, four pence accounted for that meal.

Later that day, I got their price for my bushings. It came to thirty-one hundred pence. Each.

"That seems excessive," I said. "Let's go over your expenses, and mind you, I intend to check these prices myself in the market."

The copper would cost eight hundred pence, and calamine, a compound of zinc, was three hundred and fifty pence. We had agreed, from samples that they had on hand, on a hard brass of about thirty percent zinc. The clay they dug up themselves, and they chopped their own wood by arrangement with a landowner. With transportation costs, those two items came to a hundred and fifty pence. The eye opener was the wax. It was a rare commodity, like the honey that came with it. The wax would cost eleven hundred pence, almost as much as the metal. The remaining five hundred pence for their labor and equipment did not seem excessive. Still...

Still, there was no reason why the molds themselves could not be cast off wooden forms. Both bushings could be made the same so that only one set of forms would be needed. Also, I would need four bushings for the upcoming "dry mill" that would grind grain.

In addition, I had hoped that more mills would be wanted by other landowners. We might need a lot of bushings. A lot of parts that I had planned to make of wood could be made better—much better—in brass: some of the gearing and the pump cylinders and pulleys. I wanted

some fire-heated tubs for a laundry and parts for a threshing machine, and, well, all sorts of things.

"Gentlemen." They looked up in surprise at my use of
the term. "Your prices seem fair for what you propose to
do, but it happens that I know some less-expensive techniques. Not for bells, you understand, but for the kind of
things I have in mind." As it turned out, in two years they
were selling bells again. You had to choose from three
standard sizes and had no choice of inscriptions, but they
were half the cost of the Cracow bells.

"Now, then," I continued. "It is obvious that you are
suffering under a burden of debt. It is also obvious that
you have no security at all and that your families are
hungry. I propose to purchase your establishment and pay
you all a decent salary. I also intend to pay for a number
of improvements around here. What do you think?"

"Well, that sounds fine, but there are guild rules..."
said Thom, the eldest.

"What? I thought you were the only bell casters in
Cieszyn."

"Well, we are."

"Then who is the guild master?"

"I am, actually."

"And these are your guild members?"

"Uh ... yes."

"Then to hell with your damned guild! You are three
brothers, and I am talking about hiring you."

"Can't the guild vote to disband?" the youngest, Wladyslaw, asked.

"But there's nothing in the rules—"

"And to hell with your rules! I, Sir Conrad Stargard,
by the power granted to me by my sword, do hereby
proclaim your guild null and void. Questions?"

Thom checked with his brothers. "No, I guess not."

"So. I'm not sure of local property values, but for your
house and furnace and lands, does two thousand pence
sound fair?"

I got enthusiastic nods from the younger two. The eldest said, "We also have certain rights and privileges to

clay and wood, and two thousand pence would not quite cover our debts."

"Let's make it twenty-five hundred, then," I said. "I would not want my vassals to be suffering from debt."

"Vassals? You would take an oath?"

"Of course, and I would expect you to, also. All of you and your wives, besides."

"Our wives?"

"An oath of honesty and fair work. Your wives help you, don't they?"

"Yes, but—"

"I do not touch other men's wives. Now, what would you say to six hundred pence per year each, with two hundred pence to each of your wives? When your children are old enough to help, we'll discuss it. Agreed?"

The eldest looked about. "I suppose so."

"Good. I will pay half of your first year's salary in advance, since it appears that you need some things around here. You need some clothes, but don't buy a lot. The price of common cloth is about to drop."

"How can you know?"

"Let's say that I can smell it. In addition, since I want you to apply yourselves diligently to this enterprise, once all expenses, improvements, materials, taxes, salaries, and so forth are paid, you will divide among yourselves one-twelfth of the surplus." "Profit" is not a nice word for a socialist.

Their mute agreement had turned to enthusiasm.

"Good. Now go discuss the matter with your wives. Come to me while the sun is still high, for I want your oaths. I shall be at the inn."

I was only halfway through my first beer when the six of them showed up, smiling.

"Innkeeper, I want your whole staff in the courtyard. There are oaths to be taken!"

So we had a deal, and it was in this manner that I—I can't say nationalized, since I'm not a nation, but, socialized the Bros. Krakowski Brass Works. In doing so, I was acting again, playing the role of the shrewd merchant and dirtying my good socialist soul in the process. The thing needed doing, and much of being a man is doing the things that must be done no matter how unnatural or painful they are. Surely this was a small evil compared with the naked corpses I had left in a snowy wood.

I bought the beer, called for an honest scale, and weighed out the money I owed. When I had left Okoitz, Count Lambert had been distracted with the planting and hadn't mentioned money, so I had brought along twenty thousand pence of my own. I wasn't worried; the count was honest. You see, you must either trust a person or not trust him. It is stupid to rely on oaths or marks on a piece of parchment because a thief will rob you no matter what is written down, and an honest man stays honest—within reason.

I weighed out thirty-seven hundred pence in gold—the exchange rate of silver to gold being 54 to 1—which I gave to Thom. Then I weighed out another four thousand and told him that I wanted him to buy copper and calamine at the best possible prices. We needed a wood-carver, and I told him to find one. The other two brothers were ordered to go out and bring in vast amounts of firewood and clay and start making charcoal.

There was some consternation, and then it was agreed that the innkeeper would safeguard the gold until morning, since he kept an armed guard at night.

Chapter Eighteen

THE PARTY was breaking up as Krystyana returned. She was excited about her day's shopping in the big city. As supper was served, she prattled on and on about pins and churches and ribbons and merchants and the outlandish price of dinner. I was in a good mood and said little. I heard every detail of every bargain, and sometimes feminine babble makes a pleasant background noise to relax in. Eventually she wound down.

"That's wonderful, pretty girl. Did you buy anything for yourself?"

"Well, no. I mean, you said . . ."

"Then here's fifty pence to spend tomorrow on things that *you* want." This was greeted by squeals. "Did you have any luck with dyes or a dyer?"

"I looked at them, but dyes are so *complicated*, Sir Conrad. A pound of this one can do something, but an ounce of that one can do more and—"

Pounds? Ounces? I'd forgotten the metric conversions. "I understand. Any word about a dyer?"

"I heard of one, but they called him a 'walker' because he walks on the cloth being dyed. People said that they had heard of him, but nobody *knew* him."

"Well, then you know what to do tomorrow. Keep the serving woman with you from now on. I want you to look into the price of raw woolen cloth, the kind that you make on the loom. See if you can't find a merchant willing to buy, say, a thousand yards at slightly less than the present wholesale price, for delivery next spring." If I had to play the merchant, I thought that I might as well make some gain from it. My hands were already dirty.

"I'll try, Sir Conrad."

"And I know that you'll do a wonderful job. It grows late. What do you say? One more cup of wine and then to bed?"

The next few days were busy. Thom had located a copper merchant who wanted to sell out his entire stock and move to a better—more profitable—place. We could buy copper at half price, along with some calamine, lead, and tin, if we bought his entire stock. I looked it over and paid an additional 3,250 pence. They found an out-of-work wood-carver. I looked at his work in a few churches and swore him in at five hundred pence a year. I told him that he was now a pattern maker.

Clay and wood were coming in slowly, so I told the brothers that they should hire twelve men temporarily and keep the best four on a permanent basis.

Krystyana found her walker, a Florentine who had come north to seek his fortune and had picked up a fair amount of Polish while starving in Cieszyn. He claimed to be a journeyman dyer, but on questioning him I discovered that he had never completed his apprenticeship. He had also been apprenticed as a wool sorter, a comber, a carder, and a warper. He had some experience with linen that he preferred not to discuss.

He was thirty years old and a perpetual misfit. Or maybe a diamond in the rough. I had mixed feelings about the man. "Okay, Angelo Muskarini. It is good that you have finally told me the truth. As my liege lord is about to enter the clothmaking business, it is possible that we can use you. Perhaps you know something that will help him. Look long and hard before you criticize my loom or spinning wheels! Aside from that, if you can improve the quality or quantity of his cloth, you will be very well rewarded. If you do not produce results, we shall transport you back to your garret here at Cieszyn. Understood?" It was.

I swore him in for two years at one hundred pence per year, plus food and lodging. Then I put him up at my expense at the back of the inn for two pence per day. I advanced him three months' pay for beer and such just to see how he'd do. As it turned out, he saved most of it, barring a little he spent for clothes. Sometimes when a man has spent enough time between the hammer and the anvil, he turns into good steel.

Besides explaining to the Krakowski brothers about building patterns for molds, I had to explain about grinding wheels and lathes. It is not enough to cast a bushing. It has to be perfectly round, and that is not possible with casting alone.

The wood-carver, Ivor Korenkov, found himself instructing his new employers, and the days wound on.

Krystyana made the right commercial connection. She found a cloth merchant eager to deal. It was already arranged that he would buy some two thousand square yards—Cieszyn measure—of raw wool cloth for seven-eighths of the current price, twenty-three pence per square yard. We swore the agreement before a notary, who produced three copies: one for each of us and one for himself. We left one thousand pence each with a Templar as surety, and the deal was closed.

Days later, I was still busy at the foundry, but Krystyana had nothing else to do. The story of her rebuffs at the castle had already spread, and she was embarrassed by it.

"Pretty girl, I have one more job for you. Take Angelo and the servant woman—whatever her name is—"

"Zelda."

"Zelda, then. The three of you should go and buy one thousand pence worth of dye or whatever Angelo needs. Then I want you and Angelo to go back toward Okoitz."

"But just he and I alone?"

"I'll be with you as far as Sir Miesko's manor, and that's as far as you're going. We can send Angelo alone to Okoitz."

"Why send him alone, Sir Conrad?"

"Because I'm not sure if I trust him. If I've hired a thief, I'd rather find out sooner than later."

"Why trust him at all? I mean, why take a chance with thousands of pence worth of dye and mules?"

"I have to be able to trust him because he knows things that I don't. He could pull the wool over my eyes, and I wouldn't know it."

"Pull the wool . . ." She couldn't sort that one out. "Then why are we going to Sir Miesko's?"

"Because I want you to stay with Richeza for a few weeks. Remember what I said about her being a truly fine woman? Remember her grace and charm and the way everyone feels comfortable around her? Now, compare her with those 'ladies' at Cieszyn Castle and ask yourself what you want to be like when you grow up." She thought a bit and was suddenly in tears. Her arms went around my neck. "It's okay, pretty girl."

Two days later, we set out at dawn. I was fully armed and on Anna, of course. Krystyana was sidesaddle on her palfrey. Angelo followed on a mule, leading a second mule loaded with roots, bark, herbs, and sea shells.

We arrived at noon. Richeza was charming as always, and if she was offended by my intention to leave in a few hours, she didn't show it. Gossip about our adventures at Cieszyn Castle had already reached her, and she had the insight to invite Krystyana to stay with her before I had a chance to broach the subject.

Still, courtesy forbade my immediate departure, and it was midafternoon before I was on the road again for Cieszyn. "Well, Anna, do you think we can make it before dark?"

Anna nodded her head. She'd always had the disconcerting habit of nodding or shaking her head to questions, as if she actually understood what was said. She probably picked up some clue from my body language, like the famous Clever Hans, but it was still interesting to talk to her.

"Then let's see how fast you can go, but don't strain yourself."

She took off at a full gallop and kept it up for the better part of an hour. Finally, I starting worrying; a good horse will run itself to death if you ask it. I reined her back to a walk. "Easy, girl! You'll hurt yourself."

She shook her head no, took the bit in her teeth, and galloped the rest of the way back to Cieszyn. I dismounted at the city gates to check Anna over. She wasn't even sweating! An amazing horse.

A week later, I got word that Angelo Muskarini had arrived safely at Okoitz with his charge. I was vindicated.

More remained to be done at the brass foundry than I had thought. This business of working in a pit and baking the molds with an open fire was obviously inefficient and wasteful of fuel. We built an oven of clay bricks for drying and baking the clay molds. Eventually we were to build five more.

The lathe had to be huge, and it needed bearings that had to be built before the bushings could be turned. We had to build a small lathe in order to build a big one. The big lathe was too large to be hand-powered, so we built a big barrel cage at the headstock. A man got in this cage and climbed continuously uphill, turning the cage and the part on the lathe.

I was enjoying myself, but it was five weeks before I felt confident enough of the Krakowski brothers to return to Okoitz.

During that time, though I had done the right thing by sending Krystyana to Richeza's "finishing school," I began to suffer for it. When one has had a continuous supply of sex, abstention becomes difficult. I soon discovered that my knightly right to the use of young women did not apply within city limits, and one more visit to Cieszyn Castle convinced me that I wanted nothing there.

Look. I was quite willing to tolerate honest ignorance. Most of the people I had met in the thirteenth century had been brutally poor; they'd had no chance to improve themselves. But those women of the castle had absolutely nothing to do and expended an incredible amount of effort in doing it. They were wrapped up in stupid mind games, courts of love, and "he said that she said that they said..."

nonsense. They placed an absurdly high value on the virginity of unmarried women and none at all on the chastity of those who were married.

In short, they offended *my* moral code and were not worth the bother.

There were prostitutes in town, and I tried one. She spend the first half of the evening wheedling me for more money and the second half on the streets after I threw her out.

Mostly, in the evenings I drank a lot. The innkeeper, Tadeusz Wrolawski, became my regular drinking partner. The Krakowski brothers were fine people, you understand, but it is not a good idea to socialize too much with one's subordinates. The role change from drinking buddy to willing worker becomes difficult if one must do it too often. Also, they had their wives to keep content.

"Socialism, Tadeusz!" I explained drunkenly. "This country and this century are in horrible shape because of the lack of socialism!"

"You are absolutely right, Sir Conrad! What is socialism?"

"I am glad that you agree with me, my good friend Tadeusz. All of this business of no work in Cieszyn and too much work in Okoitz and not enough to eat and no sewers and little babies dying can all be cured with a little technology and some organization."

"This sounds marvelous! What is a sewer?"

"All we have to do is to get things organized and apply a little appropriate technology. We have everything else. We have the manpower, and we have the materials. Give us nine years and we'll have things running right and beat the Mongols, besides. Have her bring us some more wine."

"Outstanding! What is a Mongol?"

"Eh? Mongols are little greasy yellow bastards that are going to ride in out of the east and try to kill everybody. They won't do it, though, if we get organized. Blow hell out of them with cannons. Brass cannons, maybe."

"These Mongols are like Tartars?"

"Same bastards. Change their name a lot."

"I have heard some horrible tales from traders from

the east. They speak of whole cities put to the sword!
Every man, every child, every animal! Not even the women
spared for ravishing!"

"Yeah. Those are the bastards. But it's not going to
happen here. We'll stop them. It's just a matter of organization. Caring about people. Technology. Socialism."

"You say 'technology.' What is this technology?"

"Why, technology is what I have going at the brass
works across the street. New lathes, new ovens, better
production processes."

"They certainly are prosperous, Sir Conrad! A month
ago they were nothing but three starving men and their
families with nothing to do. Now they work from dawn
to dusk. Their wives have bought pigs and chickens and
new clothes. They have hired a dozen new men!"

"See? Technology triumphant and socialism in action!
Another mug of wine?"

"And this technology, it can be applied anywhere? Say,
to an inn?"

"Well, of a sort. Technology is mostly sensible thinking
about the problems you face. Now, your inn here. You've
got a good building. Your rooms are clean. Your food is
good, and you make good beer. All you seem to lack are
the customers."

"What you say, at least the last part, is true."

"Okay. We agree that the physical plant is adequate.
Now, what is the purpose of an inn?"

"Why, to provide food and drink and—"

"Wrong. Your customers could buy wine from a wine
seller much cheaper than you sell it. You must buy from
the same wine seller and pay your overhead besides. The
same goes for food. The markets must be cheaper."

"But for travelers—"

"Transient business is fine, but you are not on a main
street. Local business is more important. You must serve
the *people*. There are what? A thousand men of drinking
age in town. Maybe another thousand in nearby villages.
If you could get a tenth of them to come here regularly,
your success would be assured. Once the town's people
came here regularly, the travelers would come, too."

"Yes, yes! But how do we do that?"

"Let me think." I didn't know much about managing taverns, but I had been in a great number of them in Poland and America. Some were bad and empty. Some were good and empty. Some were crowded whether they were good or bad. The biggest single factor seemed to be that people went to a given place because people were already there. Getting the first ones there was a matter of advertising—which was impossible in a world without newspapers or radios—and providing something interesting. Something different. I thought of the two or three best places I had found in Massachusetts. A combination of those.

A controls designer lives in a four-dimensional world. When things finally come to me, they come as a working, moving, solid whole. Only later do I string them out in serial fashion.

A vision crystallized in my sodden mind.

"Tadeusz, I know how to do it. You know my arrangement with the Krakowski brothers? Would you like to be socialized as well?"

"That I should be paid thousands of pence and a regular salary besides? Oh, yes my lord!"

"OK. Same deal, but I think your building is worth more than theirs. Say, 3,000p.?"

"Agreed, my lord!"

"Six hundred pence for yourself, yearly, and a twelfth of the surplus, with two hundred pence to your wife?"

"With honor, my lord!"

"Good. We'll swear you in right now."

"But the sun is not up."

"True ... But there is a full moon and that is more appropriate for an innkeeper. Agreed?"

So, under the moon, with a sleepy chamber maid and the night guard as witnesses, I swore in Tadeusz and his wife. I picked up another pot of wine and we went back to the table. The first order of business was to settle up my present bill, which I did. Then I gave Tadeusz 3,400p.

"Our first rule is that since I own the place, I shall lodge here free. Keep one room open for my own use.

"The second change is the name of the inn. 'The Battle Axe' is entirely too stern. People go to inns because they need to enjoy themselves. We need a light, amusing name. We'll call it the 'Pink Dragon'. I have a wood carver across the street; he'll make a new sign.

"Then, this room is too empty and cavernous. People like crowds. I want some curtains to divide the room in half, another set to divide the front half in half, and a third set so that only the front eighth is exposed. You are to open a set of curtains only when the space before it is so crowded that people are bumping into each other. Understood?"

"Yes, my lord."

"All your present people are to be retained. No firing except for dishonesty."

"Ah. There is the matter of certain salaries being in arrears."

"None of that under socialism. They must be paid. Figure up the amount tomorrow. Oh, yes. We'll need an accounting system. I'll send somebody to keep the books for here and the foundry. You'll think it's a nuisance, but I insist on it. What else? Your pricing! This business of having to haggle over everything has to go. We'll have to work out a reasonable set of prices for everything. Then we post those prices, and they are the same for everybody. No exceptions."

"But what if one is conspicuously wealthy and—"

"No exceptions, not up or down. Then, entertainment. From supper until late, I want some music in here. A single musician at a time will do, and hire them for only a week at a time. See what people like. And waitresses; we'll need half a dozen of them. They must be well paid, since we want the best. Say, four pence a week with another eight pence set aside for their dowries. We'll have a turnover problem. We want the six best-looking maidens available. They must be pretty."

"What! You would turn my inn into a brothel?"

"To the contrary. They must all be virgins and stay that way. See to it yourself."

"My wife would object."

"Then have your wife see to it. Part of her job will be to see to their morality. They must live here at the inn, in some of your back rooms. Customers may look but not touch. See that they are properly barricaded."

"Look?"

"Yes. They'll need some special costumes." With a fingertip and wine, I sketched out what I had in mind on the worn wooden table. "We'll have to get the wood-carver and a leather worker to do the high-heeled shoes. I can show somebody local how to do the stockings, but later they can come from Okoitz."

"You want them dressed as rabbits?"

"The people will like it. Then there is the matter of advertising. It seems that I have considerable notoriety in Cieszyn, or at least my name does. I've been busy at the brass works, and I haven't met very many people here. But in a week or two, once we get this set up, I want you to hire some old women. They are to wander around and tell about how Sir Conrad Stargard, the killer of the Black Eagle, left the ladies of the castle to move into a notorious inn where beautiful women are scantily clothed. That should get some action going."

"It will get good Christians at my door with pikes and torches!"

"Good. Let them in. Sell them some beer. If they are really organized, let the leaders verify the virginity of the waitresses. No problem."

"Uh . . . all this is going to cost money, my lord."

"Right. Here is two thousand pence to cover it. Keep a careful reckoning. Well, it grows late. I bid you good night." I took the half pot of wine to my room. The full moon was halfway to setting. God, it was late.

The next day I overslept dinner and caught a late, cold breakfast in the kitchen. My head hurt, and I had these horrible thoughts about *what I had done*.

People were cold, people were hungry, the Mongols were coming, and I was wasting valuable resources start-ing a thirteenth-century bunny club. Oh God, my head hurt.

Thinking drunkenly with my gonads instead of my frontal lobes, I had screwed up again. I tried to leave the inn quietly, hoping to avoid the innkeeper, but no such luck.

"Sir Conrad! At last you are up; I was growing worried! I have followed your orders; already the word is out that I search for the six most beautiful maidens in Cieszyn! I have explained our need to the wood-carver, and he will be available tomorrow. But he wishes, of course, to discuss the matter with you."

"Uh . . . Yes . . . I'll talk with him. You realize that for various reasons—our advertising and my relationship with my liege lord—it would be best if my name is not connected with all of this."

"But we must say, in rumors, that you stay here, my lord." Tadeusz really liked having a lord protector.

"Of course. But don't tell anyone that I have any ownership in the place. Swear the witnesses to secrecy."

"As you wish, my lord."

"Hey, the rumor campaign won't work if they know that I own the Pink Dragon."

"As you wish. I have talked with a seamstress. She will have no difficulties with most of the costumes—think; it will be like a continual carnival!—but she wants help with the stockings."

I didn't accomplish much at the foundry that afternoon, and when I got back for supper, the inn was packed. Word had gotten out that the most beautiful maidens in the city would be there. Fully a hundred young males showed up to see what was happening, along with some thirty young hopefuls. I was embarrassed, and the innkeeper expected me to do the choosing.

Stalling for time, I said, "Are you sure that all of them are virgins? Have your wife check it." I ate a meal and drank a pot of wine at the small table that had been reserved for me. I had in mind that his wife should simply ask them, but she felt obligated to actually check for an intact hymen. She passed fourteen of them. How many left because they were embarrassed, I don't know. Apparently, room and board was good wages for a maid. Twelve pence a week on top of that was fabulous.

"And now will you choose the six, my lord?"

Well, one of them was attractive, up to Krystyana's standards. The rest of them were hopeless ducklings, and I felt sorry for them. "No. Let the crowd choose one of them. You talk to them. Have them choose the best five, then the best two, and then a final vote." It seemed the fairest way, and it didn't get me involved.

"But only one?"

"Just do it all again for five more days. Remember what I said about entertainment? Well, this is entertainment."

They took in four hundred pence that night, and afterwards the crowds got bigger.

A week later, as I ate dinner, I got a visit from a local priest, a Father Thomas. I offered him wine, but he refused and immediately got down to business.

"I am worried about your actions, my son, and about your soul."

"But why, Father?"

"You have been responsible for the hiring of young women—virtuous, Christian women from good families—and parading them half naked in a brothel."

"A brothel? By no means, Father! They are waitresses at a good inn, which is the farthest thing from a brothel. They live most virtuous lives, on threat of dismissal! There is no convent that protects its nuns better than we protect our waitresses.

"Aside from the morality of it—and both the innkeeper and I are moral men—aside from it, I say, running a common stews would be bad for business. There are a lot of them in your parish, and they aren't very profitable."

"That others sin is well known. They are not the subject of this conversation."

"But why don't you try to do something about the real fleshpots? Why come to an honest inn?"

"The fleshpots, as you appropriately call them, are sanctioned by their own guild and to a certain extent by the law, if not by the Church. What you are doing is new and is best nipped in the bud."

"Father, we do nothing more than serve food and drink.

The waitresses are pretty, but that's the way God made them, and I, for one, appreciate His good work. We do offer lodging, but we do not offer bed partners."

"You dress them in a manner that encourages lechery."

"We dress them in an attractive manner that fully covers their breasts and privy members. Any man wanting to see more may simply go to the public baths, Father."

"The baths have their own guilds and sanctions. The Church will close them down in time. You evade my charge of lechery."

"Father, it is normal for men to appreciate the beauty of women. If looking at pretty girls is a sin, then every normal male in Poland is doomed to hell!

"Please go and inspect the waitresses' rooms. Talk to the girls. Prove to yourself that we are moral."

"I fully intend to make such an inspection," he said, and left.

I was just finishing my meal, washing down my cheese with beer, when the priest returned.

"Sir Conrad, I admit that the situation is much as you described it. If anything, the girls complain of the restrictions placed on them."

"The price of morality, Father." I made a mental note to see just how serious their complaints were. "While you are here, there is another matter that I would like to discuss. One of our waitresses has become fond of a local boy. I have talked with him. His intentions are honorable and his character good. Since she is employed by the inn, it seems fitting that the inn should pay her wedding expenses. Would it be possible for you to perform the ceremony?"

"Why, I suppose that this is quite possible. In fact, I would be delighted."

"Wonderful! I expect that most of our waitresses will soon be married. Virtuous and attractive young ladies don't stay single for long. Perhaps we should discuss group rates." In the next hour, I made an ally of Father Thomas.

As he left, I said, "Father, how did you know that I owned the inn?"

"The Church has its own sources of information, my son."

It was early afternoon, and only one waitress was on duty. Troubled about the waitresses' complaints to the priest, I went back to the girls' dorm, what had been "the ducal suite," even though the duke never slept there. Actually, almost no one had ever slept there since it was priced beyond the means of the usual guest. It made sense to convert it. If it was more magnificent than necessary, well, young girls like that sort of nonsense.

I had arranged inexpensive group rates at a local bathhouse—early afternoons only—for the inn's staff, at the inn's expense. Our people were encouraged to take a daily bath, and the waitresses were required to.

When I called on the girls, the five of them were in various stages of undress, with a preponderance of full nudity. They let me in without bothering to dress. Perhaps their status as untouchables, along with their recent adolescent discovery that men *noticed* them and that they liked it, was the cause of this display.

I *didn't* like it. On the one hand, I could hardly break my own rules with regard to their virginity, and, well, a really decent man simply *doesn't* take a virgin in a casual way. I think that half the world's frigid women are the results of a klutzy male on their first night. Properly done, it takes patience and warmth and a great deal of love. Back in the twentieth century, I'd had two virgins. They'd both left me as wonderful lovers. I was rather proud of my workmanship.

But just then I was horny as hell. I had been three weeks without, and the last thing I needed was five pairs of budding nipples staring at me.

"Put some clothes on, damn it! You'd think we were running a brothel here!" I shouted.

They scurried to cover themselves with towels and blankets. "We were just back from the baths," one of them said. "We were hot."

"Yeah, sure. Fourteen years old and hotter than hell. Now, what are these complaints you've been making about your jobs?"

"Complaints, Sir Conrad? We have no complaints. The pay is wonderful, and the work, I mean, it's like being at a party," the short redhead said.

"Then why were you complaining to the priest who was here today?"

"Oh, *that*," said a well-endowed blonde, managing to drop her blanket below her belly button. "We were just doing what Mrs. Wrolawski told us to do."

"Cover your breasts. Now, *what* exactly did the innkeeper's wife tell you to do?"

"She said that if we didn't act as pure as nuns in a convent, the Church would shut down the inn and we'd each be lacking our twelve silver pence per week."

"She also threatened to send us to a *nunnery* if we weren't convincing," the redhead added.

So Mrs. Wrolawski had eavesdropped on my conversation with the priest and had set things up. Well-a-day. All's well that ends well.

"Okay. But put some clothes on, damn it!"

Most of the waitresses found suitable husbands within six months. The inn paid the wedding expenses, and there was always a "new hiring" the day after. This happened at least once a month and often once a week. For most of our customers, it was their first experience with voting. In my own mind, I could never sort out the morality of it all.

I had no difficulty with the morality of a situation that occurred much later that evening. The inn had closed for the night, but I was up in my room, drinking and doodling with some ideas about a gear-cutting machine. I do much of my best thinking late at night over a bottle. Oh, in the sober light of dawn I throw out three-quarters of it, but the quarter that is left is often very creative.

My room was directly above that used by Tadeusz and his wife. The cooks lived out, the waitresses were fourteen-year-old girls, and it happened that at the time there were no overnight guests. The only men in the inn were Tadeusz, the guard, and myself when the innkeeper's wife screamed. I was shocked sober in an instant.

"Guard!" Tadeusz shouted.

"Shout all you want. Your aging guard has been detained," a sinister, gravelly voice said.

There were more shouts, accusations, and then screams as I flew for the doorway, down the hall, and down the steps. I was wearing the embroidered outfit given me by Count Lambert, and my glove-leather boots made my approach fairly quiet, at least compared with the commotion coming from the innkeeper's room.

A beefy stranger was guarding the doorway. He had a long misericord, and I belatedly realized that I had left my sword belt in my room.

I am not a master of the martial arts, but I had taken the standard military courses in unarmed combat. The important thing is to hit hard and fast. Hesitation can get you killed.

The thug came at me with a clumsy overhand swing. I blocked his dagger with my left forearm and kneed him hard in the groin. He bent over, presenting the back of his head to my clenched fists and his face to my knee.

I took advantage of this opportunity; his nose and teeth gave way with a crunching sound. He fell heavily to the floor, still gripping his knife. I don't *like* people who pull knives on me in dark hallways, so I stamped hard on his knife hand. Too hard. The bones smashed, and splinters of knuckle bones were driven through the thin soles of my boot, lacerating my foot. Pain shot up my leg.

I picked up the misericord and limped into the room, ducking my head to get through the doorway. "What the hell goes on here?" I inquired.

Two Mafia types were in the room beside the Wrolawskis. The leader of the pair grinned evilly and said, "Just a bit of guild business, stranger. Get out and you'll live longer."

Tadeusz was bleeding from the nose and mouth. His wife's dress was torn, exposing bruised, aging breasts.

"They're from the whoremasters guild!" Tadeusz said, contempt and fear in his voice.

"If your business was honest, you'd come in the daytime," I said. "Now I'm telling *you*! Get out fast and *you'll* live."

The leader signaled to his subordinate, and the man came at me with a wide-bladed dagger. He used the same stupid overhand attack as his associate in the hallway.

The misericord is a long, narrow, thrusting weapon designed to pierce chain mail. I blocked the thug's attack as before, but this time at the expense of a slash in the embroidery on my cuff. Gripping him by the shoulder with my left hand, I aimed a gutting thrust at the man's stomach. He pulled his body back, and my knife continued upward, catching him between the chin and neck. The thin blade went entirely through his brain, and a few centimeters of it stuck out from the top of his head.

Over the man's shoulder, I saw the leader hauling back to throw a knife at me. With my hands still on the shoulder and the grip of the knife, I yanked the body upward as a shield. The dead man was much lighter than I had expected, or perhaps the fury of combat increased my strength, but in all events I bashed the thug's head into a low roof beam. The misericord stuck in the wood, and the corpse hung there, the leader's knife in its back.

The leader came at me with his fists, but his sort of hoodlum lives more by fear than by fighting ability. Equally weaponless, I hit him twice, hard, in the stomach.

"Sir Conrad!" Tadeusz shouted.

Suddenly the Mafia type froze, rigid. I was too furious to stop; grabbing him by the shoulder, I chopped viciously with the edge of my right hand, once on each side of the neck, breaking both collar bones.

"Sir Conrad?" the man gasped, his arms hanging unnaturally low.

"Yeah." I was breathing hard.

"The noble knight that killed Sir Rheinburg with a single blow?"

"Among others." I was returning to normal.

"I knew him, sir."

"You look the type."

"We had heard rumors that you were associated with this inn, but the whoremasters guild felt—"

"Well, you felt wrong." The noise had awakened the waitresses, and they were clustered wide-eyed around the doorway. One had a blanket wrapped around her, but the rest were naked.

"Those girls are servants, not whores," I said. "We have nothing to do with the whoremasters guild."

"Yes, sir. That is obviously true, sir."

"So?" I said.

"I may live, sir? I may leave?"

I had to think for a minute. "Yeah. You can live. But you damn well owe us for damages."

"Of course, sir. We always pay our just debts."

"Tadeusz," I said. "What do they owe you for what they've done to your property, for the injury caused to you and your wife?"

"Who can say, Sir Conrad?" the innkeeper said. "But is this wise?"

"Name a number!"

"Perhaps five hundred pence?"

"Good," I said. "Okay, whoremaster. You owe us five hundred pence, not to mention the mess you've made on the floor and the fact that your thugs cut up and bled all over my best outfit. Get out!"

"As you command, Sir Conrad Stargard." He left with as much dignity as he could muster.

"Are you insane, Sir Conrad?" the innkeeper said. "Now they will come back!"

"I doubt it. That kind knows when it's licked."

"But they will! Girls! Quickly! Run to Sir Conrad's room. Bring back his weapons and armor!"

Six naked teenagers scurried off, the one with the blanket having dropped it in the blood pooling under the body that was still stuck to the beam.

"At least bring my wine!" I shouted. I dropped heavily into a chair. The action was over, and I was starting to get the shakes.

I got my wine, but shortly six pretty, nude girls, at Tadeusz's insistence, were stripping off my outer clothes and lacing me into padded leather and chain mail.

"This is stupid. They won't be back," I said, but I was wrong.

Once I was fully armed, we searched out and found

the inn's guard. He had a huge knot on the side of his head and was bound, gagged, and furious. He smiled at the corpse stuck to the ceiling, and when the other thug started moaning, he took particular pleasure in tying the man up.

"Yes," the guard said, gripping his sword. "Let them come back."

"Hey," I said. "If you people are that worried, why not send for the count's guardsmen?"

"Certainly, Sir Conrad," the innkeeper said. "But who would dare go out into the night?"

"Oh, hell. I'll do it myself," I said. "And have these girls get some clothes on. They act like this really *is* a brothel!"

"And leave us defenseless?" one of the girls squealed.

"Shit." I sat down and took a long pull of wine. There was nothing for it but to wait until they all calmed down and went back to bed. Anyway, my injured foot was throbbing.

The girls were passing out knives from the kitchen, which was absolutely stupid. If you don't know how to use a weapon, you are much better off without it.

In their excitement, they had forgotten my instructions to get dressed. Or perhaps running around naked with knives seemed more adventurous to them. Mrs. Wrolawski, who usually kept them in check, was sitting, stunned, on her bed.

She hadn't even made an effort to cover her bruised breasts. Her husband was sitting in the other chair in a blue funk, blood still dripping from his nose. The guard was looking for an excuse to kill somebody, the girls were working out a set of heroic passwords, the body was *still* stuck to the ceiling, and my foot hurt.

Damn, what a lunatic night! My mother told me I should have gone to the beach.

There was a knock at the door.

Everyone in the room froze. Even the previously murderous guard was suddenly sweating.

"Never mind," I said. "I'll get it."

I limped down the hall to the main door. One more

piece of insanity and I was going to scream. I did take the precaution of drawing my sword before opening the door.

"Ah. Sir Conrad Stargard, I believe," said the well-dressed gentleman before me. "Please note that we come unarmed and with goodwill. We wish to make amends for certain unpleasantries that occurred earlier this evening."

There were six of them, two men and four women. They presented Tadeusz with a purse containing five hundred pence, removed the dead and wounded men, and, with buckets of warm, soapy water that they had brought with them, cleaned up the blood on the floor.

"These, of course, are yours by right of combat," the gentleman said, presenting me with the newly cleaned misericord, the wide-bladed knife, and the leader's throwing knife. All three were sheathed. He must have brought the leader's sheath with him.

"Certain other amends will be made at the earliest opportunity. In the interim, I wish you a pleasant sleep and our assurances of our continued goodwill."

And they left.

"That's it, gang. Back to bed," I said, and took a long pull of wine.

A week later, a messenger delivered to me four complete outfits, all beautifully embroidered and one almost an exact duplicate of the one that had been damaged. He also brought a red velvet barding for Anna and a matching surcoat for me, both embroidered with gold thread.

All of it fit perfectly. I never found out how they got the sizes, but I was never again troubled by the underworld.

Chapter Nineteen

I NEEDED quite a few brass castings for the wet mills.

There was the gearing between the small, compensating windmill and the turret. I had originally envisioned a collection of wooden cog wheels, but a brass worm gear was a lot simpler and more efficient.

A worm gear is simply a screw—the worm—with threads that fit into the teeth of a gear. The problem is that for them to mate properly, the shapes of both the worm and the gear get *very* complicated. They were well beyond our ability to machine; they were probably beyond my ability to describe mathematically.

I spent an evening drinking and pondering the problem in my room. The taproom below was always too crowded and noisy to think, and even in my room enough noise seeped up from below to be disturbing. I finally hired a krummhorn player to sit in the corner and play softly. Muzak.

The next morning, I had Mikhail Krakowski make up an oversized worm and gear out of clay. This was done crudely, by hand and by eye. The teeth were very deep, and the clay was built up around turned brass mandrels to assure concentric bearings. When dry, we fitted these together in an adjustable wooden frame. The fit was poor at first, but it was possible to turn the gear by turning the worm. We then put a man to cranking the worm gently and adjusting the teeth together as the unbaked clay wore away. In three days, they were much smaller and a perfect fit. We then fired the clay worm and gear, and these became our master patterns for brass castings. This gearing gave us a 48 to 1 reduction between the small windmill and a shaft that connected to the turret. The shaft turned a lantern gear that worked on pegs set into the fixed tower. As a result, the small windmill turned 1,152 times in the course of rotating the turret once. I hoped it would be enough.

One by one, problems were solved. The bushings had been cast, one with sockets to hold the windmill blades. These bushings were being turned laboriously on the big lathe. Two more smaller lathes were under construction. We were confident that all the parts necessary for the wet mill would be ready for delivery to Okoitz in a month.

I was getting ready to return to Count Lambert when I heard an awful squealing from the foundry. I rushed over and was stopped by Wladyslaw Krakowski.

"My brother! My own brother called me a lazy pig!"

"I called you a lazy pig because you *are* a lazy pig!" Mikhail explained. The squealing was still going on.

"All right! But I'm a *tired* lazy pig, and walking in that barrel on the lathe is no fit job for a man!"

They were still arguing when I pushed past them and went to the lathe. Thom was operating it. Inside the barrel an unhappy pig was trotting madly, trying to climb the rotating wall. A brass ring in the animal's nose was tied to a wooden stick such that if it stopped running, its nose was pulled.

I stared at this for a while. Using a pig as motive power was strange, but a pig is a strong animal, and its short legs let it work where no horse could possibly fit. Would our future machines be rated in pigpower the way Americans use horsepower?

I suppose it was hard on the pig, but I can think of nothing worse to do to an animal than killing and eating it, and I am not about to become a vegetarian like Adolf Hitler.

Thom moved the stick back so that the pig could stop.

"The speed control," he said. "I think we'll have to switch pigs about three times an hour. It's cheaper than men, though."

I could see that it was time to go back to Okoitz.

I was in the saddle when the innkeeper brought me a stirrup cup and a pouch of gold. "Seven thousand pence, my lord. Your profits for the first month of the Pink Dragon," he said.

I thanked him and rode off. Seven thousand pence in a single month! That was twice what I paid for the place, back salaries and all! Well, it would keep the foundry going no matter what else happened. If I couldn't get land of my own, that foundry might be all that stood between us and the Mongols.

Anna seemed inordinately proud of her new red velvet barding. She held her head high with her neck arched and walked with a gait she'd never used before. It was a sort of hopping thing, with her left front and right rear hooves hitting the cobblestones at the same time. I guess it was impressive because a lot of people came out to watch.

But it was rough on my lower back, and as soon as we left the city gates, I urged her into a more comfortable gallop.

She ran the entire way to Sir Miesko's manor, again without working up a sweat.

Krystyana greeted me, but at first I almost didn't recognize her. Her actual appearance hadn't changed, except that she wore her hair differently. But something about her bearing, the way she held her shoulders back, the way she glided instead of clumping along like a gawky adolescent ... But there was more, much more. Something that I couldn't quite define. Somehow, a pretty duckling had turned into a swan.

"Welcome, Sir Conrad. I've missed you." She had the same calm smile that made Lady Richeza so radiant.

I was home.

I hated to leave, but I was worried about my projects at Okoitz so we set out the next morning. Halfway to Okoitz, we met Sir Miesko on the road.

"Sir Miesko! It's delightful to see you again. We have just come from your manor, and all is well."

"That relieves my mind, Sir Conrad. In truth, I worried about Richeza all winter. For my own part, I have sent Boris Novacek on his way to Cracow with half a dozen mule skinners, seventy-five mules, and a gross of barrels of wine."

"And how are things going at Okoitz?"

"Amazing! Your loom and wheels are turning out cloth by the mile, and that huge mill of yours is half up!"

"Half up! I've stayed too long at Cieszyn."

"All seemed to be going well. But aren't you being rude, Sir Conrad? You haven't introduced me to your lady."

"But you already know her. Surely you haven't forgotten Krystyana."

"What? Damn, but you're right! But her bearing, her poise—"

"It's entirely your wife's doing, Sir Miesko. Krystyana visited her for a month, and you see the results. I didn't think to buy a present for Richeza, but if you want a loom and some spinning wheels, or even the fittings for a mill, you have only to ask."

"I might just take you up on that, for you have gained a prize of great value. But now I am anxious to see my wife again, so I bid you good-bye, Sir Conrad, and you, my Lady Krystyana."

As Sir Miesko rode away, Krystyana looked at me. "He called me a lady!"

"You'd rather be a gentleman?"

'Of course not! But surely I'm only a peasant girl."

"Well, you'll always be a pretty wench to me, Krystyana."

"He acted as though I was of the nobility!"

"So, noble is as noble acts. Come on, let's get going."

"But I'm not noble, am I?"

"Do you expect to be beaten about the head and shoulders with a sword? I don't know if there *is* a ceremony for elevating a common woman, but as far as I'm concerned, you can be whatever you want to be. Let's ride."

The mill was nothing like half done, but good progress was being made under Vitold's supervision. The "basement" for the lower tank had been dug, and the new well was in. Most of the upright logs had had their sides flattened, and some of them were already in place. All according to plan. The main shaft was finished, ready for the brass collars, but here there was a discrepancy. I had assumed that the cam would be a separate piece, but Vitold had cut the cam and shaft out of a single log more than two yards across! I had allowed an extra yard in diameter to provide room for clamping the cam to the shaft, but single-piece construction let him reduce the cam diameter from three to two yards while still giving a meter's travel on the follower wheel at the end of the A-frame.

This in turn permitted raising the top of the clean tank half a yard, increasing its volume by sixty tons of water. Also, the turret could be lowered by half a yard, saving materials and work. It was an excellent improvement. Now if I could teach Vitold to read blueprints!

"You're doing a good job, Vitold."

"Thank you, Sir Conrad. We're way ahead of where I thought we'd be. It's these axes you showed Ilya how to make. The old axes needed sharpening every hour, but since he treated them, they last for *days!*"

"Hmm. Good. Tell Ilya to come to me the next time he's free."

"I'll tell him when he gets back, Sir Conrad. He's been gone for a week getting supplies."

The count's hall was humming with activity. Natalia and a girl I hadn't met were running the loom at a remarkable pace, and six other "handmaidens," most of them new, were spinning busily. Eleven huge bolts of cloth were proudly stacked in a corner, and the girls all seemed to be having fun.

Five of the count's knights were in attendance, but the count was out with a party making the rounds of his lands and the manors of his knights. The journey was partly social, visiting his subordinates; partly economic, to ensure that things were managed well; partly judicial.

The knights and barons had the right of low justice,

that is, jurisdiction over offenses punishable by fines, flogging, and up to a year's forced labor, subject to the count's review. The count reserved for himself the right of high justice, and his word could have a man hanged. For eight months of the year, he was out riding circuit half the time.

Except for Sir Stefan, who was still making himself unpleasant on my behalf, the knights were essentially a decent lot, if somewhat extroverted. They tended to spend their afternoons in fighting practice, their evenings in heavy drinking, and their mornings sobering up.

I spent some of my afternoons with them, but they were slow to pick up on fencing, and I wasn't worth much with a lance and shield until I discovered that if I held my lance steady, Anna would guide us—and it—into the target.

Evenings were like being back in the air force again. They were especially pleasant since Sir Stefan had the dusk to midnight guard shift. We sang songs, told stories, and swapped lies with boisterous good humor. Yet I always had to watch what I said so as not to violate my oath to Father Ignacy, and much of their conversation revolved around hunting and hawking, of which I was ignorant. Then, too, they were very heavy drinkers. While I like to drink, too much of it spoils lovemaking, and sex doesn't give you hangovers.

Following local custom, the knights had left their wives at home to manage things. There were now a dozen ladies-in-waiting, six of them new since Mary and Ilona had been pronounced pregnant and married off. This left us with plenty of variety, although Krystyana was still the best-looking of the bunch.

The other knights were courteous to Krystyana, but at bedtime they paired off with other girls. After a few nights, I got to sleeping with Krystyana regularly even though there were quite a few I hadn't sampled. I just didn't want her feelings hurt.

I looked up Angelo Muskarini, the Florentine walker. "You have strange things going here, Sir Conrad." "How so?"

"You told me not to criticize your loom and spinning wheels. Your loom looks crude, but it makes more cloth— and faster—than any that I have ever seen. And your spinning wheels are amazing! They make a hundred times the thread that a distaff can!"

"Better than the wheels in Florence?"

"There are no spinning wheels in Florence, nor any in Flanders, either. This is a new thing under the sun!"

Huh? I'd thought that they had spinning wheels in the thirteenth century. Oh, well. "I'm glad that you approve. So what's so strange about our goings-on?"

"Because, Sir Conrad, you are doing everything else entirely wrong! You have the finest methods for spinning and weaving that I have ever seen, but you aren't even sorting your wool! Your ideas of combing and carding are a joke, and no one here has ever heard of warping, or dyeing, or fulling!"

"Well, we're new at this. Talk to Vitold and Ilya about any special tools you'll need and figure out what you'll need in the way of dyeing vats and so on. The count wants a dozen looms going by winter, which means a dozen of our six-station spinning wheels. We'll need enough of the rest of this stuff to keep them fed. How are you doing for dyes and other chemicals?"

"I have plenty for now, but with a dozen looms—"

"Figure out what you'll need for a year and we'll place an order with Boris Novacek. I still owe him a favor."

I spent some of my time watching the mill go up, although Vitold really didn't need any help. Mostly I worked on the scale model of the dry mill.

The basement of that mill was to be eight yards deep and insulated with two yards of sawdust. It was to serve as an icehouse, a communal refrigerator. Come winter, two-thirds of its volume was to be packed with snow, the rest in storage shelves. According to my crude estimates, the snow should last at least twelve months. We would be able to store some of the vegetables and meat from the next harvest through the winter.

In external appearance, the dry mill looked like the wet mill, except the circular work shed was missing. The only attendant building was to house a threshing machine. The dry mill's construction was lighter, because it didn't have to support twenty-five hundred tons of water.

Internally, it was designed quite differently. The ground floor had a huge, three-yard grindstone, which was turned by a shaft connected to a ten-yard solid wheel just below the turret. Four circles of carefully placed vertical pegs rose from the wheel, and on the shaft above it were eight matching rows of radial pegs. The shaft was offset by a yard from the center line of the mill. Between these sets of pegs was a movable lantern gear with sliding concave brass rollers to mate with both sets of pegs. By moving the lantern gear, the miller could get four different speeds, both forward and reverse.

The space between the gears and the stone was mostly taken up by twelve grain hoppers. Each had a chute at the bottom to direct grain to the hole in the top of the stone. Outside, a system of pulleys and dump buckets filled the hoppers.

One of the knights, Sir Vladimir, seemed to have some mechanical ability. He got interested in the model and started helping me with it. After we had worked together for a few hours, I asked, "What's wrong between you guys and Krystyana?"

"Why, nothing. Everyone has been most polite to her."

"You've been polite, but you haven't taken her to bed. Do you think that I have some exclusive right to her?"

"No, it isn't that. It's just—oh, I don't know."

"But she's the prettiest one there."

"I know, but—well, it just wouldn't seem right. She doesn't *act* like a peasant girl. You don't just grab a lady and drag her to your room—"

"I've never seen a wench here who needed dragging. Anyway, you know she isn't noble. Her father is a peasant right here in Okoitz."

"I know, I know. But you've asked me and I've answered you, so let's let the matter drop," he said. "Now, explain again why it is necessary for the rollers on the lantern gear to be able to slip sideways."

After about a week of monogamy on my part, Krys-

tyana sort of withdrew. I put this down to feminine mood-
iness and continued my sampling for a week.

Ilya the blacksmith returned with five men and fourteen pack mules loaded with hematite, a red iron oxide.
A small placer mine some thirty miles away made a limited
amount of bog ore available. Ilya had spent much of the
winter preparing to make charcoal from the branches of
the trees we had cut, but somehow I had never realized
that he actually made his own iron out of ore and fuel.

To make charcoal, Ilya and his helpers cut and split
wood, which he piled in a single huge stack. As soon as
the weather broke and the ground thawed enough for
digging, the stack was covered with a full yard of dirt.
Only a small hole was left at the top and an even smaller
one at the bottom. Then he lit the stack. Over the next
few days, he dug sampling holes to see how the burning
was progressing. When the wood was completely charred,
he filled in all the holes, let the fire smother, and went
off for iron ore.

"Got a hundred pairs of hinges that I promised people,
Sir Conrad, plus I figure you'll need some iron for that
thing." He gestured toward the half-completed mill.

"You're right, Ilya. Later on we'll talk about a saw
blade. I saw those axes you made. Nice work. I'm amazed
that you made so many of them in only five weeks."

"Five weeks? That didn't take me five days! Those are
the same axe heads we used last winter, only I cemented
them. Cementation didn't change the shape of the iron
bars I made into steel, and the old axe heads already
looked like axe heads. I took the handles off and put them
in the count's last pickling crock with plenty of charcoal
and heated it up. Didn't go a whole week, though. A kid
I had keeping the fire going fell asleep the third night, and
the crock was cold in the morning. I still haven't found
the bastard; he's been hiding from me. But those axe
heads hardened up all right, so I guess it's okay."

"Congratulations, Ilya. You have just invented case
hardening. What you have is steel on the outside and iron
on the inside. Not a bad thing for an axe."

"Heh. Thought it might be something like that. This saw you want, does it have to be steel?"

"It sure does."

"Then you better find me some more clay pots. There is not one left in Okoitz, and the cooks are not happy. Neither will be the count if he gets a taste for sauerkraut."

"I know just the place. There's a brass foundry in Cieszyn where they use a lot of fire clay. Some of the workers should be coming here in a few weeks to deliver fittings for the mill. I would have sent an accountant to them by now, but I think I need the count's permission to swear the kid in. Maybe you know him, Piotr Kulczynski."

"Know him! That's the bastard that let my fire go out. You're going to be shy one accountant if I find him!"

"Not a chance, Ilya. You hurt that kid and I'll hurt you. Like I said, I need him. Anyway, he taught you something about steel, so call it even."

"Well, seeing as how it's you asking, I'll let the kid off. I'll be busy making iron for a month, but after that I'll need those crocks."

Ilya actually made wrought iron in the same crude forge that he used for everything else. He layered charcoal on the bottom of his forge higher than the nozzle of his bellows. Then he carefully put lump ore on the side away from the bellows and more charcoal on the near side until the forge was heaped high.

He started a fire and worked the bellows gently for two hours, adding a mixture of fine ore and charcoal as the mass in the forge was consumed. Then he called for assistants, who worked the bellows hard. After three hours of this, constantly adding ore and charcoal, he dug into the burning mass with large pincers and pulled out a glowing spongy mass.

This was immediately placed on the anvil, and three burly men beat on it vigorously with sledgehammers. Ilya kept turning the mass so that it was shaped into a crude rod.

When the rod cooled, it was put back into the fire; another spongy lump was fished out, and then the process was repeated. Two men were still working the bellows and adding ore and charcoal.

Each rod was pulled and beaten and reheated four times before being set aside to cool. By the end of the day, six men working twelve hours had consumed forty kilos of ore and two hundred kilos of charcoal. But they had made less than ten kilos of wrought-iron bars.

"You know, Ilya, once we get the wet mill built, we'll have machines to work the bellows and a trip-hammer to beat your iron. We'll build you a bigger forge, and you'll be able to make ten times the iron working alone."

"Bellows that work themselves? Hammers that swing on their own accord? You might as well tell me that fishes can fly!"

"I know of one that does."

"Sir Conrad, if you hadn't been right about steel, I'd call you the greatest liar in Christendom. As it is, well, you tell me what you want and I'll make it. But I'll believe those hammers and bellows when I see them!"

Krystyana was still acting standoffish, so finally I asked her about it.

"Sir Conrad, it's not that I'm putting you off, it's just ...oh, you'd call it a superstition."

"Try me, pretty girl."

"Well, it's something that Lady Richeza told me about."

"Yes?"

"Well, she said that if you count the days after your ...your time and sleep alone from the end of the first week to the middle of the third, you won't get pregnant. I know it's silly, I know it's superstitious, but I don't want to get pregnant and I don't want to marry a peasant and I don't want to be old at twenty and dead at forty and—" She was in my arms, crying uncontrollably.

Once I got her calmed down, I said, "Don't worry, pretty girl. You don't have to be anything that you don't want to be. As to this abstention during certain times of the month, well, in my country it's called the rhythm method, and the Pope has approved it. It works most of the time."

She cried some more, and after that I settled down to a program of fifteen days a month with Krystyana and the rest of the time spreading myself around.

I had a model of the cloth factory built by the first of May. We were running out of room in the bailey, so I made it a three-story building, as high as the church.

The top floor, with a high, peaked roof, was filled with a dozen looms. The middle floor held the spinning wheels and the combing and carding equipment. The ground floor was for washing and dyeing, with additional space for storage. I added a treadmill-powered lift to carry materials up and down.

I wished that I could have done something about windows, but glass was hideously expensive. Even a few small glass windows would have cost more than the rest of the building put together. The lack of glass or decent artificial light was serious. It cut our available man-hours by a factor of three at least. Poland is at a high latitude. In the summer, it can be light for eighteen hours a day. But in the summer, except for two months after planting, most people had to spend most of their time in the fields.

In the winter, nothing could be done in the fields. There was often less than six hours of daylight, and that was useful only to those who worked outside or next to an open window. Oil lamps burning animal fat were hard to work by, smelly and expensive. The animals of the thirteenth century were skinny, and fat was scarce. In Cieszyn, a kilo of fat sold for twice the price of a kilo of lean meat.

Farming occupied six months out of the year. Two months in the late spring were available for other work, but without a good source of light the four winter months were largely useless.

Although electric lights were out of the question, kerosene lamps were possible. The world's first oil wells were drilled in Poland by Ignacy Lukasiewicz, who built the first petrochemical plant and invented the kerosene lamp. But I saw no possibility of getting our technology to that level in the next five years.

Beeswax candles? It would take thirty candles to light

the factory poorly. I estimated that it would take six hundred beehives to produce enough wax to keep them burning all winter.

In short, I was designing a factory that could be operational only two months out of the year.

When I explained the problem to the count, he solved it in moments in his own typical way. He simply told each of his 140 knights to send him a peasant girl or two from just after Easter to just before Christmas. The girls were paid in cloth, and everybody was happy. But I get ahead of myself.

Chapter Twenty

COUNT LAMBERT returned on the morning of May 1, which was yet another holiday. With him were about thirty knights and a number of dignitaries, one of whom was Sir Stefan's father. I thought it best to leave Lambert with his guests until I was summoned.

In the early afternoon I was watching an archery competition; the peasants were shooting at targets about fifty yards away with a skill that was about equal to that of modern archers.

Suddenly, Count Lambert was standing beside me. "Well, Sir Conrad, are you going to teach us the proper way to shoot arrows?"

"Not I, my lord. But I know a man who could."

"Indeed? And who is this man?"

I told him the story of how Tadaos the boatman had shot the deer.

"A single arrow into a deer's head at two hundred yards from a moving boat? You saw this yourself?"

"Yes, my lord, and helped him eat the venison."

"Hmm. I could use such an archer to train others. Could you get him here?"

"I could write Father Ignacy and ask him to tell the boatman of your needs. Perhaps he will come."

"Do so. I will affix my seal to the letter. Now then, I

have talked to this Florentine cloth worker you sent me. Does he really know his trade?"

"I think so, my lord, but we won't know until we see his cloth."

"Hmm. You swore him to yourself. Would you transfer his allegiance to me?"

"Gladly, my lord. I engaged him for you. But could I ask a favor in return?"

"Name it."

"There's a boy here, Piotr Kulczynski. I would like him to swear to me."

"Certainly, Sir Conrad, if the boy and his father are willing. In fact, as long as someone is not sworn to me, you really don't need my permission. Even sworn, a man always has a right of departure, provided his debts are paid. What do you want with him?"

"He's a bright kid, my lord, and has picked up accounting very quickly. I want him to keep an eye on some commercial interests I have in Cieszyn."

"Do these commercial interests include ownership of the Pink Dragon Inn?"

"Yes, my lord. Do you object?"

"Not in the least. It's just that some remarkable rumors have been circulating about your adventures in Cieszyn. Did you really seat one of my peasant girls at the head table in my brother's castle?"

"Yes, my lord. I'm sorry if I've offended you, but—"

"Sir Conrad, my only objection is that I wasn't able to see the expression on his wife's face." He laughed. "That bitch has always hated me.

"Well, come along. I want to introduce you to my liege lord, and I want you to explain your mills and the new cloth factory."

As we entered the castle, Sir Stefan was talking heatedly with his father. I couldn't hear them, but twice he pointed at me. As my American friends would have put it, the shit was about to hit the fan.

Duke Henryk the Bearded was one of the most remarkable men I had ever met. He was almost seventy years old, and his face was cracked and wrinkled like old timber, yet his back was straight and strong. His thick white hair brushed his shoulders, and his thick white beard was huge. It was wider than his chest and extended below his sword belt.

But more important than his appearance was his—I don't want to say aura, because that implies something mystical, and this was an immensely practical man—but a feeling of power was almost tangible about him, as if, had he decided to walk through a wall, the wall would have apologized and scrambled out of his way.

Even more impressive, though in a totally different way, was his son, who would eventually be called Henryk the Pious. Young Henryk was just over forty and approaching the height of his powers. He could read and write and did a lot of both—rare among the nobility. Whereas the father was a tough politician, the son was a prince, every centimeter of him. His bearing and his look and his tone of voice were a chant that said, "Duty, justice, order, and restraint; honor, vigor, and discipline."

We looked each other in the eye, and I knew that this was a man I would follow into hell, fully confident that he could lead me out again. I had found Poland's king and my own.

Henryk the Bearded looked at me and said, "So, you are Sir Conrad the Giant. I have heard much about you."

"I hope nothing too bad, my lord."

"Mixed. But all of it is impossible, so most of it is lies. Your loom works faster than anything the Walloons own. They brought nothing like your spinning wheels. Now, tell me about these mills you're building."

The mill tower was now up, the tank floors were in, and the circular shed was completed. Work was under way on the turret. With the five-story-tall structure and my two-meter models, I was able to explain what I was doing, yet their questions kept me hopping. Our two visitors might be statesmen and warriors by profession, but they were not stupid when it came to technical matters. They went over things point by point almost as thoroughly as Vitold did.

After the mills, we started on the cloth factory. The

looms and spinning wheels were already understood, and I referred them to Angelo the Florentine when they asked about the dyeing vats and the combing and carding equipment. They jumped on me when it came to the washing line. After all, everybody understood washing.

"Why twelve tubs? Why not one big one?"

"A single big tub would have to be brass, with a fire under it. Using a dozen small tubs, only two tubs need to be heated. The rest can be of wood. Also, wool needs not only to be washed but to be rinsed several times. With a single tub, we would not only have to heat three tubs of water for each batch of wool, we would have to throw away a lot of cleanser with the rinse water."

"Explain that."

"We call this the reverse-flow system. The wool moves from north to south along the line of tubs. The water moves from south to north, overflowing from one tub to the next. The water comes in cold and clean and goes out cold and dirty. The wool comes in cold and dirty and goes out cold and clean."

I could see that I wasn't getting through.

"Let's follow some wool as it goes through the tubs. Dirty wool is dumped into the first wooden tub, and a worker stirs it with a wooden fork. The water is only warm, and it's dirty. Most of the cleanser has been consumed, but some dirt is easily removed. Excess water goes out this drain, and fresher water flows in through this pipe from the second tank.

"The wool is scooped up and into the second tub, and more raw wool is dumped into the first. In the second tub, the water is hotter and cleaner.

"This goes on until the sixth tub, which is made of brass. It is set in stone, and there is a fire beneath it. The water is very hot. Cleanser is added here.

"The seventh is the first rinse tub. The water is warm, and cleanser that is washed off the wool flows with the water into the sixth tub.

"Tubs eight, nine, and ten are additional, progressively hotter rinse tubs. The eleventh tub is also of brass and is heated boiling hot.

"The twelfth tub contains fresh, cold water. Its purpose is to cool the wool while warming the water before it flows into the boiling rinse tank.

"The washing line is followed by these draining and drying racks."

"Hmm. So the same water is used many times, and fuel is saved. Interesting."

The reverse flow is one of those beautifully simple things that were invented remarkably late. It was first applied to heat exchangers in the 1930s and was Albert Einstein's major contribution to engineering. Since then, it has been applied to hundreds of industrial processes.

"Sir Conrad, you keep saying cleanser. Aren't you using soap or wood ashes?"

"Soap is a boiled mixture of ashes and grease. The wool already has grease on it. It is what we are trying to remove. Raw ashes have a lot of solid particles that would make the wool dirty.

"Instead, we leach the ashes first. We put them in a barrel with a cloth bottom and run hot water through them. The water that drips out contains sodium hydroxide, lye, which is a stronger cleanser."

"So there is a worker at each tub?"

"Probably not, my lord. Working all day over the two boiling tubs would be arduous. We plan to have each worker follow a given batch of wool up the line."

This grilling went on for hours before Duke Henryk called for beer and I could slake my very dry throat. We were seated in the count's hall.

"Sir Conrad, as you have described the washing line, it seems to me that it can wash more wool than your wheels can spin."

"True, my lord. It will be free much of the time for other things. Washing clothes, for example."

"You have explained what you are doing but not why you are doing it."

"Why make cloth, my lord? So that people can wear it!"

"No. I mean, you are a foreigner among us. What do you want? Is it money?"

"I have plenty of money, my lord. More than I want for myself. And I am *not* a foreigner. I know that my accent is strange to you. I grew up in ... another place. But all of my ancestors were Poles, and I am a Pole, and this is my country."

"Indeed. I am told that you may not discuss your place of birth, and I will not press you. But *why* are you doing what you are doing?"

"Because Poland is divided and backward and weak! Because our people are cold and hungry and illiterate! They die like snowflakes touching a river.

"And because the Mongols—the Tartars—are coming! They want to kill all our people and turn our fields into grazing lands for their war-horses!"

"Calm yourself, Sir Conrad. It is good that you are concerned with the lot of our people. These mills, these looms of yours, they are good things. I will see that their use is encouraged. But as to the Tartars, why, Genghis Khan died five years ago, so why worry about them?"

"Genghis had sons, and his sons have sons. They will come."

"When?"

"In nine years. A little less than that."

"Hmm. You know their plans so far in advance?"

"They will come, my lord."

"If you believe that, then why are you wasting your time on these peaceful pursuits? Why are you not building weapons of war?"

"I will build weapons, my lord. But who will use them? In Poland now it takes a hundred peasants and workers to support a single fighting man, a knight. When the Mongols come, they will come with every man in their tribes under arms. By numbers alone they will overwhelm us. My machines will give all the people the time and the weapons to train for war. Poland can survive only with a citizen army!"

"You would arm commoners? That would upset the social stability."

"You are right, my lord. But there is nothing as stable

as a dead man. He just lies there and doesn't move at all."

"You are a strange man, Sir Conrad the Giant."

And so I was dismissed. As I walked away, I knew that I had blown it. I had gotten so wrapped up in technical details that I had forgotten what it was that I should have been trying to accomplish. I was like the engineer who became so involved in fighting alligators that he forgot that his job was to drain the swamp.

It didn't matter what the duke thought of my mills and factory. They were already being built, and he would not be likely to stop them, no matter what he thought.

The important thing I needed was his approval on a grant of land. Without my own land, everything I had done so far would be trivial.

And I had come across like a lunatic prophet of doom! I couldn't have done worse if I'd been carrying a sign proclaiming the end of the world.

I was in a black mood when I learned that the Krakowski brothers had arrived with a packtrain loaded with my brass mill fittings. City folk didn't pay much attention to most of the country holidays. When there was work to be had, they worked. The collars were so big that they had to be slung between two mules each, like sedan chairs.

I called Vitold, Ilya, and Angelo away from a sort of soccer game and introduced them to the Krakowski brothers. We discussed our mutual needs: the fittings for the dry mill, tubs for washing and dyeing, axles and bushings for wheelbarrows.

Fortunately, the Krakowski brothers understood my technical drawings, and I had a thick stack of parchment for them to take back.

It took Vitold a long time to grasp what a wheelbarrow was all about, but he agreed to make a gross as soon as the sawmill was done. They would help in getting in the harvest.

Then there were the clay crocks for Ilya's steelmaking. The brothers agreed to make them but insisted on understanding the cementation process. They already had the clay and the charcoal and the ovens. They were impressed by Ilya's axes and wanted to get into the cementation business themselves. I gave them my blessing.

They had the idea of casting brass into molded clay forms and a hint from me about stacking up small clay forms and casting many objects at once. They were already selling belt buckles and door hinges by the gross.

I called over Piotr Kulczynski and swore him to fealty before the group. It took a while to make the brothers understand that Piotr was not their boss—they could run their business as they saw fit—but they were expected to keep him informed on all financial transactions, and he would be reporting to me.

It was understood that Piotr was to live in my room at the inn and keep the inn's books as well. I gave him a letter to the innkeeper confirming this.

Finally, Thom Krakowski brought up a delicate subject. Despite the fact that they were working for me, I had agreed that they should get one-twelfth of the profits of their work. He therefore felt that I should buy the present fittings and the order I had just placed, just to get it on the books so that they could figure up their bonus. I would get much of this back as my profits for ownership.

I had to agree that this was fair but stipulated that they would be paid from the surplus from the inn. This was agreed on.

Their bill came to 19,500 pence.

It was growing dark, so I invited all present to a quick meal in the count's kitchen. We were halfway through the meal when Lambert came in.

"Sir Conrad! Where the devil have you been? There was a high place for you at supper that stood empty!"

"I'm sorry, my lord. I didn't know that I was invited. The brass mill fittings came in, and there was much to discuss."

"I saw the brass. I've never seen so much brass in one place in my life! You paid for all this?"

"Well, yes, my lord. When I left for Cieszyn, you were distracted with the planting, so I thought it best to take my own money along."

"But you agree that the mills are mine?"

"Of course, my lord."

"Then I owe you your expenses. What were they?"

"The present fittings, plus those for the dry mill, the tubs for the factory and the dye, the mules, and the Florentine came to...uh...about twenty-three thousand pence."

"Twenty-three... Come talk with me in my chambers, Sir Conrad."

When we got there, he said, "Twenty-three thousand pence is a huge amount of money, Sir Conrad."

"Yes, my lord."

"Hmm. You wouldn't wager on your chess playing. Would you wager on your mill? I would bet you that your wet mill doesn't work. Double or nothing. Do you agree?"

"If you wish, my lord. But I'm stealing your money. The mill will work."

"We shall see. For now, come to the hall. People want to meet you. I should mention that throughout supper Sir Stefan and his father, Baron Jaraslav, have been damning you to all and sundry for a warlock and a witch! I believe they've called you everything but a Christian."

"Sir Stefan? But why isn't he on guard duty?"

"One of his father's other knights is doing his stint so he can be there to blacken your name. I don't like my vassals acting this way. I know it's not your fault, except had you been there they wouldn't have been so blatant about it. What the duke thinks is anybody's guess."

As we entered, Lambert whispered, "Here we go. *Keep your temper!*"

As we walked into the hall, conversation was suddenly muted. People had been drinking and socializing after a feast. Now half of them were staring at me, and the rest were obviously trying not to.

Bluff it through! I thought, shouting to myself. You can do it, you can do it—I think I can, I think I can, I think I can... Head high, smiling, I swaggered in at Lambert's side, almost convincing myself that I wasn't scared.

Sir Vladimir saved me. Cutting through the crowd, he said, "Sir Conrad, what's this I hear about your attacking six thugs from the whoremasters guild and killing the lot of them?"

"Just lies, Sir Vladimir. There were only three of them, and I believe two lived."

A knight I hadn't met said, "You were completely unarmed when you attacked?"

"Well, yes. You see, there wasn't much time. A friend was in trouble, and had I gone back for my sword, well, who could tell what would have happened?"

"A friend of the whoremasters guild? Was she pretty?" a third knight said.

"Hardly. It was a he. The innkeeper of the Pink Dragon, although his wife was also being abused."

"But how was it possible for one unarmed man to defeat three with knives?" the second knight persisted. An interested crowd was gathering. Except for Lambert's ladies, this was an all-male group. They were all professional fighters, so by their standards anybody talking about bloodshed and mayhem had to be all right. *I was winning!*

"It wasn't three at once," I said. "I was able to get them one at a time."

"But even one man is hard to believe."

"Okay. Hang up your cloak and I'll show you." As I've mentioned, I'm no black belt, but I did learn a few simple throws in the service. With the sheath on his knife, we went through a few judo throws in slow motion.

I didn't actually reenact my fight in the hall of the Pink Dragon. I wasn't sure how these knights would react to kneeing someone in the groin, and I wanted to play the good guy. The first time you find yourself lifted into the air in judo is a memorable event, and it looks impressive. Three or four of them lined up to try me. The others were watching and drinking. I was becoming socially acceptable.

"You see," I said to a fellow in blue who was lying at my feet. "Had I thrown you down hard, you would be momentarily stunned. I could do all sorts of things to you. I could stamp on your chest, for example."

"Try me," a voice said from behind me.

I turned to find myself facing Duke Henryk the Bearded.

"My lord it . . . it doesn't seem fitting," I stammered. *Good God*. He was my boss's boss, and he looked to be seventy years old. Not your usual judo partner!

"Try me," he repeated, holding his knife high with his right hand.

"Yes, my lord." Taking it slow and watching carefully to see that I didn't hurt him, I started through the same throw that I'd shown the others.

"Hold!" he said. I froze.

I felt a sharp prick at my ribs. Looking down, I saw that the duke held a dagger in his left hand. Where it had come from, I didn't know.

"What do you think now, Sir Conrad?"

"My lord, I think that had I met you in that dark hallway, I would be a dead man."

The room exploded in laughter, but it was laughter of a friendly sort. It was no dishonor to be bested by one's superior.

Contented, the duke sheathed his knives—one in his boot—and walked away.

The evening went well, I thought. Sir Stefan stayed to one corner of the room with his father and a half dozen knights. Sir Vladimir told me that they were the baron's liegemen. No hope of support there! I avoided them and circulated.

Conversation that evening centered mostly on hunting and hawking, so I didn't have much to contribute. Krystyana was a perfect hostess, and a lot of her newfound poise was rubbing off on the other girls, especially Janina, Natalia, Annastashia, and Yawalda. They were treated cordially, but they got a lot of side glances.

Later I found myself standing with Lambert and the duke.

"It's an interesting thought you've brought up, Sir Conrad," the duke said. "That it is possible for an unarmed man to defeat one who is armed."

"My lord, please understand that I am not a master of unarmed combat. I'm hardly an apprentice. *I* certainly believe that in a fight one is much better off armed. It is just that a warrior should remain a warrior even if he's naked."

"Interesting. You say *you* believe the obvious. Is there anyone who doesn't?"

"I've met one, my lord. He insisted that weaponry was unimportant compared to mental attitude and training. He was a master of the martial arts, a black belt from Japan."

"Ah, yes. It is said that you have traveled widely."

"Yes, my lord. Perhaps more widely than you can imagine. But I made a vow—"

"I know, son, and I won't push you. Still, a man must think. You, Lambert. Where do you think our Sir Conrad has come from?"

"My lord, I had not intended to speak on this, but since you ask, I must answer. Know that I have been watching this man carefully since Christmas. I have pondered long as to his origins, and I am confident that my guess is the right one."

"Then what is it?" the duke asked.

"I think that he is an emissary from Prester John, the Christian king of that most distant and fabulous empire."

Naturally, I was astounded by this. I'm not sure that I kept my jaw from sagging. *Prester John!*

"Remarkable," the duke said.

"Think about it, my lord. We have here a deadly knight who is distressed by the sight of blood. A master of the technic arts who didn't know how a smith makes iron. A man who treats warriors and children just the same. Where else could he have come from but the most civilized empire in the world?"

"Sir Stefan would say that he came from the Devil," the duke noted.

"There has been bad blood between them, my lord. I have explained—"

"So you have. But why would Prester John send a man to us?"

"Perhaps because of the Mongols," Lambert said. "It is said that they have conquered half the world. Perhaps they press him and he is in need of aid."

"Then why didn't he send an emissary instead of an engineer?"

"Perhaps he did, my lord. Whatever Conrad's instructions were, well, I've explained the gist of his oath."

"So you have. Well, Sir Conrad. It grows late. We are hunting tomorrow. Will you join us?"

"I would be honored, my lord." I don't like blood sports, but hunting at least has the virtue of putting meat on the table. Anyway, when your boss's boss invites you, you go.

The duke and Lambert drifted away.

We were to hunt for wild boar and bison, the misnamed buffalo of my American friends. There were, of course, wild bison in thirteenth century Poland. They still exist in modern times on carefully tended game preserves.

I sent word to the Krakowski brothers to go home and take Piotr Kulczynski with them.

The next morning at dawn, I was on horseback with armor and spear, along with two dozen other knights. The duke sent me back to get my shield, since this was also part of the paraphernalia required.

As we rode out, young Henryk dropped back from the front column and rode at my side. "A remarkable coat of arms, Sir Conrad."

"Indeed, my lord?"

"A white eagle on a red field. That is very similar to the insignia of the dukes of Poland."

"Consider it a symbol of Poland, my lord."

"And the eagle wears a crown. Do you claim to be a king?"

"No, my lord. I'm saying that Poland needs a king."

"Hmm, 'Poland is not yet dead.'" He read my motto. "Are you saying that Poland is dying?"

"It's lying in a dozen pieces, my lord. That's a fair start."

"You know that my father and I are working to unite those pieces."

"I know, my lord. When you weld them back together, I will change my motto."

He laughed. "Done, Sir Conrad! In ten years I'll watch you paint out that motto yourself."

"Gladly, my lord. But do it in nine."

We stopped for an early dinner and then spread out at two-hundred-yard intervals to sweep through the forest, driving the animals toward the mountains. Lambert was on the far right, and my station was next to him, with Sir Vladimir to my left. They had deliberately put me between two experienced hunters, which was fine by me.

After a few hours I found myself facing a large bull bison a hundred yards away. Anna immediately broke into a gallop. Anna was trained to pass to the right of a charging knight so that one's spear went over the horse's neck at the knight to the left, but it was easier to use a spear on the right if one had to strike downward. I signaled her to pass on the left. The bison charged at us, not to slightly miss, as a knight would, but directly at us, to ram!

I was bracing for a crash when Anna abruptly side-stepped at the last instant. Surprised, I managed to get a slashing cut into the animal's shoulder. It was bleeding, but it was not mortally wounded.

The bison had had enough and took off at a dead run, angling in front of Lambert. Anna, of course, raced behind it.

"After it, Sir Conrad!" Lambert shouted, and blew a signal on his horn, which I didn't understand. I'd been given a hunting horn, but I didn't know how to use it.

Anna was faster than the wounded bison, but he was built lower to the ground than we were, and he knew it; he charged through the thickets and under low branches. We lost sight of him.

I found tracks along a game trail and followed them for half an hour. By now we were into mountainous country and the trail seemed to lead between two cliffs, about two hundred yards apart, into a valley beyond. The valley contained about a square kilometer of flat land and was devoid of bison, wounded or otherwise. We worked our way up the sloping walls toward the bald mountains above, but it was soon obvious that I had lost the animal.

I was tired, and Anna probably needed rest, although

she didn't show it. I dismounted, took a long drink of water from my canteen, and gave the rest to her. I sat down and fell another yard into a hole.

It was not actually a hole but a cave, and the floor sloped downward at a forty-five-degree angle. I was sliding on my back, headfirst into the darkness. My shoulder hit an obstruction. I yelled and flipped over and skidded on my armored belly, feet first, for about twenty yards and then hit water. The cave was narrow, only about a yard across, and had I still been going headfirst, I might have ended my story right here, by drowning.

As it was, I was able to wedge myself between the walls and work myself out before I ran out of air. Climbing up in slippery armor was a miserable job, but I managed it. I looked around. It was not a natural cave at all but an abandoned mine!

When I finally got out to greet my anxious horse, I threw myself on the ground, exhausted.

Shortly, I heard a horn blowing from the entrance of the valley. I got up, managed to get a squeak out of the horn slung on Anna's saddle, and then sat down again, carefully avoiding the hole.

Count Lambert rode up. "Sir Conrad, what are you doing up here?"

"Trying my hand at drowning, my lord."

"Drowning on a mountainside with no water in sight? By God, you *are* all wet! Another of your arcane arts?"

"No, my lord. I simply fell down a mine shaft."

"Ah, yes! I remember that shaft. It was dug in my grandfather's time. They used to dig coal out of it and burned limestone from that outcropping to make mortar."

"The coal seam ran out?"

"No, there's plenty of coal down there. But when you have two men mining and thirty more passing water buckets, there's not much profit in it. That mine is *full* of water."

"I noticed, my lord."

"Well, we got your bison two miles to the east. You followed a day-old trail up here. I gather that you don't know much about hunting."

"No, my lord. I've never hunted before in my life."

"There are a lot of things that you don't know much about. Since we're alone, it's time we discussed them. I'm talking about Krystyana."

"What about her?"

"Understand that playing a joke on my sister-in-law is one thing. Encouraging a peasant girl to take on the airs of the nobility is quite another. Aside from the offense this gives my other vassals—yes, and my liege lord! Do you realize that Henryk asked me why I had a noble-woman working like a servant?—aside from that, have you thought about what's to become of her? Is she going to be content to settle down as a peasant's wife?"

"No, my lord. She wouldn't be."

"Do you plan to marry her yourself?"

"No, my lord."

"Then why have you encouraged her to rise so far above her station?"

"Well, she's a good girl, an intelligent girl who wanted to better herself, and I didn't think—"

"That's just it! You didn't think! What's more, it's spreading. Three or four of the others are starting to imitate her. You started this, Sir Conrad. What do you plan to do about it?"

"I don't know, my lord." He was right, of course. I'd set the poor kid up for a nasty fall. I'm good with technical stuff, but I am not a wizard when it comes to people problems. Best to change the subject. "You know, if there is still coal in this mine, I could build pumps to empty the water. We could make mortar here again."

"Ah! I see where you are leading. That would take you out of Okoitz, and you could take the girls with you. Well, why not? You've given my workmen projects that will take a year or two to complete, and it's time you had your own lands, anyway. What if I gave you this valley and the land for a mile around it?"

"A mile, my lord?" God! He was giving me some eighteen square kilometers of land!

"You are right, of course. This soil is rocky and poor. You'll need more. The top of that mountain is the boundary of my brother's land. We'll make that your southern boundary. We'll extend you to Sir Miesko's land on the east and to Baron Jaraslav's on the north and west. That will give you lands about six miles across. You should be able to eke out a decent living on it, in sheep if nothing else. In return, let's see. I'll want you to come to Okoitz for two days a month to oversee your improvements there. And if you get this mine working, I'll want a hundred mule loads of mortar a year. Agreed?"

"Yes, my lord. You are most generous!"

"Good, then it's settled. Leave tomorrow and take the girls with you. Now let's return to the hunting party."

"Will the duke approve your grant?"

"That is a very good question. I don't know."

I had taken first blood on the expedition, which was apparently some sort of honor even though Sir Vladimir had actually killed the bison. All told, the knights took four bison and six wild pigs.

The meal that night was braised pork—sort of a shish kebob—and bison stew.

Because of the first-blood thing, I was seated at the high table between Lambert and the duke. I was the only mere knight up there. All the rest were at least barons. Baron Jaraslav sat to the duke's left.

The high table was just that. It was a third of a yard higher than the rest of the collapsible trestle tables in the hall. We had a correspondingly higher bench to sit on.

Krystyana and company did the serving. Once the meal was well under way, Lambert announced that he was minded to grant me a fief but that it required the duke's consent to be binding. While Lambert spoke, Sir Stefan was in the crowd, talking angrily to the knights at either side. Apparently, he had again found a substitute for guard duty. Then Baron Jaraslav began muttering in the duke's ear.

Lambert outlined the proposed boundaries of the fief. As he finished, Stefan struck his stein on the table so hard that it shattered, spraying beer over a dozen knights. "You'd grant that black warlock lands adjoining ours? Damn you!" he shouted.

The room was suddenly totally quiet.

Lambert turned and struck Stefan with an icy stare. I'd seen many facets to Lambert's personality, but never before that of a cold, deadly killer. "You would raise your voice to your father's liege lord?" Lambert asked in the silence. There were swords in his voice.

"I—I spoke rashly, my lord."

"Yes, you did."

"I . . . apologize, my lord." Stefan knew he was in trouble. He came from his bench and walked stiffly to the front of Lambert's table. He went to his knees and made a full Slavic bow, with forehead touching the rushes on the floor. "I regret my words and beg forgiveness, my lord."

"Sir Stefan, this is the second time your temper has offended me. A true knight knows his place and his duty at all times. He does not give way to fits of temper. You need some cooling down. Perhaps some additional meditation in the evening air will help. I extend your tour of guard duty by an additional three months, from now until Michaelmas. On the night shift!

"Go now and stand your post."

Sir Stefan rose stiffly. "Yes, my lord." He left without a word. The room was silent after he left.

"Well," the duke said after a bit. "Returning to the matter of my consent of this grant, I must think on it. The thing is perhaps being pushed too quickly, but you will have my answer before morning. For now, Lambert, can you provide music?"

The peasant band had been waiting in the kitchen and was soon performing. The music didn't help me a bit. I've never been much good at waiting.

I couldn't help overhearing Baron Jaraslav's advice and comments to the duke.

"To allow evil into our own ranks . . . foreigners taking the lands of our fathers . . . worse than the Duke of Mazovia inviting in the Knights of the Cross . . ." The duke's replies were inaudible, but my stomach tightened and I wasn't able to eat much. I drank more than I should have, but I stayed on beer so as not to get too drunk.

When the meal ended and the tables were being taken down, Baron Jaraslav and the duke went to the duke's chambers.

"I think it doesn't look good," Lambert said to me. "Perchance I erred in punishing Sir Stefan, but, damn, a lord has to maintain discipline."

"I appreciate your aid, my lord. If this doesn't work out, perhaps we'll think of something else."

"I've thought on simply having you develop that mine on my own lands, just as you are building the mills. We could work out some informal arrangement. But it would border on my deliberately circumventing the wishes of *my* liege lord."

The knights who had been on guard duty at Okoitz had learned the waltz and polka and were demonstrating them, with the ladies' help, to our guests. They called me to join them, but I was too tight. It almost hurt to smile. During a lull in the music a page summoned me to the duke's chambers.

With a profoundly acid stomach and no Alka-Seltzer due for seven hundred years, I followed him up the steps.

On entering, I bowed low.

"Sit down, boy. I have things to ask you. First, I want to know more about this guise. Whom did you make this vow to and where can I find him?"

"He is Father Ignacy Sierpinski, at the Franciscan monastery in Cracow, my lord."

"I will talk to this Father Ignacy. My second question is, Why do you want this land? From what I've heard, you know as little of farming as you do of hunting."

"I want the land so I can build an industrial base."

"A what?"

"Hear me out, my lord. You have asked me why I wasn't building weapons. I intend to build them. I can make armor that no arrow can possibly penetrate. I can make swords as good as the one I carry. Have you seen what it can do?"

"I've heard stories. Go on."

"I can build weapons that roar like thunder, strike like lightning, and kill your enemies half a mile away.

"And I intend to make these arms and armor by the thousands. By the hundreds of thousands if I can."

"A hundred thousand suits of armor? Why, I doubt if there are fifty thousand knights in all of Poland."

"Not the knights, my lord, the peasants."

"And just how do you suppose that a peasant could afford armor?"

"Obviously they can't, my lord. The arms will have to be supplied to them."

"Do you expect *me* to pay for this?"

"Of course not, my lord. I will have to do that myself."

"I know that you are wealthy, Sir Conrad. But even your wealth could not equip a hundred men, much less a hundred thousand."

"I said I would make the weapons, not buy them. The money I have will get me started. After that, I will have to come up with salable products to meet expenses. Mortar and bricks, certainly. Perhaps pottery. Cookware, pots and pans. Maybe even glass. At this point I am not sure of specifics, but I know it can be done."

"Very well. If we assume that you really can build such arms and that the peasants will wear them, it is still useless. A mob of peasants, no matter how armed, is still a mob. Fighting men could cut them up regardless of weapons. Believe me. I've seen it too many times."

"Training is necessary, of course. But techniques exist that can turn a bunch of farmers into a fighting unit in four months' time. I've been through it myself, my lord."

"Indeed. What does all this have to do with my original question? Why do you want that land?"

"I need to have someplace to do these things. I can't do it in the cities. The guilds would never permit me the innovations that I will have to introduce."

"You did well enough with the guilds of Cieszyn. You abolished one and have another louting to you."

"My lord, that business with the whoremasters guild was simply stupidity on their part. I never wanted anything to do with them. As to the bell casters, they were only three brothers who were starving to death. I wouldn't have that kind of luck in Cracow.

"I can't do it here. These people are primarily farmers. I need full-time craftsmen."

"I see. You are dismissed, Sir Conrad."

Shaking slightly, I went back down to the party and drained two mugs of beer.

Shortly, I saw Lambert being escorted to the duke's chambers. A thorough man, the duke.

The party was breaking up. It must have been approaching midnight, because I saw Sir Vladimir stumble out to relieve Sir Stefan. He hadn't been at the feast, and from the looks of him he had slept in his armor.

The duke came down and looked at me. "There is more to gain than to lose. I'll be watching you, boy, but you can have it."

I came close to fainting.

Privately and somewhat curtly, the count informed five adolescent girls that they were leaving with me, the ones he thought were acting above their station in life. That night Krystyana was happy and excited about the coming adventure. She didn't realize that she was being thrown out.

I didn't regret my actions. I intended to raise a million bright kids "above their stations," and damn these Dark Age rules!

Yet personally, I was somewhat sad. I had been happy at Okoitz, but my job there was done. Good things must end, and perhaps the future would not be so bad.

For a penniless immigrant who had arrived only six months before, I had done fairly well. We now had the start of a decent school system, the beginnings of a textile industry, and the glimmerings of an industrial base.

If the seeds I'd brought worked out, we had the makings of an agricultural revolution.

We had steel, a fairly efficient brass works, and a profitable if embarrassing inn.

And now I had a hundred square kilometers of land to work with, land that would someday be the industrial heart of Poland.

It was a magnificent challenge, but still, leaving is a sad thing.

Interlude Three

TOM PRESSED the hold button.

"Enough for today. They're waiting the banquet on us, but I'd hate to make them hold the ballet."

"Okay," I said. "But first tell me what went wrong."

"Wrong with what?"

"With Conrad's plans. He seems to be an intelligent, competent engineer. He had the backing of the authorities. He had raw materials and a good work force. Where did he fail?"

"What makes you think he failed?"

"Well, he had to fail! He's trying to start the industrial revolution five centuries too early, which obviously didn't happen."

"Ah, the catch is in that word 'obviously.' Son, I've been showing you this record for a reason. You know that subjectively I'm over eight hundred years old. There are limits to what even our medics can accomplish. You are ninety now, and I think you're mature enough to get involved with the firm's decision-making processes.

"But decisions shouldn't be made without complete information, and for us there's never a reason for anything to be rushed. Time, after all, is our stock in trade. Let's go eat."

"But—"

"But nothing! You want to keep the dancers waiting?"

As we left for the banquet hall, Tom put his hand on my shoulder and said, "What tickles me is the way Conrad keeps on talking about building socialism while at the same time taking all of the actions a nineteenth-century capitalist would approve of. Buying businesses, making them profitable, reinvesting the money . . ."

About the Author

Leo Frankowski was born on February 13, 1943, in Detroit. By the time he was thirty-five, he had held more than a hundred different positions, ranging from "scientist" in an electro-optics research lab to gardener to chief engineer. Much of his work was in chemical, optical, and physical instrumentation, and earned him a number of U.S. patents.

Since 1977, he has owned and managed Sterling Manufacturing & Design, the only mostly female engineering company in the Detroit area. Sterling designs electrical and fluid power controls for automatic special machines. It also produced Formitrol®, a stretchy metal that is useful in fixing rusty cars.

He is active in MENSA, the Society for Creative Anachronism and science-fiction fandom. He is an officer in two writers' clubs, and his hobbies include reading, drinking, chess, kite flying, dancing girls, and cooking.

A lifelong bachelor, he lives alone in Sterling Heights, Michigan.